ISLAND OF DOOM

THE HUNCHBACK
ASSIGNMENTS
4

Also by Arthur Slade

OTHER BOOKS
IN THE HUNCHBACK ASSIGNMENTS SERIES

The Hunchback Assignments

The Dark Deeps: The Hunchback Assignments 2

Empire of Ruins: The Hunchback Assignments 3

Jolted: Newton Starker's Rules for Survival

Megiddo's Shadow

Dust

Tribes

ARTHUR SLADE

ISLAND OF DOOM

THE HUNCHBACK ASSIGNMENTS
4

This is a work of fiction. Names, characters, places, and incidents either are the product of the author's imagination or are used fictitiously. Any resemblance to actual persons, living or dead, events, or locales is entirely coincidental.

 Published in the United States by Wendy Lamb Books, an imprint of Random House Children's Books, a division of Random House, Inc., New York. Originally published in hardcover in Canada by HarperCollins Publishers Ltd., Toronto, in 2012.

Wendy Lamb Books and the colophon are trademarks of Random House, Inc.

Visit us on the Web! randomhouse.com/teens
Educators and librarians, for a variety of teaching tools, visit us at RHTeachersLibrarians.com

Library of Congress Cataloging-in-Publication Data
Slade, Arthur G. (Arthur Gregory)
Island of Doom / by Arthur Slade. — 1st ed.
p. cm. — (The Hunchback assignments ; 4)
Summary: Modo, the shape-shifting, masked spy, and fellow spy Octavia Milkweed learn that Modo's biological parents are still alive but when the Clockwork Guild find Modo's parents first, Octavia and Modo chase them across Europe and North America to the Island of Doom.
ISBN 978-0-385-73787-6 (hardback) — ISBN 978-0-385-90697-5 (lib. bdg.) — ISBN 978-0-307-97574-4 (ebook) [1. Disfigured persons—Fiction. 2. Shapeshifting—Fiction. 3. Spies—Fiction. 4. Europe—History—19th century—Fiction. 5. Islands of the Pacific—History—19th century—Fiction. 6. Science fiction.] I. Title.
PZ7.S628835Isl 2012 [Fic]—dc23 2012006130

Printed in the United States of America
10 9 8 7 6 5 4 3 2 1
First Edition

Random House Children's Books supports the First Amendment and celebrates the right to read.

For Tori and Tanaya,
with all my love

ISLAND OF DOOM

THE HUNCHBACK ASSIGNMENTS

4

PROLOGUE

Resurrection Men

William "Mad Dog" Middleton faced the gallows rope with a jaundiced eye. He'd lived thirty-six years, the last five in Sumpter, Oregon, during the dregs of a dying gold rush. In a fit of cold anger he'd murdered three prospectors for their meager findings, and now he was about to hang. It was that simple. He'd never been maudlin and felt only a slight annoyance as he stared back at the gathered crowd: faces he recognized from the saloons, from brawls, all eager to watch him swing. Life had been harsh. He had been harsh. He was happy to go.

His heart didn't skip a beat when the hangman placed the rope around his neck. "Get it done" was all he said, his last words. The trapdoor opened, and one minute later a doctor pronounced Middleton dead. The law had been upheld along with his neck.

Middleton's journey didn't end there. The sheriff, who was also the coroner, barked at the gravediggers, "Take him up to Stoney Cemetery and throw him in a hole!" They placed his large body in a wagon and drew it to an unmarked grave in the half-frozen ground outside Sumpter. It was shallow because of the frost and stones. There was no one to mourn him. The men who threw the dirt did their job quickly and left before nightfall. There were other new graves. Some Chinese laborers who had died of consumption, and the miners whom Middleton had shot. He lay only yards away from his victims.

A full moon appeared in the sky, the type William had preferred when he hunted deer. Three men arrived. They were small, wiry, and dressed in black, faces covered by balaclavas. They unearthed Middleton's body, placed it in a coffin, covered it with ice, and adjusted several dials on the lid. They were professional resurrection men from the Far East, the finest at their job.

The body was transported by cart to a train and settled beside the first-class baggage, the closest Middleton had ever come to riding in luxury. At the coast, he was loaded onto a midsized paddle steamer alongside several other coffins from America and Canada. There had been three other hangings in the Rockies. One coffin contained the recipient of a bullet—a common cause of death on the frontier. There were stakes to be claimed, cattle to be rounded up, and land to be purchased, all of which often led to arguments that ended in gunfire.

William wouldn't know it, but his coffin was next to the

body of a magistrate and sometime novelist named Duncan McTavish. He'd been locally famous for his wit, his loquacity, and his love of money. He'd poisoned his wife to inherit her fortune and instead had been hanged. If he and Middleton had both been alive at the same time, they wouldn't have been able to find much to converse about. Since they were dead, this presented no problem.

The steamship was named *Triton II*, and it navigated the Pacific without the flag of any nation, the caskets rattling in its hold. Most smaller ships would hug the shore for safety as they traveled, but this one ran on compressed coal and an engine that would be the envy of the Royal Navy. It sped directly west, cutting through the waves.

Two evenings later the vessel arrived at an island and was met by armed patrol ships. Messages were relayed by lantern, and the ship was guided into a port as large as any in London. The eyes of the resurrection men widened, for in the center of the island was a fortress of glass. The moon painted it a glowing yellow. They knew that inside that palace was the man they referred to as the dragon master. This man was a visionary, renowned for the magnificence of his ideas and philosophies—philosophies that the resurrectionists happened to agree with. And as it turned out, the dragon master paid rather well.

It was the middle of the night, but gas and electric lamps lit the work of the soldiers building barricades. Others were hauling wagons of dirt from excavations. Several gray-clad soldiers helped the resurrection men unload the caskets and carry them to a cave a short distance away. The resurrectionists returned to their ship and the search for more flesh. And there on the cool stones lay William "Mad Dog" Middleton's coffin, his body as dead as ever.

Shortly thereafter, four men in white coats came out and lifted each coffin. Middleton's was brought into the cave and set beside a worktable littered with flasks, surgery tools, and electrical cables. One of the assistants awakened an old man dozing on a cot in the corner.

"Your supplies have been delivered, Dr. Hyde, sir," the assistant said.

The doctor nodded, shook the sleep out of his balding head, fumbled to put on his glasses, and approached the coffins. The first one he opened was William Middleton's. When he saw the size and the condition of the corpse, he smiled.

He began his work immediately.

1

A Most Mysterious Letter

A courier in a gray bowler hat and a frock coat approached a tall brick house on the outskirts of Montreal, Quebec, unaware of the professionally trained eyes watching him from a bedroom window. He was measured, weighed, and classified in the space of a few heartbeats.

"Five feet six inches," Modo whispered. "One hundred and forty pounds. Twenty-five to twenty-seven years old." He was alone in the room and had reverted to his childhood habit of talking to himself. "Slight limp indicates hip difficulty, perhaps from poliomyelitis." Modo's years of espionage training made the measuring of the man a rather easy task. It would be even simpler to jump down from his second-story window and dispatch the courier with a blow or a sleeper hold. Now, that would make him wet his britches!

Modo carried out this surveillance to break the monotony

of his day. He hadn't had an assignment for months and consequently his skills hadn't been tested by either Tharpa, his weapons trainer, or his master, Mr. Socrates. They continued to train Octavia, his fellow agent and friend; every day she was in the courtyard huffing and puffing and practicing martial arts or shouting her way through elocution lessons with Mrs. Finchley. But Modo was persona non grata—an unwanted agent.

Three months ago he had twice disobeyed a direct order from his master to send innocent Australian natives into battle. Mr. Socrates had not forgiven him his trespasses.

Modo threw himself back on his bed and opened his copy of *Middlemarch.* The arrival of the courier would likely be the most exciting thing to happen this week. Occasionally, to entertain himself, Modo would go through the painful process of shifting his deformed body and face into one of the many personae he had perfected, such as the Knight, the Doctor, and others. He would wander out to the market to practice his French, though the Quebecois spoke a different dialect than Parisians. He did enjoy this little city in the Canadian wilderness with its French citizens, Irish merchants, and British magistrates. It was like several small countries all rolled into one. But he always returned to Montreal House and his life in limbo.

He scratched at the little finger on his left hand. It often itched; the skin was fresh and pink now, but in a few weeks it would shed. He had lost the finger to an enemy saber only three months before, and, to his great and absolute surprise, it had regenerated itself: proof that he was the oddest, strangest human being to have ever walked the earth.

He tried not to think of the woman who had wielded that saber, Miss Hakkandottir, one of the leaders of the Clockwork Guild. The Guild was an organization bent on the destruction of everything British, as far as Modo could tell. The Permanent Association, his organization, was bent on preserving Britannia. Modo had last seen Miss Hakkandottir fleeing into the jungle. He hoped she'd ended up in the gullet of a particularly nasty crocodile. He imagined the beast spitting out her metal hand and couldn't keep from chuckling.

Alas, even if she were dead, someone else would rise up to take her place. The Clockwork Guild was not a small organization; it could strike anywhere in the world with ease. After all, it was most likely the Guild that had burned down Victor House, Mr. Socrates' home in England, forcing them to flee here.

At least the Guild had left them alone for several months. Modo turned a page in his book and tried to disappear back into the world of *Middlemarch*. Would Dorothea ever marry Ladislaw? He was tempted to flip to the end, but stopped himself. He'd done that with *Wuthering Heights* and regretted it still.

There came a hard knock on his door and before Modo could say "Enter," or even reach for his netting mask to cover his monstrous face, Mr. Socrates was standing at the side of his bed. His master had dark circles under his eyes, and his white hair was longer than usual. He looked as though he'd aged ten years in the past few months. The stress of hiding from the Clockwork Guild was obviously keeping the poor man up all hours of the night.

Modo had been raised by Mr. Socrates. Or not raised, but

trained, for Mr. Socrates had never been a parent. He'd bought Modo from a traveling curiosity wagon. He'd never changed Modo's diapers or soothed his bruises. He'd given orders for Modo to be shaped, from age one, into a secret agent at Ravenscroft, his secluded country home. Modo didn't leave the house for thirteen years.

"May I help you?" Modo asked.

Mr. Socrates extended his arm. At first Modo thought he wanted to shake hands, but then he saw what his master was carrying: "This most mysterious letter has arrived for you," Mr. Socrates said.

Modo took the envelope, briefly touching his master's hand. How he wished, just once, that hand had patted his shoulder or his head in a gesture of kindness.

Modo cast aside these silly feelings and examined the letter. His name was written neatly along the front, and below that was the address of Montreal House. "But how can this be addressed to me? No one is supposed to know that we're here."

"Not entirely true," Mr. Socrates answered. "Since our *great retreat* from London, I've cut off the majority of communication with the other members of the Permanent Association, but I have left a few trusted channels open." So, Modo thought, the Permanent Association still operated! The secret organization had employed him for most of his life; its single goal was to keep Britannia ruling forever. One woman and six men, including Mr. Socrates, had created and now controlled the association. Even Queen Victoria didn't know of its existence.

Modo's master jabbed a finger toward the letter. "This was delivered to a trusted courier by a French contact."

"But what would the French want with me?"

"Ah, that is the question of the hour. I'm here to discover the answer."

Modo held the envelope up. "It's already open."

"Of course it is!" Mr. Socrates replied, lowering himself into the chair across from Modo's bed. "Several eyes have studied it along the way. But the letter is in a code that no one, including me, has been able to decipher. Open it."

Modo pulled the single page out of the envelope and unfolded:

20-22-11-22:
33-23-28 32-18-21-21 12-15 30-32-29-27-29-20-30-15-11 25-20 16-11-7-24 13-25-22-20 21-13 11-30-29 30-18-15 30-20-31-33-12-31-20-21 30-8-10-23-23-17-22 . . .

"But it's just numbers," Modo said after scanning the first couple of rows. "Without a key it will be impossible to crack. Have you tried the Vigenère cipher?"

"Do you think I am a fool? That was the first code we applied. The day the French discover that we cracked their cipher will be a bad day for our intelligence gathering. No, whoever sent it has likely used a key only you would be able to decipher. They would know that you are part of the Permanent Association and that other eyes would attempt to read the missive."

Modo paused. Had he heard that right? *You are part of the Permanent Association.* Perhaps his exile was nearly over.

Another knock at the door. An unusually busy morning!

As was his habit, he drew his netting mask from the bedpost and pulled it over his face. He barely had his eyeholes straight before Octavia entered in her exercise outfit—black pantaloons and a black sweater. Her sandy blond hair was tied back, sweat still on her brow.

"Please, Octavia!" Modo exclaimed. "You really must wait for permission to enter!"

"Oh, Modo." She waved away his protestations as if she were shooing flies. "Since when did we have such haristocratic stuffery between us?" He gritted his teeth. Yes, he had shown her his real face once, and he couldn't stand the guarded look she'd given him. Now he thought of the event as the "yours is not the face I've dreamed of all my life" incident. Sometimes she seemed entirely oblivious to his feelings. "I've heard that a letter arrived for you."

"Where did you hear that?" Mr. Socrates said.

"Tharpa told me."

Mr. Socrates raised two doubting eyebrows. "He would not impart that sort of information."

"Well then, I spied the delivery boy and saw you climbing the stairs through the picture window. You only go upstairs to lecture one of us, sir."

"Mmm. Perhaps I've trained you too well. Please have a seat."

She chose the end of the bed, nearly plopping herself down on Modo's feet.

Modo was searching for something clever to say when another person came through the door: Mrs. Finchley, in a long gray dress. "Oh, is it an official meeting?" she asked. "Would you like tea?"

"That won't be necessary, Mrs. Finchley," Mr. Socrates said. "Please return to your duties."

"Actually, Mrs. Finchley," Modo said, "would you kindly telegram the gendarmes or whatever it is they call their constables here? My room is becoming rather crowded with vagrants."

She gave him a smile on her way out. "I shall send an urgent message."

"Where's the letter from?" Octavia asked.

"France," Modo replied. "I don't know anyone in France."

"There is that French spy." Octavia brushed a hand through her hair. "What was the little viper's name? Coquette? I mean, Colette Brunet?"

"Impossible," Modo said.

The penmanship had neither a masculine nor feminine appearance and it contained no flourishes, no hint of personality, as though the person had intended to mask his or her personal style. But the last two sets of numbers had the same number of characters as Colette Brunet's name. He recognized that immediately—her name had come to mind often recently. Perhaps because of the French spoken in Quebec. If it was her name, deciphering the message would be relatively easy: each number likely corresponded to a letter in the alphabet. He just needed to know one of the words. Two would make it even easier.

"Octavia is correct," Mr. Socrates said. "Use your faculties, Modo. I did not spend countless hours training you for nothing. Decipher the letter."

"Now?" His heartbeat sped up. Nervousness? No, something else. Colette had written to him. *To him.* Colette, who had fought alongside him on the submarine *Ictíneo.* She had been brave and feisty and—he could not lie to himself—bewitchingly beautiful. But when their battles were done, their enemy vanquished, and his defenses down, she had asked to see his face—his real face. They had been adrift at sea; they might never see land again. When he took off his makeshift mask, she had paled and turned away in disgust from the sight of him, then asked him to cover his face. He had relived that moment far too many times. He was stronger now, but it would always hurt.

"Translate immediately," Mr. Socrates commanded.

Modo grabbed a pen and paper from his desk. If C equaled 10, then O would be—he counted—22. He wrote out the alphabet. *A* = 8; *B* = 9; etc. It was Colette! But when he went to decipher her last name, it was not Brunet, but *Csvofu.* What could that mean? Ah, it came to him. Every word had its own code. Instead of A equaling 8, it was 9 this time. Guessing that the pattern repeated itself, he was able to decipher the first word of the letter: *20-22-11-22: Modo.* He began to write it out, calculating rapidly, his mind so focused on the task that he forgot the peering eyes of Mr. Socrates. He didn't even notice Octavia turning up the gas lamp. Soon the words were coming to him almost as quickly as reading regular text. As he deciphered he felt astonished.

Modo:

You will be surprised to hear from me, but the situation warrants this communication. I have been well since we met and I often think of you. Perhaps,

I could say, it is an obsession. I cannot rid my memory of your face and of my failure to match your inner strength. But my regrets should be of no great matter to you. The important thing is that I have found your parents in France, though I do not know their exact location. You were born in the village of Nanterre, a short distance from Paris. I assume this information will be a revelation to you. I also have dire tidings: your parents are in great danger and I cannot protect them alone. Come to me. The moment you receive this missive you must depart. I shall be in Le Hôtel Grand at noon every day for the next fortnight, or longer, if necessary. I shall wait for you with eagerness.

Your bonne chance *friend,*
Colette Brunet

"Well, what does it say?" Mr. Socrates asked. "Tell us, Modo."

Modo looked Mr. Socrates directly in the eye. So much in those few sentences. He tried to find the most important point and surprised himself when he said, very simply, "If her words are true, then I am French."

"You were born in France, yes," Mr. Socrates agreed gruffly. "I brought you back to England when you were no more than a year old. I rescued you from a curio cage in a traveling oddity show."

Modo sat stunned. He had known about the curio cage, but had always assumed he had been found in England.

Anytime he asked about his parents, Mr. Socrates had one reply: "That is not necessary information." Modo had long given up on knowing about them.

In one breath he regained control of his emotions. "Then I was born in Nanterre," he said. And if that one piece of information was correct, then the remainder of the letter was most likely also correct. Colette had somehow, for some reason, located his parents and they were being pursued by enemies. There was far too much to consider; Modo felt as though the constellations in the heavens had suddenly begun spinning in several directions at once. He took another calming breath.

"You're French?" Octavia said. "That explains so much."

"It's no laughing matter!" Modo retorted.

"You're British now," Mr. Socrates asserted. "If not by birth, then by education."

"My parents are alive."

"I always assumed so," Mr. Socrates said defensively. "Remember, Modo, that they abandoned you. Enough of this piecemeal information. Read us the letter."

Modo sat up straighter and put his feet on the floor. He cleared his throat and read, struggling to keep his voice from cracking. When he was done, Octavia was the first to comment: "I'm most curious about the *bonne chance* friendship. She was a shyster."

"She was not," Modo said.

"The question remains," Mr. Socrates said, "as to whether or not she actually wrote the letter. It may have been forged by another agent or agency."

Modo lowered the paper. "But it sounds like her, the way she speaks."

"Cadence and personality can be easily mimicked," Mr. Socrates reminded him. "You of all people should know that. You make your living as a mimic."

"I like to consider myself more than just a mimic," he shot back. "Besides, she said '*bonne chance* friend.'"

"Is that what she called herself?" Mr. Socrates asked. "*Bonne chance* is a common enough French expression."

"No. It's what she said to me before . . ."

"Before what?" Octavia asked.

He remembered the event clearly. He and Colette had thought they were going to die in a metal pod many fathoms below the surface of the Atlantic.

"Before she kissed me. For good luck," he added quickly.

Mr. Socrates smiled, the wrinkles around his eyes becoming more pronounced. Then he let out a rattling laugh. "You forgot to add that little detail to your report. It seems you have learned more about life than I was aware of."

"It was inconsequential," Modo insisted. He glanced at Octavia. Her face was as serene as a doll's, but he thought he saw a glint of anger in her eyes. She already knew he'd kissed Colette. He had assumed she had forgiven him long ago. Or maybe he was dreaming, and her reaction was only wishful thinking on his part. Perhaps it didn't matter to her at all.

"So, we have established a likelihood that it's Colette Brunet who wrote the letter," Mr. Socrates said. "Why would she look for your parents?"

Modo shrugged. An obsession, she had said. With him.

Consumed by her guilt, it seemed. Was she seeking forgiveness for turning away from him?

"The French government obviously knows that you exist, Modo," Mr. Socrates said. "She certainly would have told them. They could be seeking your family, perhaps in the hope that you have brothers or sisters who share your abilities."

"Or, more likely, it's the Clockwork Guild who wants my blood," Modo said. He felt a chill. He had meant to say bloodline, but somehow *blood* rang more true.

He had rarely thought of his mother and father; they were only formless shadows who had abandoned him—the uncaring parents in so many of the fairy tales he'd read. In any case, he'd had Mr. Socrates and Mrs. Finchley to care for him.

Despite that, these two people were being pursued by the agents of an evil guild. He had seen what unspeakable things the Clockwork Guild had done to poor street children to create a weapon to destroy England's Parliament buildings. If they did indeed find his parents, would they be any less cruel?

"Yes," Mr. Socrates said, breaking Modo's reverie. "The Guild could very well be in pursuit. I hadn't properly considered the possibility of your having siblings. I'm sure I would have received reports—I paid a great sum of money for the information that brought you to me."

"You paid for me?"

"Uh, no," Mr. Socrates said. "I paid for information that led to you." Then he paused. "That isn't quite true. I did indeed purchase you from the owners of the curio carriage."

Modo spoke slowly, deliberately, so as not to allow his voice to crack. "How much did you pay?"

"That's immaterial, Modo. If I hadn't paid for you, you'd

still be in that caravan or in some cabinet of curiosities, or perhaps you'd be dead."

Modo was getting dizzy. He felt behind him for the headboard, just to touch something solid. It was all too much to take in. A sibling—a brother or sister as ugly as him? Or perhaps not cursed by this affliction at all?

"I know what you're thinking," Mr. Socrates said.

"You do?" Modo himself had no idea what he was thinking.

"You can't go to France," Mr. Socrates said matter-of-factly. "You're too valuable. I'll send orders to my agents there."

Valuable? Modo thought. So the old man didn't hate him. "You have French agents?"

"Of course. It's a smaller organization, but the Association can still infiltrate where it needs to."

"I understand, sir," Modo said, even though he wasn't certain he believed him.

Mr. Socrates took the letter from Modo's hands and, leaning heavily on his walking stick, made to leave the room. He turned in the doorway. "We will discuss this further tomorrow."

Octavia followed him and seemed to leave in a huff.

Modo stared at the wall, unable to move.

French. He was French!

2

The French Connection

Colette Brunet could not imagine a church more spectacular than Notre Dame de Paris, but she padded quickly alongside it without a glance or a moment's pause to admire the way the moonlight reflected off the stained-glass windows. She had dressed as a young man, pulling her dark hair back and up under a sweeper's cap, and created a bruise around her eye with purple makeup to distract any onlookers from noticing her unusual eyes. Few Parisians had Japanese blood. Her hand was on the pistol inside her long dark jacket as she followed the limping movements of her target: Father Alphonse Mauger. The priest was striding at a surprisingly fast clip, considering his chubbiness. He looked furtively over his shoulder. Twice she had to throw herself out of his line of sight.

She believed Father Mauger was working with the Clockwork Guild, an organization she had only learned about nine months earlier while hunting for a foreign submarine. That mission on the Atlantic had been amazing and eye-opening, but it had cost her much more than she could have imagined possible. She had stood on the ship *Vendetta* as it was pulled down into the Atlantic. Now, she felt the same horrible sensation as her career was sinking. No longer was she first among *les espions*—the French secret agents at the Deuxième Bureau. The agency had picked her brain about her mission in the Atlantic and become fascinated by Modo, salivating at the thought of an agent who could change his shape. Every bit of information she had given up felt like a betrayal of Modo, but if she hadn't shared it she would have betrayed her country.

Then the bureaucrats—desk sitters!—who'd been jealous of her quick ascent in the ranks pulled out their knives. They cast doubt on her stories of an underwater city. They pointed out her divided loyalties; she was, after all, *ainoko,* half Japanese and half French. They whispered lies and scribbled lies until those lies had acquired the ring of truth.

Then one day, two burly gendarmes came to her desk, grabbed her by the shoulders, escorted her to the front gates of the bureau, and tossed her to the curb. She was warned that if she betrayed any secrets of her country she would be imprisoned, tortured, and shot.

Father Mauger entered the cathedral. If she was correct, he was carrying the original documents that revealed the last known location of Modo's parents; the Catholic Church was even more enamored of paperwork than the Deuxième Bureau. She couldn't think of Modo without a shudder, not of fear or revulsion—though his horrid appearance had haunted her for these many months—but a shudder at her own failure. She had not been strong enough to face his face. Fate had given her a chance to forge a true friendship with a fellow agent, a man more amazing than any she had ever met, and she had turned away. How spineless!

Her former employers had sent agents to England who were desperately searching for Modo and any relatives he may have had. She had been on the team up until the moment of her dismissal. She'd decided to take on the task herself, sifting through hospital files and copies of birth records for any mention of a "freak" child, reading nearly every outlandish article in every newspaper published in England: reports about boys in India with three eyes; Siamese twins; a girl with four arms. Colette found no mention of a shape-changing child.

It wasn't until she visited the Bibliothèque Nationale that her first break came. There she had struck up a relationship with a librarian who had a particular and somewhat distasteful interest in *phénomènes de cirque*—circus freaks. He had dropped a massive collection of clippings and diaries onto her desk. She sifted through it to discover an account of a monstrously malformed boy from Nanterre who had been mentioned in *Le Temps* in 1858. It was the right year, assuming Modo was near her age. The article made her reconsider her assumption that Modo had been born in England. After all, the British were known to scour the world for spies. Could Modo have been born in France? *Mon Dieu!*

She discovered a transcript of an interview with a midwife who had helped deliver "a demon straight from hell but born of woman's flesh," so she pursued the midwife to Nanterre. The woman's name was Marie. She had three teeth and had taken to drink in her later years. Her harrowing account of the birth made Colette cringe; the midwife had actually screamed at the sight of the *monstre petite* as it was pulled into the world. Colette left that meeting with a possible last name for Modo's parents: Hébert.

The next day the midwife had died, drowned in the Seine. Colette would've thought it an accident, except a week later the librarian from Bibliothèque Nationale fell from the roof of the library to his death. The Deuxième Bureau rarely resorted to such crude methods. She suspected another organization was on the same path, might even have someone on her trail. It was the British, perhaps. Or the Russians.

She made discreet inquiries and followed the trail of rumors, until she discovered that a family of potters named Hébert had once lived in Nanterre. No one had seen them for years. She learned that they indeed had had a child who was believed to have been abandoned, though no one had ever set eyes on the infant. Perhaps it had been left at Notre Dame; this was a common occurrence, since many believed their cast-off children would have the best chance of a future if left at the greatest church in the land.

And so, a week earlier, she had visited the church, but Mauger, the archivist, had not allowed her so much as a peek at his records. This surprised her, since she'd had little trouble getting similar information from other churches. So she waited outside the church for him to leave, then followed him through the streets of Paris. After several hours of surveillance she had spotted him meeting with a white-haired man. She'd read their lips from a distance and was only able to decipher the date they planned to meet again: this very day.

The priest appeared anxious as he entered the great doors of Notre Dame, stopping in the doorway to look about with feigned nonchalance. Colette waited behind a statue until he entered, then sped through the doors. Hiding behind columns, she crept down the nave of the church. The moonlight shone through the massive stained-glass windows, splashing colors across the marble floor. She trailed Mauger into the Chapel Sacrament and outside again as he crossed the short distance to the stone archives building.

She couldn't follow him directly inside; the building was too small. She hunted around the periphery for another entrance, thankful that the priests didn't keep guard dogs. Who would want to steal church records? The only other door she found was secured by a large, ancient lock.

Seeing a darkened window on the second floor, she climbed spiderlike up the side of the building, gripping the rough edges of the stone. Her arms and legs were strong; every morning she performed a vigorous exercise regimen designed by her late father. She grabbed the windowsill and it broke off, pieces of stone clattering to the ground. She would've fallen if not for a firm grasp on the protruding and solid nose of a gargoyle. "*Merci,*" she said, smiling at it.

She found a more secure piece of sill on her second attempt. The window opened easily and she slipped in, stepping onto wood that creaked. As her eyes adjusted she saw that she was standing on a desk, musty volumes stacked beside her. She lowered herself to the floor, crept across the room, and opened the door a crack.

Light. Two figures, one of them Mauger, were visible at the bottom of a set of stairs, their voices distant mumbles. Colette opened the door enough to slip through and peer over the railing. She was surprised to hear them speaking English.

"Seventy-five hundred." It was Mauger's nasal tone, his French accent now very clear.

"Don't be uffish," a reedy voice warned. "I humbly suggest you provide the information free of cost." Colette thought she heard an Irish lilt to the man's words. She'd never seen such white hair; it glowed in the low light. He was thin, his tan suit very stylish.

"I—I will take sixty-five hundred. But no less. This is very important information. You're not the only agency who has requested it."

"But I am here; the other agencies are not. And what if you receive nothing?"

Father Mauger was holding a paper in his right hand, which was clearly shaking. "That was not the agreement. And why did you bring this . . . this man with you?" He motioned toward a gray pillar that Colette quickly realized wasn't a pillar but a brute of a man, standing dead still.

"Is the name on it?" With a serpent's speed, the thin man snatched the paper from Mauger's hand, then read it. "Names. Addresses. Perhaps this is helpful."

"Fifty-five hundred?" Mauger pleaded. "Mr. Lime, please. I have risked my position."

"It is Lime. Not Mr. Lime." He signaled to the larger man,

who didn't respond. "Ah, such mush for brains! Can you not obey a simple gesture? Fine. I shall use words: Typhon, please separate the dear father's head from his body."

The monstrous man grunted an answer and batted aside Mauger's feeble attempt to block him. He wrapped one hand around the father's neck.

"No! No—" Mauger's words were cut off as he was choked.

She couldn't let the priest die! Colette cocked her pistol and charged down the stairs, leaping high and landing several feet behind her targets. She pointed the gun at Lime's heart.

"Release him!" she commanded.

Lime smiled as though he'd expected her all along. His teeth glittered in the light of the gas lamp. "Why?" he asked.

"I'll shoot you if you don't."

With his back to her, the beast Typhon continued to choke Mauger.

"And what will that accomplish?" Lime asked. "Will it stop the moon shifting in the sky? Will it silence the music of the spheres?"

He wanted to wax philosophical while she pointed a gun at him? He was mad.

"Drop the paper, too," she added. "Now."

Again, that smile. His glinting teeth, if her eyes weren't deceiving her, were made of sharpened metal. "A girl dressed as a boy tells a man what to do." With some drama, he held the paper high and dropped it. By a lucky current of air it floated through the several feet between them. She lunged and grabbed it, not allowing the pistol to waver.

"You won't leave this room alive," he said quietly. "Your

bones will be broken. Your brains stomped to gruel. Your thoughts will leak onto the earth."

"You must be a failed poet. That's not how this will play out."

"I will it to be so and so it will be. Can the tides of destiny be stopped?"

Madness could only be met by madness, Colette decided. She fired, intentionally missing Lime by inches and shattering a lantern behind him. Lime didn't budge, though he did open his sneering lips to say, "Release the priest."

Typhon dropped Mauger and the archivist fell to the ground like a sack of stones.

"That's better," Colette said. "Now back away from the priest."

Lime smiled again. "Please, Typhon," he said to his companion, "kill the frumious girl in an egregiously painful manner."

The massive man turned, his eyes dead. Collette froze as he lunged; it was as though a mountain was falling toward her. Then she heard her father's voice: *Always be ready to fight!* She lurched backward, pulling twice on the trigger. The first bullet struck the wall. The second, a stack of books. *Steady,* her father's voice whispered. *Aim for the center of the chest.* The third bullet hit the man in the sternum, but he didn't even stagger. The fourth and fifth bullets punched two holes in his greatcoat, right near his heart. Then she was pulling the trigger madly, the hammer clicking uselessly as the giant thrust out an arm to grab her. His skin was slightly greenish and stitches snaked up the side of his neck. His eyes were cold, unseeing.

She ducked and he snatched her fluttering scarf and pulled, yanking so hard that she was lifted into the air. The scarf unraveled from her neck and she rolled across the marble floor, letting the piece of paper go. She'd landed close to the door.

Something struck her hard in the back of the head. White birds flapped in all directions. No, not birds, she realized as she scrambled to her feet, but pages from a book.

I was almost brained by a book! She nearly chuckled. Then, without a backward glance, she tore open the door and fled into the night.

3

Such a Playful Language

Lime chose not to pursue the young woman. She would not dare return. There was no sign of companions. He had known of her existence; both the librarian and the midwife had mentioned being interviewed by her, but neither had any idea who employed her. The woman's East Asian appearance made guessing the exact country of her origin rather difficult; could it be that even the Chinese were after the same information? It didn't matter. She might alert the gendarmes or her masters, but his work would be long done and he would be back in his hotel room drinking tea and nibbling chocolates.

Typhon continued to lumber toward the door, following Lime's initial command. *Stupid brainless lump*, he thought. "Stop, Typhon," he commanded. The thing turned and its eyes caught the lantern light, giving even Lime a chill. "Come to me." The creature slouched back, a slight drag to one leg. It stood right next to Lime, so close that the formaldehyde stink was overwhelming.

"Stand *there*!" Lime shouted. "There! There! There!" He pointed at a spot a few feet away and Typhon eventually stomped into position. Of all the tools his masters had given Lime, this one was a sledgehammer.

It had taken Lime several months of research and inquiries to thoroughly assess the numerous accounts of monster children, first in England, then Germany, and later, France. The French, he was beginning to believe, were especially prone to storytelling. Nonetheless, Lime had managed to gather those stories and shape them into the truth. Sometimes it had required a few coins, other times more violent means. He had always been gifted at following leads.

At the behest of the Clockwork Guild, he was pursuing the parentage of a young man named Modo; he didn't know who Modo was or why the Guild was so fixated on him, other than the reports that he apparently possessed wondrous capabilities: uncanny strength, a quick mind, and the ability to somehow shift his shape into the appearance of another. Lime had assumed the shape-shifting to be a fabrication, but the more he read and researched, the more he was beginning to believe the stories might be true.

He scooped up the paper Father Mauger had provided and read its contents. It was a signed document granting a nameless child to the church. It included the old residence of the parents and their intended new residence. As they had chosen to fill out the papers instead of simply abandoning the child on the church steps, they were probably religious and unlikely to lie to the church, especially in writing.

The priest had crawled into the shadows. He was the last loose end. But what sort of trouble could he cause? No, he had too much information. Though the other buyers he'd mentioned were likely fabricated in an attempt to raise the price, one could never be certain.

"Father Mauger," Lime said, "please show yourself."

The room was silent.

"Father Mauger," he repeated, "I promise not to harm you. You are more valuable to me alive."

"You promise?" The voice came from behind a desk several feet away.

"I do, Father," Lime said. "*I* will not harm you. That is my solemn vow."

The priest crept out from behind the desk and into the light, what little there was of it. He was pale and shaking with fear. He swallowed.

"Typhon, please vigorously break his neck," Lime commanded.

"But you said you wouldn't harm me!" the priest squawked.

"I won't." Lime shrugged. The joke was an old one. He was surprised how many fell for it. "But Typhon will. English is such a playful language."

4

Through the Window

After his third sleepless night, Modo began to think he was trapped in a reenactment of *Macbeth*, for he was seeing ghosts and hearing screams. Every time he closed his eyes the gaunt featureless faces of his parents rose up. They were crying out in pain, metallic hounds pursuing them. Or they were tied to torture racks.

The nightmares were particularly vexing. Over his lifetime he'd given little thought to the man and woman who'd abandoned him. Now they were popping up in his head, pleading for his help. How dare they? They'd sold him to a traveling freak show. Sold him!

He owed them nothing.

He also knew Colette would be waiting in Paris, sitting alone at a restaurant table. He had cared deeply for her and had taken a great risk in showing her his face. It had turned out badly.

He owed her nothing.

He punched his pillow, sending feathers into the darkness. The truth was he had never shirked any duty, large or small. Yes, his appearance was likely the reason his parents had abandoned him. And it was definitely the reason Colette hadn't been able to say goodbye face to face.

If there was one lesson he had learned from the Rain People of Australia, it was that beauty truly was in the eye of the beholder. They had accepted his ugliness, even seemed to worship him as a god. But the gift the tribe had given him was perhaps the greatest gift of his life: they had looked at his face without reservation and with absolute love. They had seen him for who he really was.

His was not a face that the "civilized" could love. But that was their problem.

Modo sat up. For all their faults, his parents didn't deserve to be in such danger. *It's my task,* Modo thought. *My duty!* Besides, he wanted to prove his parents wrong; they should never have given him up. He pictured himself breaking them out of a jail cell and how they would beg his forgiveness. Faceless and nameless, they still shared the same flesh, the same blood. And that blood was French!

It had been something more than a small betrayal, Mr. Socrates not telling him that the blood in his veins wasn't English. Modo felt weakened by this new knowledge, for he believed that British blood and intellect were what got important things done in this world. He'd been trained to serve

England, in fact had served the country well, and yet, he was not really English.

He stepped gingerly onto the floor. It creaked as he dressed. The thought crossed his mind that he should go directly to Octavia, though it was inappropriate to enter a woman's room at night. He thought of gently poking her shoulder and asking her to make the journey with him. But how could he ask her to both betray Mr. Socrates and risk her life? These were his parents, not hers. And the journey would be easier without her. He had not shown her his face again since their return from Queensland. He didn't want her to see it. She desired a handsome prince; she'd admitted as much. His friendship, of course, she wanted. But not him.

He must go it alone. He stuffed a wallet in his pocket, knowing it held twenty Canadian dollars and enough British pounds to buy third-class passage on a steamer. He slipped a stiletto into his belt. Into his haversack he tossed a pocket lucifer; the electric device had proved quite handy and cast a surprisingly bright light. He also threw in spare netting masks, along with a few trousers and shirts. He would need very little.

He decided to slip out the window. He approached it, wincing at each complaint of the floorboards. He had opened the window several times in the past week, but this time it wouldn't budge. He applied his strength and the wooden frame squeaked noisily. He was strong enough to tear it open, but that would wake up the entire household.

He tiptoed into the hallway and paused in front of Octavia's door, lifting his hand to knock gently, but then lowered it. She would be angry that he'd left without a word, even angrier when she learned he was going to France to see Colette. *You must be your own man*, he told himself.

He stopped at the hallway window, the crescent moon drawing his gaze. He opened the window easily and climbed silently out onto the roof tiles. The pitch was not too steep. Freedom was only a short climb to the ground.

"Are you leaving us, young sahib?"

Modo nearly fell off the edge of the roof. "Tharpa?"

"Yes, it is I."

The words seemed to float in the air, coming from no particular direction. Then he saw his weapons master leaning against the dormer wall, hidden in shadow. "H-how did you know I'd be out here?"

"I have come to know you well over these past fourteen years. Restless sleeping for three nights in the room next to mine has come to mean something. The news of your parents isn't something a young man like you can ignore, and so I took the liberty of nailing your window shut."

"Ah, you know me too well."

"I know your heart." Sometimes Tharpa seemed more mystic than human. "I repeat my question: Are you leaving us, young sahib?"

"No," Modo said, "I was only . . . Oh, all right, then. Yes, I am."

"Ah, then Mr. Socrates wins."

"Wins?"

"We had a wager."

"A wager!" Modo lost his footing momentarily.

"Yes. I said you would not leave without permission. He believed you would."

The very fact that they'd foreseen his departure as though he were as predictable as a windup soldier was most distressing.

"You bet on me?"

"Just a small sum. Do not worry for my financial loss. Now, I suggest you go back through the window. Mr. Socrates awaits you in his office."

Modo shook his head in frustration and stepped back inside the house, followed by Tharpa. It was as though he'd been caught stealing sweet biscuits. *To these men I'm still a child,* he thought. Trudging down the stairs to the main floor, he saw light under the door of Mr. Socrates' office. Tharpa knocked gently.

"Enter."

Modo blinked at the brightness when he opened the door, but strode into the room, holding his head high. Mr. Socrates gave him a tired smile.

"So, you were slinking out," he said.

"I wasn't slinking."

"You were leaving without permission. When I was a soldier, desertion was a capital crime. In India we would tie deserters to the mouth of a cannon and let the cannonball do the rest."

"That's barbaric," Modo scoffed.

"It was. I myself was not in favor of it. It did inspire discipline, though."

"Well, this is not the army."

"No, Modo, what we do is more important than what any company of soldiers does." Mr. Socrates lifted his sterling-silver letter opener—a miniature saber—from the desk. "They are a hammer. We are the surgeon's knife."

"I've not been a knife—or should I say an agent—for some months now. It's clear I'm no longer of use."

Mr. Socrates sighed and rubbed his temples. "What's clear to me is that I have made a mistake."

Modo raised his eyebrows. Had Mr. Socrates ever admitted to a mistake before?

"And what's this mistake?"

"I have let my emotions—my anger at you—get the better of me. You have been trained to a keen edge and you grow bored with inaction. I should have kept you busy with tasks and goals. Instead, a missive from France arrives and its contents stir you up. You become obsessed. That is clear. I must purge you of your obsession."

"Purge me?"

"Yes. I've decided to send you to France."

Modo couldn't stop himself from blurting: "You'll send *me*?"

"Yes. It's just a small assignment, really. I've booked steamer passage for you and Octavia first thing in the morning. I've decided that it's important for us to discover whether you have any living relatives. I have no idea what the Guild or the French would want with them, if indeed they are seeking them. It would take years to train another agent as skilled in transformation as yourself. I suppose our rivals could be looking at the long game. Or they have some goal that I cannot surmise. You are to be my eyes and ears again. Just don't become overly emotional."

"Emotional?"

"Yes. You shouldn't think of the people in question as your parents."

"And who are my parents then?"

Mr. Socrates pressed his lips together, a look of confusion crossing his face. "You don't need parents, Modo. You have done very well with the appropriate guidance and training. A trip to France is your chance to free yourself from the past."

Could one ever be free of the past? Modo wondered. It seemed to slink after him wherever he went.

"Does Octavia know that she's been assigned to this mission?"

Mr. Socrates shook his head. "She'll know in the morning. She'll be pleased to be doing something more exciting than eating croissants in Montreal."

Modo wasn't so sure of that. In fact, when he pictured Octavia and Colette in the same city, a certain queasiness set in.

5

Setting His Mind to the Task

Mr. Socrates stood in his office, slowly spinning a small globe, his fingers tracing the Atlantic, France, the Mediterranean, and India. He'd visited all these places and would do so again in a heartbeat. But here he was trapped in a house in Montreal, like a fox backed into its hole.

With Modo and Octavia gone, he was left with Tharpa, Mrs. Finchley, and the newly arrived Cook and Footman, whom he'd summoned from their hiding places in England. How his great dream of the Permanent Association was shrinking. Yes, he had fellow heads of the Association who had their own agents, but they had sworn to cut off all contact with him and retreat from active duty. It seemed the best course of action until they discovered how the Clockwork Guild had tracked down the location of one of their safe houses.

Despite the retreat, he wished to strike a blow against the Guild. But his special dragoon project at the Pacific naval base was an egg not quite ready to be hatched. No one—not even the Queen or the Lord Admiral—knew of it.

He rang the bell on his desk. A moment later Footman opened the door. The Chinese man was perhaps the best hand-to-hand fighter Mr. Socrates had ever employed.

"Please find Cook and accompany him here. I have orders for both of you."

Footman nodded and gently closed the door.

Mr. Socrates was beginning to fear that he had become too emotionally invested in the boy—no, not boy, for Modo was a young man now, fifteen or sixteen, and as such, rebellious. It was to be expected. *Were you not rebellious with your own father?* he mused. Mr. Socrates had struck out on his own, joining the army at age sixteen and attempting to conquer the world. What he wouldn't give to have that vitality in his bones again.

He lifted the gray photo of his wife from his dresser. He had carried it all these years, had even stowed it safely in his kit bag on his adventures through the Queensland jungle. His memories of her were as faded as the image itself. She had died during childbirth and he had lost his child minutes later, a boy with a weak heart. Mr. Socrates had cradled the dead weight of his son in his arms. The world was a hard place, but when he looked at the image of his beloved he tried to remember he had once been a softer man. Had once felt the pangs of love.

And so what of Modo? The agent had unequivocally disobeyed him. Twice. And yet Mr. Socrates found that he didn't have the resolve to punish him properly. The young man was such a spectacular talent, possessed such an impressive intellect. He had devoured every book handed to him, understood concepts far beyond his age. And his shape-changing abilities made him the greatest asset the Association had ever had.

He didn't want to lose Modo to whatever half-wits had abandoned him. If he'd attempted to prevent Modo from leaving Montreal, the young man was damnably dutiful enough to have tried to rescue his parents himself. Mr. Socrates had no choice but to give Modo the needed support.

And if there was a last secret to be gleaned from Modo's parents, if it was true they'd been located, then it was necessary to keep them from the myriad enemies of England. What havoc hostile forces could wreak if they had their very own shape-changing agent.

If it was the Clockwork Guild that was pursuing Modo's parents, then it was dire news indeed. The organization had constructed a giant of metal and flesh to attack the Parliament buildings, had sailed halfway round the world in a warship more powerful than any other on the seven seas, and had swooped through the Australian skies in a massive airship. Mr. Socrates could not imagine what it would be capable of with an agent similar to Modo.

No, it was better that Modo nip whatever was developing in the bud. He had sent the girl because, despite her smart mouth, she did have a vested interest in keeping Modo alive. And there was no one else he could spare.

He had to discover more about the Guild. He had to be proactive and to strike at its heart, once and for all. Britain was a big target, and the Clockwork Guild must have a large operation to have built such impressive war machines. These things didn't materialize out of thin air. They required foundries, docks, and treasuries jammed full of money.

But where had they been hiding all this money, all the armaments? What country would grant them sanctuary?

Cook entered the room, Footman beside him. Cook had been a pleasure to have in the house; while Mrs. Finchley had been adequate in the kitchen, he was excellent.

"I'm sending you on a hunt for documents," Mr. Socrates said.

"Paperwork, sir?" Cook asked. "Would rather you asked me to charge up some enemy hill."

Mr. Socrates laughed. "It will have to be a hill of paper. And please, before you go, make some of your famous asparagus soup and roast pork with dinner rolls. It would be nice to enjoy that at least one more time."

"It'll be an honor, sir," Cook said. "I won't forget the sweet cream butter."

6

Yet Another Fraudulent Marriage

Octavia laughed as Modo stumbled under the weight of her luggage, bumping the guardrails of the gangplank. He regained his balance and they boarded the SS *Ottawa. Serves you right, silly man,* she thought, *not allowing me to carry even one piece.*

She held the second-class tickets in her hand, wondering if such a lowly fare was a sign that Mr. Socrates was becoming a miser. Or perhaps he wanted to teach them some lesson or other. At least it wasn't steerage. Those poor people traveled like cattle.

Octavia and Modo were led by a gruff steward to a cabin near the aft stairwell. Inside was a bed, a minuscule writing table, and, Octavia noted with satisfaction, a tiny water closet—they wouldn't have to use the public toilet.

"Well, husband, we've been in worse digs than this," she said as Modo closed the door.

"It'll do," he answered. "It needs airing." He went to the porthole and opened it. He was wearing the Doctor's face—that was how Octavia referred to it—one of only a few he had shown her. She found it familiar and distant at the same time. His real face, the disfigured one, still burned in her memory.

"Are you enjoying our second fraudulent marriage?" she asked.

"One marriage to you was enough. A second is a trip through Dante's *Inferno*."

She didn't like his tone and didn't know what he meant by Dante, though the inferno reference she assumed to be something hellish.

"Oh, you will feel the inferno," she promised. "I was far too kind as a wife last time, hiring a drunk captain and scouring the Atlantic as you drifted to certain death in a diving bell."

"I'm sorry, Tavia," he said, "I was just trying to be clever. It's true. I owe you my life for finding me adrift on the ocean."

"You owe me thrice over by my count. And last night you were going to leave without me."

"How do you know that?"

"I heard your exchange with Tharpa."

"Don't you ever stop spying?"

"My window was open. It's not my fault I have such good ears."

He sighed with a huff. "Truth is, I didn't think it likely that you'd go with me. After all, you don't speak French."

"*Au contraire, je suis le tout!*"

"You just said, 'I am a muddlehead.'"

"I did not! *Tu es le muddlehead.*"

She began to giggle, Modo smiled his handsome Doctor smile, and they both laughed.

"Modo," she said when they had caught their breath again, "why don't we watch our departure from the deck? The air would be good for us and our humors."

"Then let us go, dear wife."

He offered his arm and she took it, surprised that he held it all the way up the stairs, as though they really were married. As second-class passengers they had access to the promenade, so they watched as the *Ottawa* left the dock, bound for Liverpool. From there they would board another steamship, headed to Le Havre. It was the quickest route from Montreal to Paris, for there were no steamships that went direct.

Octavia was sad to leave Montreal. For a small backwoods city it had heart, with the Scots, the Irish, even a few English all working for a new life in a new land. And the Canadian French were so different than the French in France. Rougher around the edges and more likely to swear. Of course, she based her judgments of the French on that tart Colette. They had met in Iceland.

All morning, despite the cold, they read under blankets on their deck chairs; at lunchtime, they had chicken sandwiches in the second-class saloon. After their meal, Modo withdrew his handkerchief and wiped his forehead, saying, "I must return to the cabin."

Octavia knew what this meant. He could no longer maintain the visage and shape of the Doctor. These transformations could be held for only a few hours at a time.

"I'll wait here," she said. "I'd like to visit the ladies' saloon. Perhaps there'll be some action there. You know, needlework, gossip, penning morose diary entries."

He managed a smile and bowed, grimacing briefly, then turned abruptly. She recognized the sweat on his brow, the look of . . . of pain, that was it. It actually hurt him to change. And she wondered at his lifetime of changing, of learning to be a chameleon. How much did it hurt him? He had spent so many hours manipulating his bones, his very flesh, all for the service of Mr. Socrates and Britain.

He had once revealed his true appearance to her but had not done so since. She preferred it that way. It had taken all of her willpower to look him in the eyes in the Australian rain forest. She hoped she would be able to do it again but didn't want to be tested yet.

She spent a few hours in the saloon reading *Pride and Prejudice* as the other women played the cottage piano. Back at the cabin she opened the door slowly. Modo was seated by the porthole, wearing his mask. His shoulders and back, so perfectly proportioned as the Doctor, now looked lumpy and malformed. He was staring out at the ocean.

"I have returned, husband," she said jauntily.

Modo nodded. Without taking his eyes off the water, he said, "If you had the chance to see your parents again, would you?"

"No," she answered without hesitation. She sat on the end of the bed. "I'm not as sentimental as you, Modo. Remember, they left me at the orphanage with a note saying *burden*."

"Do you think I'm a fool for traveling all this distance to attempt to save my parents from a mysterious threat?"

"I'd expect nothing less of you. You're far more noble than me."

He laughed. "I can't tell if you're serious."

"I am. And there's always the chance that you have brothers or sisters. That's the one thing I wish to know, whether I have a sister or a brother. You know, someone as clever and quick and handsome as me."

"If it be so, watch out, world!" He smiled, then became serious. "It's good to have you along, Tavia. It feels . . . well, there's no one else I'd rather share this journey with."

"You're not going all maudlin on me, are you, husband?"

"Never!"

"Good. I suggest we dine on the upper deck tonight. As you know, I can eat more than ten men. I plan on making those piano-playing ladies roll their eyes."

7

A Clockwork Mind

In the Central Pacific, on the island of Atticus, Miss Hakkandottir entered the main doors of the Crystal Palace, walking briskly past the saluting guards. She strode into the copper-plated elevator and barked, "Observation deck," at the soldier operating the controls. The elevator rose in swift silence. Despite her dark mood, she found the interior of the palace, viewed through the glass doors, impressive. Her eyes were drawn beyond the twenty-eight-foot fountain to the hundred-foot brass clock that towered over the inner plaza. Its face was a clock within a triangle—the symbol of the Clockwork Guild.

In earlier days it had bothered her that he'd chosen to replicate the British Crystal Palace in Sydenham Hill. The British had built it for the Great Exhibition and had raved about its majesty for more than twenty years now. She would have gladly crashed an airship into it, just to see them all moan and gnash their teeth.

But as this palace had been brought piece by piece to the island and raised to the heavens, it grew into a building that made the original look like an oversized greenhouse. It was beautiful, yes, but more important, it was a hundred times more practical than England's flimsy structure. First off, it was nearly impregnable, made not of glass but of a quartz as impenetrable as any stone. And should there be a siege, its airship dock meant it could be resupplied for months.

The soldier slid open the elevator door and Miss Hakkandottir marched onto the observation deck, a room with translucent white quartz walls that glowed in the sunlight. Round observation windows faced all four directions across the Pacific. The roof was retracted and the sea breeze played with her red hair and gently wafted the six-foot-wide feathered wings hanging from the iron rafters. They were symbolic of some Greek story or other, but since it was an imaginary tale it wasn't important for her to recall it.

The Guild Master stood in the center of the room, surrounded by twelve operators sitting at quadruplex telegraph machines and handing him strips of paper. He was not a tall man, but he was wiry and strong. He wore a gray military uniform without any insignia and simple gold-rimmed glasses. He could easily have been mistaken for a library custodian. Miss Hakkandottir knew much better. He was the greatest tactician in the world.

He pushed up his glasses and continued to read. This was how he kept his eyes on the world. The world! From here he gave orders to agents in all four corners of the earth, purchased metals or armaments, bought and sold stocks, all without a moment's hesitation. He'd formed a perfect plan in his head and each command spoken, each message sent, brought the plan that much closer to fruition.

Miss Hakkandottir didn't know exactly what the plan was, but she suspected it was larger than bringing the pompous British Empire to its knees. She sometimes wondered if it was the Guild Master's intent to control every single government in the world. A foolish thought, for who could exert such power? Even Alexander the Great had failed to accomplish it.

Though the Guild Master was small and lean, Miss Hakkandottir feared him. For his mind could outpace hers a hundred times over. And though his face was pleasant, behind those glasses his eyes were ice. Rarely did he express anything resembling an emotion. Many years before, when she'd been captain of a Chinese pirate ship, she'd first been summoned to his Hong Kong lair. It had stunned her to discover that this nondescript white man was at the heart of a massive criminal organization that ran half of China and nearly all of the opium trade. Even then he had an aura of power.

She knew nothing of his earlier life. He could be Danish or French or Russian. Even British. He had no accent, and she'd lost count of how many languages he spoke.

She waited. It was best not to interrupt him during his work. He wrote a final missive and spoke to a telegrapher in German. Then the Guild Master turned to her.

"Ah, Ingrid." His tone was flat. His eyes, such a consistent dark brown that they appeared almost black, examined her. "You've been so helpful over the years."

She tensed. "Am I about to be retired?"

He let out a dry chuckle. "No. I only experienced a moment of sentimentality. I apologize. I have also been disappointed by your mistakes: the sinking of the *Wyvern* under your command is a fine example."

The loss of that ship had nearly broken her heart. The Guild Master had allowed her to name it so that it truly belonged to her, though he'd expressed some regret that she'd chosen a name that wasn't from the Greek pantheon. How she'd loved those iron decks and perfect guns. But now it languished at the bottom of the Atlantic. All due to Modo. "I should have done better."

"Ah, that is true. My design for the *Wyvern* was tempered by my hubris, though. I should have closed the interior compartments so that a blow to the hull would not have allowed all the lower chambers to fill." Had he just admitted a mistake? She almost fell over. "But don't forget, Ingrid, you lost our henchman Fuhr in the Thames and allowed our mechanical giant to be captured by the British, and you failed to retrieve the God Face in the jungle. A disturbing pattern of losses."

She squeezed her metal hand into a fist. "Am I here to be chastised?"

"No. I seek only to remind you that you are not perfect."

"I am aware of that."

He nodded. "Do you have any thoughts about the disappearance of Mr. Socrates?"

"He is hiding in one of his lavish homes. Do you want me to hunt him down?" The mere thought of it made her heartbeat quicken, her bloodlust rise. How she would love to corner Alan Reeve—or Mr. Socrates, as he fancied himself now—and skewer him right through the heart with her saber. After all, he'd been the one who'd cut off her hand. She should perhaps thank him for that, since the metal hand was her greatest gift. But she still remembered the pain of the blow during the sword fight. He would pay for that.

"You're dreaming of revenge, aren't you?" the Guild Master said. His eyes were measuring her again. "Don't deny it. You get a crinkle between your eyebrows when you dream of such things. I've toyed with the idea of flushing him out, along with the rest of the Association. We shall remove the members of the Association from the board one by one. But at this point, I don't want to take any resources away from Project Hades and the myrmidons."

She'd heard him mention this project several times and she knew that the bodies arriving daily at the island were part of it. She also knew that *myrmidon* meant "warrior"; she'd asked Dr. Hyde for the definition. She was growing tired of having to know every single Greek myth. If only she understood the grand plan behind it all.

"What is it you want me to do?" she asked.

"There've been interesting developments in France. Our search for more—how shall I put it?—flesh is progressing at a satisfactory rate."

"And why do you mention this?"

He paused, deep in thought. She knew better than to ask another question at this point.

"I was going to send you there," he said a second later, "but I have reconsidered. Lime is progressing nicely, and you and your airship skills are needed here. Our assembly of the myrmidons is of the utmost importance."

"You want me to transport bodies?"

"Yes. An airship is faster than boats. I have ordered you a larger airship, though construction will not be finished for three months. We'll make do with our older airships. Soon we'll have more than enough material."

"Is this a demotion?" she asked, then quickly added, "Sir."

He smiled. "No. You enjoy being in the air and your efforts will help the Hades project come to . . . well . . . to life." Another dry chuckle.

"If these are your orders, then I will follow them. But there is little challenge to transporting the dead. Would you prefer I bring them back alive? That would be simple enough. I would need only a dozen or so Guild soldiers. And irons."

"Ah, Ingrid, that is an intriguing idea, but far too time consuming. And I need the extra soldiers here. You may head southwest now—there are materials in New Zealand. I shall contact you en route if your orders change."

"Yes, sir."

Then she left him and made her way to the airship tower near the dock. The *Hera* could make the journey to New Zealand in four days. She commanded her pilot to start the engines and her crew to load supplies. The sooner she was in the air, the better she would feel.

8

Operating on Instinct

Modo sat at a table in the open-air section of Le Grand's café, wondering if his shivering was from the breeze or nervousness. Octavia seemed aloof this morning, though they had shared the occasional word about the weather or how different Paris was from London. She'd said she didn't like the smell of the city and he'd said it was no worse than the Thames. They'd said little since.

Their fellow diners were all engaged in animated conversations. Modo was pleased to find that he understood most of the French he overheard. He noticed too that everyone was very fashionable; he'd never seen such an array of ladies' hats in England. Everything in Paris was remarkably stylish, from the people to their fiacre carriages; even the tables of the café were a fancy wrought iron topped with glass.

He searched the crowd for Colette, expecting her to appear at any moment. He'd decided to shift into what he called the Knight face, the one that she'd seen before, so she'd be able to recognize him.

"I like the Doctor face better," Octavia suddenly said.

"Better than what?"

"Than this one," she said. "It was more sophisticated."

"Well, I'm sorry that I don't look sophisticated enough for your taste."

"No, it's me who is sorry, husband." She didn't seem to be sorry. He could only presume it was the impending arrival of Colette that was responsible for her change in mood. It had been a good journey here. She'd even exclaimed how beautiful Paris was when they first stepped off the train from the port of Le Havre. But since they'd woken this morning she'd been nitpicking. In all his years of education, why hadn't he thought to ask Mrs. Finchley to explain the female mind?

They continued to wait in silence. At a quarter to one Octavia began tapping her teaspoon on the table.

"Must you do that?" Modo asked.

"Ah, sorry, husband. I forgot how jangled your nerves are."

"I am not jangled!"

But he was and he knew it. Had Colette given up on waiting here for him? He'd traveled as quickly as possible after receiving the letter. Of course, she had probably assumed he'd be traveling from England, not Canada.

"Your French mistress is late," Octavia noted.

"She's not my mistress, Tavia."

"Well, you certainly were in a hurry to cross the Atlantic to see her."

"You know why I—"

"Modo, I thought you would be alone," a young woman's voice interrupted him.

Modo and Octavia turned to see Colette standing behind them. She was thinner, wearing a black hat and dress, as if on her way to a funeral. She held a tan briefcase. A colored ribbon tied back her hair, but her eyes had dark circles under them and her cheeks looked sunken. "A pleasure to see you again, Miss Milkweed," she said, her accent clipping the consonants coldly.

"Yes," Octavia agreed with mock geniality, "a most welcome pleasure."

"And it is wonderful to see you, Modo." She grabbed Modo's shoulder with a firm grip, and her voice softened. "It has been far too long since I last set eyes on you."

"It has?" Modo said. "I mean, it's wonderful to see you."

"Are the two of you married again?" she asked.

"Yes," Octavia answered.

"Only for show," Modo added. "Please join us."

Colette walked around them and sat down, waving over a waiter to order coffee. "I've not had fish for eleven months now," she said, laughing. It was, of course, a reference to what she and Modo had been eating on the *Ictíneo* when last they'd met. "Strictly beef and chicken."

"You could do with adding a few pounds," Octavia said, feigning concern.

"I appreciate your suggestion," Colette replied, dusting a few crumbs off the table, "but I like to stay lean and hungry."

She was as beautiful as Modo remembered, and yet she'd lost more than weight—a certain vibrancy, perhaps? Her air of invincibility?

"I avoid fish," Modo admitted, giving her his full attention.

Colette leaned toward him. "Let us get to the matter at hand, shall we? The French secret service is looking for others who are like you, Modo. It is a top priority."

Octavia set her cup of coffee down right between them with a clatter and said, "Who would be leading that search? You?"

"I—uh—am a member of the team."

"So this could just be an elaborate trap to capture Modo."

"It's exactly that," Colette said, narrowing her eyes to slits. "With a snap of my fingers armed agents will sweep down and surround us. They'll haul you, Miss Milkweed, off to jail, cotton stuffed in your snide mouth, and drag Modo to our interrogation rooms on Rue de la Mercy." She lifted her hand and snapped her fingers, drawing the attention of a nearby waiter. She waved him away, laughing bitterly at his confusion. "I do not expect to gain your trust, Miss *Weed de la Milk*. But I do hope that Modo will remember our previous, shall we say, adventures and the pact we made."

"And what sort of pact was that?" Octavia glared at Modo.

"Umm . . ." He looked to the sky and cleared his throat. He scoured his brain for the answer. Octavia was often vexing, but Colette's presence made him doubly vexed. He could barely think straight. "Did we swear to help each other survive?"

"Yes, you remember!" Colette said. "Good. Good. It was

not an oath I took lightly. I come not as an agent for my country, Modo, but as a friend to you. I owe you."

Owe me? For what? Modo was confused. Couldn't she meet his eyes for longer than a few seconds at a time?

"Your parents are living in the country; I've been able to ascertain that much."

Modo's heart sped up and this disturbed him. It was important to keep his emotions in check. "Please tell me what you know."

"I've done a great amount of research, Modo. I discovered accounts of your birth. I even interviewed a witness."

"A witness to my birth?" Modo asked, flabbergasted. "A relative?" Maybe he had an aunt. Or even a grandmother.

"No, not a relative. A midwife. Her name was Marie."

"What did she say?"

"She . . . uh . . . verified that you were born. And that you were . . . well . . . she was affected by your appearance."

Just as you were, Modo thought.

"How can you be certain she was describing Modo's birth?" Octavia asked.

"I am certain—unless there is more than one child with Modo's unusual abilities. How old are you, Modo?"

"My age? I can't be certain. I'm sixteen, at least."

"No, Modo. You're fifteen. Your birthday is November 1, 1858."

"You're only fifteen!" Octavia exclaimed. "I thought you were older than me."

"I'm wiser," Modo snapped. Then he couldn't help himself: he smiled broadly. He had an actual birth date! He'd never once celebrated his birthday. "May I interview this midwife? Was she a friend of my parents? What other information does she have?"

Colette sucked in her lips for a moment and stared into her coffee cup. "I'm afraid interviewing her will be impossible: she's dead. Drowned in the Seine." Modo sat back, dazed, but Colette went on. "And a librarian who was a great aid to me in my research also died, after falling off the roof of the library. One wonders how he got there. And finally, a Father Mauger, who was the records master for Notre Dame de Paris, is also dead."

"Death certainly likes to follow you around," Octavia said.

"Who committed these murders?" Modo asked.

"Two foreign agents, Lime and Typhon. I know for certain they killed the priest. I can only assume they murdered the others. The leader, Lime, spoke English."

"They were British?" Modo asked.

"Well, Lime spoke with an Irish lilt. He seemed somewhat mad: spouting poetry and such, even as I pointed my pistol at him."

"That sounds Irish to me," Octavia said.

Colette set down her cup and tapped a finger several times on the table. "I am certain that they were members of the Clockwork Guild."

"How did you come to that conclusion?" Octavia asked.

"Instinct."

"Instinct? Are we to trust your flighty instinct?"

Colette wagged her finger. "Only one of you was invited,

my dear. And I have learned to trust my instincts. Furthermore, the methods of these killers were more than brutal; one of the hallmarks of the Clockwork Guild."

"What exactly were they searching for?" Modo asked.

"Information about you, my friend. They've retrieved your submission forms from Father Mauger."

"My what?" Modo said.

"The Notre Dame submission forms from 1858," Colette replied.

"Which are?" Octavia said.

"Forms that parents sign giving their children up to Notre Dame. Most just abandon their offspring on the steps, but there are a few who want to officially hand the child over to the church. These papers may have contained valuable information. Shortly after your birth, Modo, your parents changed their names and left Nanterre. The question is for where? And what are their new names?"

"What was my—their last name?"

"It was Hébert. They were potters."

Modo paused. Potters! His parents made cookware? How . . . how normal. He had pictured his father as a doctor or a military officer, something impressive. But a simple potter?

"Well," Octavia said, "since these enemy agents have all the information, are we stuck just twiddling our thumbs?"

"No. There are other French agents besides me who are working on this case. They have put together an index of names and occupations of residents in the villages surrounding Paris. There's a high probability that Modo's parents' new names are on that list."

"Why don't you just go take a look at their list, then?" Octavia asked.

Colette let out a long sigh, and for a moment, Modo thought he saw her eyes become moist. She straightened her shoulders and set her jaw. "I have been discharged from the agency."

Octavia shot Modo a glance.

"But why?" Modo asked, averting his eyes from his colleague. She was too quick to jump to conclusions.

"They considered the *Ictíneo* assignment a failure," Colette admitted, "and no one would believe me about the underwater city of New Barcelona. We don't have submarines capable of diving to that depth. They even insinuated that I was imagining the Clockwork Guild. And they . . . well . . . let us just say I was not always the best agent after that. They no longer trusted me."

"They are wise men," Octavia said.

Colette stood up, as if to leave. Modo stood up too, putting his hand on her shoulder. "Please sit. Octavia, despite her demeanor, wants to get to the bottom of this as much as I. Don't you, Tavia?" He shot her a glance and she gave him a grim nod. "How do we get this information from your former comrades?" Modo asked.

"That's where your spectacular talents come in." Colette's voice was suddenly energized again, the vitality that Modo remembered returning to her face. She placed her briefcase on the table. "I would like you to assume another persona, break into a building, and steal the information."

"Whose persona?" Modo asked.

"And which building?" Octavia added.

"The Deuxième Bureau, our spy agency. And the person I want you to impersonate is Directeur Bélanger, the agency's head."

Modo met Colette's eyes. She was clearly enjoying the shock on their faces.

9

A Slight Skip of the Heart

Colette gave directions to the fiacre driver, then allowed Modo to hold the carriage door for both her and Octavia. The folding roof was open, letting in the warm September sun. As they sat on the cushioned bench, a luxury Colette was extremely thankful for, she pointed out a few of the sights, hoping that her descriptions weren't too forced. *He is here! He is right here across from me!*

The moment she'd seen Modo there had been a slight skip to her heartbeat. He was wearing the face she'd known on the *Ictíneo,* but something about it had changed, or her memory of it was different. She was also surprised that she had difficulty meeting his eyes. She remembered them with utmost clarity. Once, in jest, she had called them soulful, but it was a word she would use again, this time with sincerity. In Paris. She'd been waiting for him for so long, checking at Le

Hôtel Grand every day. As the weeks passed she'd begun to believe her letter had not been delivered.

She had imagined his arrival often, with anticipation and a little fear. What if she broke down again? But, mercifully, that hadn't happened. And now it was as though no time had passed, even though it had been almost a year since their last meeting.

"Enough of this tourist talk," Octavia said. "We need to get to the meat of our visit to your fair country."

"What a . . . pleasant way of putting it," Colette whispered. "Then let us get to the meat." Colette remembered well Octavia's protectiveness of Modo, or rather, her possessiveness—that was a better word. "We are nearly at the bureau."

The carriage turned down the Rue de la Mercy and she thumped brusquely on the side of the car. The driver stopped in front of a tall iron fence. Beyond it was a structure Colette knew all too well. From the outside it appeared to be an ordinary seven-story rectangular building; the architects had taken pains to make it look exactly like a textile factory. In reality it was the very heart of French espionage; from here the bureau's tentacles ran throughout Europe and across the oceans.

Inside those walls Colette had spent far too many hours sifting through paper, searching for clues, taking orders from oafs whose minds worked at half the speed of hers.

"This is the building you will enter, Modo." She spoke quietly so the driver wouldn't overhear. "It is the Deuxième Bureau de l'État-major Général, or in English, since I know Octavia doesn't understand our beautiful language, it means

'Second Bureau of the General Staff.' It is the center of our military intelligence."

"Hmmph." Octavia gave a dramatic sniff. "It's rather plain."

"That is the point." Colette spoke slowly, as though explaining something to a child. "Did you expect a big sign saying *French Spies Inside*?"

Colette was pleased to hear Modo chuckle. Octavia looked out the window. Colette opened her briefcase and pulled out her dossier. "I have a photograph of Directeur Bélanger, though it is ten years old, so you'll have to age yourself appropriately."

Modo examined the photo. "I assume you also have his height, a description of the type of clothing he typically wears, jewelry, his manner of carrying himself, and his personal habits."

"It is all listed in great detail."

"And, while I am Mr. Bélanger, would you like me to reinstate you to your position?" Modo asked, cheekily.

Though Colette enjoyed that he could be so flippant at such a time, she could not imagine working for the agency again. "I am done with them. I do hope your French has improved."

"It is adequate. But there are many other more worrisome and unpredictable matters. For example, Bélanger would know most everyone in that building. Whom do I acknowledge? Which individuals are his close colleagues? There are too many relationships to understand, faces to know on sight. Normally I spend weeks memorizing the interactions of my targets."

"Monsieur Bélanger is—how do you English say?—gruff. He ignores everyone—his wife, his agents. He even kept *le président* waiting for several hours once."

"He sounds typically French to me," Octavia said.

Colette continued. "Your mission will be less complicated if you enter the building at night. Most of the staff are finished by early evening. You'll stride right in and take the papers and return to us with a canary-eating grin on your face. Did I say that right?"

Modo smiled. "Yes, you did!" That face, Colette thought, that face was so handsome and yet she knew what lay beneath it. No, she reminded herself, the beautiful face was the mask.

She managed to return the smile as she handed him the dossier. "First we'll go to a tailor," she said.

"Well," Modo said, "with the two of you picking my clothes I should be the sharpest dresser in all of Paris."

10

The Root of All Evil

It was perhaps the most boring week Mr. Socrates had endured. He'd spent nearly every waking moment in his office ferreting through information brought to him by Cook and Footman in the hope of gleaning some telling detail about the Clockwork Guild's location. Mrs. Finchley would bring him tea and meals, clearing the plates without him even noticing. Tharpa would cajole him into a short constitutional to clear his mind. Data gathering was something Mr. Socrates had always abhorred during his life in the military, but it was a necessary evil of his job. From data came conclusions and from conclusions came action.

A few months earlier he'd have had his team of trusted "ferrets," as he called the clerks who worked for him, sift through the newspapers and documents. Instead, he was reading shipping records, passenger lists, market trends, even patents. He wanted to know the prices of metals and the places where they were being bought. Fools often said that money was the root of all evil, but Mr. Socrates knew better. It was metals. If there was anything that drove the vital mechanizations of war it was metal. First for swords. Then cannons. And finally iron-hulled ships.

He did stop to read the papers: the *Montreal Gazette*, the *London Times*, and the *New York Post*. There were the usual stories of terrible railway collisions, of political campaigns, addresses to Republicans, even an article that graded butter. He paused over a story about bodies disappearing along the Pacific Coast. If he'd had more agents, he might have pursued it further. Most likely it was resurrection men selling cadavers to medical establishments. There was so much to learn about the human body and not enough dead bodies to go around. He set down the paper, and his mind cleared.

In time his boredom grew to excitement, for a pattern was beginning to emerge. A large purchase of metal from Ontario had been made by several companies with Greek names. Did the Clockwork Guild not have a penchant for using Greek names? It was perhaps a reference to the past glory of that civilization. The metal had been shipped to an unknown destination in the Pacific.

He worked even longer hours. He read accounts of metal leaving from Vancouver, from Seattle—and spotted a large shipment three years ago to a Chinese buyer in the Yellow Sea. That piqued his curiosity, for he knew that Hakkandottir had once been employed by the Chinese triads, the pirates and brigands who fought both the emperor and the

British empire. He'd dealt with many of them, Hakkandottir included. He knew she'd not easily give up those ties.

Sixteen years ago he had met her in a sword fight on the deck of a two-masted junk and severed her hand. At the time he'd been pursuing the leader of a triad, someone known only as 489. It was a number from Chinese numerology that referred to the dragon master, the leader. Mr. Socrates had been reassigned to India, but his fellow servicemen had never discovered the identity of that triad leader. Why hadn't it occurred to him before? The elusive 489 could have formed the Guild. The organization did not have the structure of a triad—it was something much larger—but would take the same skill set to control. It was entirely possible.

He remembered the junk, the ship of Hakkandottir's that he had captured. It had been steam-powered, with an engine he'd never seen before.

Was it all connected? *Oh, Alan, you fool. Of course!* Their nest was in the Pacific; as far from British might as possible. Now the only difficulty was to pinpoint exactly where they were.

It became clear what he must do. It was a big world, made smaller by train and steamship. He summoned Cook and Footman. By the time they were standing before him, he was practically vibrating with excitement.

"I'm about to ask the two of you to charge full steam up a hill," Mr. Socrates said.

"I was hoping so, sir," Cook said. "I'm ready, willing, and able. Just point me in the right direction."

Footman only nodded in agreement, but Mr. Socrates was certain he saw excitement in the Chinese man's eyes.

11

The Heart of the Agency

It had been relatively simple for Modo to take Directeur Bélanger's form. Modo had paid for a room in a nearby hotel and rested for several hours. He then removed his mask and composed the face while staring at the man's photograph. Colette had fetched clothing from a haberdashery, while Octavia quizzed him about the upcoming mission. When he emerged, dressed in a dark suit and a long jacket, belt cinched tight, he was amused by Colette's shocked expression.

"*Sacré bleu!*" she said. "You have captured the image of Directeur Bélanger."

"It's a stunning gift, this shape-shifting." Modo had meant this to be lighthearted, but he was suddenly aware that it sounded like bragging.

"*Très excellent* is what it is!" Colette said.

"I prefer when he looks younger," Octavia added.

"Young or old, the disguise lasts for only a few hours, so let us hasten away," he said. Within minutes they were in another fiacre and, shortly after that, had returned to the Bureau.

Despite the plain facade of the stone building, Modo felt as if he were looking at a fortress. The fence was taller than any of the nearby ones and there were several guard stations and plenty of gas lamps, making the courtyard relatively bright. He wiped the window of the fiacre, for their breath had fogged the glass.

Smoke rose from three smokestacks protruding from the roof of the building. In the short time Modo had been watching he'd seen three tarp-covered wagons stop at the gates, present papers, and then continue up to a large delivery door that led into the lower section of the building. Were the tarps hiding arms or stacks of files?

"Are you certain you want to do this?" Octavia asked. "I don't know that we can trust her."

"I do have ears," Colette said.

"I want you to hear," Octavia answered. "This could very well be a trap."

"Why this whole complicated ruse, then?" Colette asked. "If it were a trap I could have agents swoop down on us at this very moment."

"Modo is the strongest man I've ever met. To even stand a chance of capturing him you would need to draw him into your lair first."

For a moment Modo thought Octavia was having him

on, but her face said otherwise. She really was bragging on his behalf. Well, it was the truth. Even Tharpa couldn't beat him at arm wrestling.

"I know you find this hard to believe, but I trust her, Tavia," Modo said as he patted Octavia's hand. "She may have been a French agent, but her word is good as gold, that is one thing I learned on the *Ictíneo.* And I need this information. *We* need it. I believe Mr. Socrates would agree with me."

"There is no time like the present," Colette said. A light flashed to life inside the carriage and Modo was momentarily blinded by it. She'd shone what looked like a pocket lucifer directly at him.

"You have a battery-powered lamp?" Modo asked. "I didn't think the French were so advanced."

"Oh, *la petite lumière*? It is an old technology. The English are not the only ones with batteries." She peered at his face. "It continues to amaze me how much you look like Bélanger. Now, you remember the map I drew for you?"

"I've memorized it."

"Then you will recall that the office you want is in the center of the fifth floor? And that it belongs to Lucien Quint?"

"Yes, of course I do. You need not repeat the instructions," he snapped. Perhaps he *was* getting nervous. "I have the plan in here," he said softly, tapping his skull. "You have prepared me well." He paused. "Both of you."

"Then we shall begin," Colette said. She knocked three times on the ceiling of the fiacre and the driver drove up to the front gates and stopped. Modo opened the door and stepped down onto the street.

"*Sois agressif!*" Colette whispered. "Remember to be gruff. Not your usual polite self."

"Indeed I shall," he replied gruffly, then smiled.

"Take great care," Octavia said. "Don't go running around like a bull in a china shop."

"The two of you are acting like mothers," he hissed, then turned away before either could get another word in. Truth was, he'd be happy to be out of the wagon, away from them.

He strode to the front gate. Behind him, he heard the fiacre pull away.

"*Arrêtez-vous!*" the guard commanded.

"*Arrêtez-vous, Monsieur,*" Modo said, correcting him.

"*Mot de passe,*" the guard said.

"Ashenden!" Modo barked, for Colette had given him the password. The name had no meaning that he could discern, though he found it odd that they used a British surname.

The man nodded and said in French, "Welcome back, sir."

Modo, pleased his appearance had fooled a guard, didn't give the man another glance. He carried on to the main entrance, passing a second guard station. Two hounds growled and their master pulled back on the leashes. "Shut those hogs up," Modo spat in French, then opened the door to the Deuxième Bureau.

He marched smartly down a brightly lit hallway. Of course the French would have electric lights; they liked showing off the latest advances. Modo found this new type of lighting to be garish, not nearly as warm and natural as gaslight. He tried to set aside his worries that the brightness would make it easier to spot any mistakes he'd made in his transformation.

How many papers about England, about Queen Victoria, about Mr. Socrates, about Modo himself would be filed in this very building? If he had hours to spend he could uncover a lifetime of secrets. But there was only one secret that Modo wanted to uncover tonight.

He encountered another agent, who saluted, but Modo just stomped by. A guard at the door to the stairwell also saluted, but Modo didn't even look at him, giving the air of a man in a hurry. He burst into Bélanger's office and closed the door, then immediately exited out the office's back door and climbed the stairs to the fifth floor.

Room 5498 was exactly where Colette's map had indicated it would be. He opened the door and charged in, just as he imagined Bélanger would do. This was a mistake, as he banged his knee on a desk. He cursed and flicked the brass switch for the light. It flickered to life. This room was smaller and bursting at the seams with perfectly piled papers, folders, and files.

He went to the desk Colette had told him about and discovered that the file drawer had been locked. It took him more than a minute to pick the lock with two small pins he had in his vest pocket. He chastised himself for not practicing enough recently. The lock eventually clicked and he pulled open the drawer; all the papers inside had been neatly placed in labeled folders. Ah, the bureaucrats were good at this sort of thing.

He found a thick file marked *Subject Modo: 24601* and began to read its contents. At first there was very little of interest or import, only conjecture on his whereabouts. Someone had seen him in India. India! He laughed. He'd never been to Tharpa's homeland. Then he went back to the drawer and thumbed through several more files, stopping at one marked *Ictíneo/Brunet/Modo.* He opened it and skimmed the pages until his eyes found this: "Agent Brunet insisted that an agent with the code name 'Modo' was able to change his shape and his facial features. Her description led Investigator Quint (47b321) to doubt her sanity, but after several tests by doctors she was certified as sane. Quint searched records in England . . ."

He folded up the page and stuffed it into his pocket. Perhaps there was something else in the file, but it would take days to read through it all. He was here for one file only.

He noticed an envelope had been clipped to the back of the file. Curious, he opened it. Inside were several pages, including a handwritten note in French: "Copies of pages 1 through 8 appear under *Brunet, Colette: 15901.* It is important detail for file *Modo: 24601.* Agent Brunet complains of nightmares and is easily excited. Her discovery of the *Ictíneo* was exemplary, but the loss of the *Vendetta* leads us to conclude that ultimately she failed in her mission. She complains of dizziness and lack of sleep, and when interviewed by the physician she blames this on seeing the face of the English agent Modo, a face she describes as being 'gargoyle ugly.' She has mental fatigue compounded by physical exhaustion, and an extended stay in a sanatorium is recommended. When Brunet is released again, she should be put on light duty only."

Mental fatigue? Blames this on the face of the English agent Modo? Gargoyle ugly? So seeing his face *had* marked her. The deaths of hundreds of her comrades, the weeks spent as a prisoner on the *Ictíneo,* the fight for their lives: these were all hardships, but none were listed as contributing to her illness. It was seeing *his* face. His true and ugly self. *That* was what had broken her. He skipped ahead where three sentences had been underlined:

Brunet has become extremely delusional and is no longer in full control of her faculties. She was sent to Laroque Sanatorium for three months, but the stay did not improve her condition. She was declared unfit for duty and released from employment on July 7.

She'd spent time in a sanatorium! He'd seen the inside of Bedlam, London's most infamous home for the deranged. The people there had been totally cracked. This information threw everything into question. Had anything Colette said so far been the truth? Were his parents actually alive? Was he even French? No, that part was true. Mr. Socrates had confirmed it. And the French agents were looking for his family, so there had to be something to it.

Why was she helping him? Out of pity? Did she feel she owed him?

He put the documents in his jacket pocket. He stole several other papers that he hoped would contain something about his parents. He began to comb through the remaining papers, madly hoping to find his parents' current residence.

The door swung open and a man walked in. "Directeur Bélanger!" the agent exclaimed in French. "I didn't expect to see you in the office this evening."

Modo closed the file drawer with a bang, keeping his voice gruff. "Since when do I report to you?"

Colette had described Quint as thin and pale, and this man fit that description, though the electric lighting made everyone look pale. "Is there something I can help you with, sir?"

"No, Quint. Nothing." Modo kept his sentences short. The more French he spoke, the greater the chance of a gaffe. The agent would know Bélanger's voice well, but Modo had discovered that people would believe their eyes before they'd believe their ears.

"I understand, sir. May I have a few seconds of your time?"

"I'm extremely busy."

"I just need to ask you about the Modo case. I've made great headway on the location of his family. And I have an important request."

"What's that?"

"I would like Colette Brunet to be arrested."

"Brunet? Why?"

"Because, sir, she has betrayed her former position. I have proof she has been continuing to research Modo, even after her removal from the Bureau. She has recently been associating with foreign spies."

Modo stood up. "How do you know this?"

"For the past few weeks I've had her followed."

"Under whose orders?"

"You gave me full rights, sir. Remember? *Do what is necessary* were your exact words."

"Quint! Don't be impertinent!"

"I apologize. But I must tell you that these spies she has been dealing with are British."

"British? Have you proof?"

"Yes, sir." He paused, a glimmer of a smile crossing his face. "You are the proof."

Modo stiffened. How could the man have guessed? "I don't follow."

The agent reached into his coat and removed a pistol from his pocket in a swift, well-rehearsed motion. "I am not Quint. My dear directeur may have hundreds under his command, but he would recognize me. I can't believe you are here, that you have come to us."

"Put away that gun! What madness is this?"

"I've been doing much of the fieldwork on your case for eight months now. I've interviewed Brunet. I've read the reports of your ingenious robbery of the French Embassy in London. Do you think I'd miss the connections? But never did I imagine that you'd walk right into my office."

"Put down that gun at once. You are mistaken!"

"Am I? Then tell me my name." Colette hadn't mentioned any other agents.

"Put away the gun, you fool!"

"Modo, enough of this," the man said calmly, this time in English. "I am impressed. You do look very much like Bélanger, except shorter. I was handpicked and trained by him. He comes from southern France and has a Meridional accent. Oh, and Quint retired three weeks ago; I inherited his office."

Modo sat down and shrugged in a friendly manner. "You've caught me. Congratulations. What is your name?"

"Philip Laroche. It is a pleasure to meet you. I am—how do you English say?—an admirer of your work."

"So what do you intend to do with me?"

"Ah, you'll know soon enough. For now, we have a room where I would like to take you for questioning. It's a quiet place on the lower floor of the building. I'd like to inquire about so many things. This Clockwork Guild, were they just a figment of Brunet's imagination? And the Association de la Permanence that controls you. And this Mr. Socrates. So much to review. You'll be detained for some time, but your favorite meals will be served. We aren't barbarians. It will be a pleasant and polite series of conversations, I promise." He waved his pistol. "Now please stand up or I'll shoot you."

12

Transporting the Dead

In her thirty-seven years Miss Hakkandottir had seen hundreds, if not thousands, of bodies, and now she was carrying load after load of cadavers to the island. She had been at it for weeks. There were three more coffins resting in the car of the airship *Hera* as she floated across the Pacific. This last batch had been from New Zealand, brought to her by desperate prospectors who had yet to find a vein of gold. Another hanged man, his neck stretched too long. Someone who'd died in a mine by suffocation, the body in pristine condition; a particularly happy find. And a man who'd ingested poison after losing all his money in a card game. He was an odd shade of yellow.

Designed by Dr. Hyde, the ice coffins showcased his trademark ingenuity. Despite the humidity and warmth of the Pacific, the ice melted slowly so the bodies stayed cold, in the same state they had been not hours before their deaths.

Miss Hakkandottir's orders had been to keep the coffins closed, but curiosity got the better of her and she opened them one by one to gaze down on the faces of the dead. Hardened, muscular men who had lived tough lives. The combination of gases and cold kept them looking as though they could snap their eyes open at any moment. She mused about what she'd look like when she was dead and shrugged it off. Death was not something she dwelled upon. *Fearlessness is better than a faint heart,* her father had told her many times. The hour of her death had been written long ago; she could not prevent it.

It was an important but boring task to transport the dead back to Atticus. She had brought a total of one hundred and seven bodies to the catacombs of the Clockwork Guild's lair. There was something sacred about the job. She laughed. Sacred? When had she ever been concerned with spiritual matters?

The trip took three days. She did love being airborne. From here she could look to the northwest, where the giant shipyards on the coast of China were building three new steam-powered Guild battleships: the *Hydra,* the *Gorgon,* and the *Medusa.* They would be larger and more powerful than the *Wyvern,* her last battleship. No navy would be able to stand in their way. Each ship would be accompanied by a fleet of steam-powered Triton boats. Any and all nations would tremble at the sight of this armada.

She had no desire to be the captain of a seafaring vessel—

if she was to be captain of anything it would be in the air. No nation—not England, not Germany, and not France—had an airship with as much weaponry and speed as the *Hera*. With enough coal and food she could strike London and vanish into the night before they even knew who had dealt the blow She imagined having a hundred airships at her command. No. A thousand! The stunned world would be in awe of her.

"I want a perfect landing this time," she said to the pilot. The wind was blowing out of the northwest, and the crosswind would make it difficult. "Yes, Captain," the pilot replied. She noted that his hand was steady on the wheel. Good. Only the best of the Guild soldiers could work with her.

Below them three small Triton boats were cutting through the water at a speed she estimated to be over twenty-four knots. In a short time there would be a hundred of them. The Guild Master had some plan or other at play, but he was always so secretive about his grand intentions. Even Dr. Hyde, whom she could twist into whatever shape she desired, had been secretive.

The pilot lowered the flaps and a gust of wind banged the *Hera* against the dock, a rattling that made the ship shudder. It was enough to set Miss Hakkandottir's nerves on edge. She grabbed the pilot with her metal hand, ignoring his pleading, and lifted him over the side of the open car. "You'll land perfectly next time." Then she dropped him. He fell several feet before grabbing onto the landing rope and slipping down it to the ground. She was disappointed. Not even a broken leg.

As the soldiers began unloading the cargo, she climbed down the net ladder and strode across the island to Dr. Hyde's cave. The Crystal Palace glowed with the red light of the setting sun; the dull Pacific evening was still warm and humid. She felt as though she was being watched from the palace's observation deck. That was how the Guild Master wanted her to feel: watched. He had numerous telescopes and would often look down on his creations; perhaps he was watching her right now as she marched up the hill and into the cave. She straightened her shoulders.

Dr. Cornelius Hyde was under the gaslight holding two tubes in almost the exact same position she had left him in nearly a week earlier. The man, old as he was, rarely stopped working. If she were to make a sudden noise, he would startle and drop the tube, smashing it and destroying the contents. She had done that only once before and set his work back by days. So she cleared her throat lightly until he looked up.

"Ah, Ingrid. It is such a pleasure to see you."

"And you as well, Cornelius. I have brought you more fine specimens. How does your work go?"

"It is frustrating, Ingrid. Typhon was such a success. He made me feel I was born to design human beings." He paused. "That does sound somewhat mad, does it not? But I see so much potential!" He lifted his hands to emphasize his point. "Every molecule. Every cell is connected. Run through with veins and nerves. And with Typhon I was able to animate it all using that metamorph's finger."

"Metamorph?"

"Agent Modo. Metamorphs—like a tadpole to a frog

and back again. Remember how he changes shape? There is something about his cells, his blood that, combined with the right electrical impulses, brought Typhon to life."

"You do remember who brought you his finger, don't you?" she said slyly.

"Of course, Ingrid. I praise you every day for that. But I need more of his tissue." He pointed at the empty cages where several chimpanzees had once been. There was also an aquarium on four wrought iron legs. Inside it was a large octopus that had seven arms. "All other attempts have failed. The secret is in his flesh."

"Would you like me to bring him here, piece by piece?" she asked.

"Ah, if only you could. But the Guild Master has promised me more material very soon. Typhon was only the beginning, Ingrid." He grabbed her by the hand. "Imagine if you could live forever in a larger and more powerful body. Imagine that? Never breaking down."

"It would be glorious," she admitted.

"Well, it is within my grasp. We are marching toward a beautiful and brave new world."

Perhaps he was mad, but he hadn't been wrong yet.

13

A Stronger Woman

Inside the fiacre, Octavia's eyes moved from the window to her pocket watch and back. They had asked the driver to stop in an alley, where they had a good view of the whole bureau. The building and grounds looked to be quiet, guards standing upright at their posts. No alarms had sounded since Modo had disappeared inside. The two young women spoke in hushed tones. "Remind me how long you expected this little adventure to last?"

"According to my calculations it would take Modo three minutes to enter the building, four minutes to reach Quint's office, less than a minute to pick the lock. He'll need at least ten minutes to find the proper files. Then he has to retrace his path back to the gate. Therefore, I estimate twenty-five minutes. Though we should allow him at least ten minutes' leeway."

"Thirty minutes have passed," Octavia said. "Any moment now he should be walking out that door."

"You care about him deeply, don't you?" Colette said

Octavia was about to say something glib, but when she saw the look on the young woman's face she fell silent. Colette seemed sad, even forlorn. As much as Colette raised her hackles, Octavia couldn't help admitting, "I do. There are few like him."

"There are none like him," Colette replied. "I've never met anyone I was so willing to trust. Not since . . . well, my father was the only other man I trusted so completely."

"Your father?"

"He died in Japan. Many years ago."

"I'm sorry to hear that."

"It is in the past. And we cannot change the past." Colette rubbed her fingers together nervously. "Though perhaps we can atone for mistakes we have made. Perhaps." Octavia was surprised at the candor in her voice. And the bitterness. "I have no country to serve now. Modo is my country. I must prove that I am worthy."

What kind of statement was that? Was she professing her love for Modo? Or her allegiance? "What do you have to prove to him?"

"Everything," Colette said. "I asked you once, in Reykjavík, if you had seen his face. His real face. You answered no. Has that changed?"

"It's none of your business," Octavia said. Colette's dark exotic eyes, her prying questions, her grip on Modo—these things were becoming such an aggravation.

"Well, I will make it my business. I was coy with you then.

I said it was a matter of confidentiality. But the truth is, I have seen his face. I could not look at him for more than a moment without feeling an absolutely uncontrollable revulsion. He is such a brave man. He is, despite his occupation, guileless. And I rejected him. And it . . . it marked me."

Octavia found herself holding her breath. She'd had a similar feeling when she had seen Modo's real face. It was so different from what she had expected. So twisted. So raw. And, perhaps, not what he deserved. He was such a grand young man that he deserved to be beautiful.

"I too have seen it," Octavia admitted.

"And did you look away?"

"I did not." She remembered that night, that moment, in the Queensland rain forest clearly. Every cell, every nerve, every instinct had been telling her to look away. Such ugliness. She'd wanted to touch his face, knowing the pain he'd felt his whole life, but could only put her hand on his shoulder.

Colette grabbed Octavia's hand and squeezed it. "You are a much stronger woman than me," she whispered. "You are so very brave. I could not look. I failed him. It is as simple as that. I am not accustomed to failure. I do not accept it."

"So how do you reverse this failure?"

"I must admit, I do not know. Will he ever accept me as, well, as a friend? Will he accept my loyalty? He is my country. My country. Just being around him. You know what it is like. I envy you." She paused. "He must love you, you are so beautiful."

"I—I don't know."

They were silent. The horses snorted, and the fiacre creaked as the driver stirred in his seat, perhaps shivering in the cold. He would wonder what they were doing, but they'd been careful to cover their faces when they hired the carriage so that he wouldn't be able to identify them later. Only Modo had been visible, and he, of course, would soon look completely different.

Did Colette really see him as her country? Did that mean she would fight for him? Octavia didn't understand her own feelings. In her own way she too had turned from Modo's face.

"It has been forty minutes," Colette said, her voice steady now. "I fear that something has gone awry."

"What do we do? We don't have an alternate plan."

"We cannot charge in there. Modo is a brave and clever man. He'll have to find his own way out. And once he does, we will be here to rescue him."

14

The Strength of Seven Men

"You'll open the door to the office and proceed down the hall," Laroche instructed.

Modo nodded and gave the French agent a friendly smile, one that he hoped would be disarming. He nearly chuckled to himself, as *disarming* was exactly what he had in mind. Laroche was holding the gun in an easy manner that indicated he was completely comfortable with the weapon. That was dire news. Modo stood slowly, opened the door to the office, and began to walk down the empty hallway.

"Good, good work," Laroche said, as though encouraging a child. "Now, please stay five paces in front of me. We will go to the end of the hall and turn left."

Modo did as told, judging the distance of the man behind him by the sound of his footsteps, picturing the gun at his back. Laroche was no fool and had been well trained—

he would not come within striking distance. The chance of turning and quickly knocking the gun from his hand was extremely low and would most likely result in several bullet holes in all the wrong places. Modo glanced around for something he could throw.

"Please look straight ahead," Laroche said calmly. He spoke English without an accent, indicating that he had worked in the field for a number of years. "I assume you are searching for an object to use as a projectile. I should inform you that I won the bureau marksmanship competition seven years running."

"Recently?" Modo asked. "Or was that in your younger years?"

The man laughed again, a pleasant sound. "Well, it was some time ago, I admit that."

He was gray-haired, yet young enough that he might have only recently been assigned to a desk. Perhaps that was why Colette hadn't mentioned him. Or was it that she didn't have control of her mental faculties? What other major details had she missed?

"Is it true that you're as strong as ten men?" Laroche asked.

"Only seven men," Modo answered. "Ten French men, perhaps."

Laroche laughed. "You mock me, but I know that you are French too."

"But British by education." Modo was surprised to hear Mr. Socrates' pronouncement come out of his own mouth. Maybe there was some truth to the old man's words. How

Tharpa would be shaking his head at him now. Falling into the hands of the enemy. Or, at the very least, suspicious allies.

"Please open the stairwell door and proceed down the stairs."

The offices they had walked through were deserted and so was the stairwell. That, at least, was in Modo's favor. He could jump down the stairs and flee. Laroche might get off two shots. Of course, at such close range he wouldn't miss. Modo decided to walk slowly down the stairs.

"A bit faster, please," Laroche said. "I'm so looking forward to our conversation. Your disguise is almost impeccable. I am extremely impressed."

"I'll make a note of that in my diary."

They crossed a landing, then continued down more stairs. Light appeared beneath each door they passed; the agency was busy this evening. Soon they were on the main floor. The steps leading down into the basement and the walls around them were made of stone, like a real fortress.

A lone light cast fractured beams across the stairs. In the shadows it might be possible to make a quick attack that would give Modo the extra seconds he needed. He listened, not daring to turn. Before he could decide on the best course, the metal door at the bottom of the stairs scraped open and two burly men stepped through it. They looked up and were just beginning to salute Modo when instead they reached for the pistols at their hips.

"Halt," Laroche said in French. "This is not as it seems. This man is an impostor. A prisoner."

"Listen carefully," Modo said calmly, also in French.

"Draw your weapons and shoot Laroche. He has captured me and turned against France. He is a traitor."

The guards' hands were frozen on their guns. One moved slightly, making the keys on his belt jangle. "Shoot him! That is an order!" Modo barked.

The guards drew their guns. Laroche fired, his bullet sparking off the stone wall, making the men duck. Modo smashed his way between them and hurtled through the doorway. There were more rows of desks and several hallways. A collection of French spies looked up from their paperwork, mouths gaping, clearly alarmed by the pistol fire. He dashed past them, shouting, "Intruder! Intruder behind me! Bar the door!"

He chose a hallway, sped to the end of it, and turned awkwardly down another. A shot rang out, knocking a painting off the wall. Even in his mad running he was impressed that they had artwork hanging in the bureau. There was an uproar behind him, but he couldn't make out a word of it, except that Laroche was swearing at such a volume that his voice rang clearly above all the others. Modo flew by a row of occupied cells. Some prisoners were in rags, looking as if they hadn't seen the sun for years; others were in dapper gray jackets, as if they'd been arrested while dining.

A way out! There had to be a way out! He was beginning to feel like a trapped rat. *Get me out of here now!*

He took a deep breath. *Calm yourself.* It was Tharpa's voice—he was always there in the background. Modo pictured the front of the building. There had been loading doors that led to the underground level. They were on the west side, so he veered to the left, down a narrow hall, and plowed through the door at the end, knocking it off its hinges.

He found himself in a giant storage room. Crates stood along several walls; one lid had been pried off to reveal a collection of guns. Modo recognized them as chassepot rifles, the main armament of the French forces. He could use one to fight his way out, but he'd be surrounded and shot in the space of a few minutes. Stealth was still the best option. He passed another crate jammed with ceramic dolls, of all things. What purpose they served he couldn't imagine.

At the end of the room was a ramp leading to the loading doors. When he reached the top of the ramp, he discovered that the doors were locked and barred. He put his back to them and strained, swearing and pushing until the bars snapped and the doors flew open. He charged out into the dark shouting, "*Intrus! Intrus!*" He couldn't think of anything else to say. His French was failing him.

A siren sounded, screaming from the top of the building, then the barking of dogs; the guards had let loose the hounds. He ran past the nearest guard station and the dogs turned their snouts toward him and leapt into action.

Behind him, from the upper floors of the bureau, someone used a voice trumpet to shout, "*Fermez les portes! Fermez les portes!*"

They were going to close the gates! He was still fifty yards from the exit. He could see the guards swinging the gates closed. He was sweating madly now, his hair disheveled. They'd shoot him before they even recognized him as Bélanger.

"*Arretêz-vous!*" a guard shouted. "*Arrêtez-vous!*"

"*Je suis Bélanger! Je suis Bélanger!*" Modo repeated as he ran full speed down the lane.

But the guard at the front gate raised his rifle and pointed it directly at him, forcing Modo to stop and wait for the hounds that would tear into his flesh at any second.

15

Mad Horses and an Englishwoman

The siren sent a shiver down Octavia's spine; the barking of dogs doubled her fear. She stared out the fiacre window but could only see the guards running back and forth across the courtyard. "Something has gone dreadfully wrong!" she said.

Colette shoved open the door and shouted, "*Allez vers la porte!*" The fiacre began to roll down the street toward the gates, but it was clear from the carriage's slowness that the driver was apprehensive. Colette banged her fist on the ceiling. "*Dépêchez-vous!*"

The fiacre picked up speed, then slowed again as they neared the gates. Octavia spotted a man running across the courtyard, dogs pursuing him. It was too dark to tell if it was Modo, but who else could it be?

"The driver's a white-livered muffin face," she muttered. "I'll jaw with him."

She pushed open the door, and without so much as a glance at the cobblestone street below, in fact with a joyous beating of her heart, she grabbed onto the top rail, climbed the side of the carriage, and plopped down next to the driver. "*Sacré bleu!*" he exclaimed. She would have laughed at the look of shock on his face if she wasn't in such a desperate hurry.

"Through the gates!" she shouted, pointing madly at the bureau gates. "*Donnez la porte!*" She didn't know if those were the right words. "Through the gates right now!"

"*Non! Non!*" he shouted back.

"Well, off with you, then!" She gave him a shove. He tumbled from the driver's seat and bounced along the street. Octavia grabbed the reins and shook them, shouting, "Go! Go!" She had only a thimbleful of experience with horses, but she knew they answered to the whip, so she grabbed it from the holder and snapped it above their backs.

The man who'd been fleeing was now standing about twenty yards from the gates, two soldiers pointing rifles at him. Another soldier was holding a pair of hounds by their leashes as he approached the man from behind.

Octavia turned the fiacre toward the gates. The horses had worked themselves into such a frenzy that they were frothing at the mouth. She began yelling, "Mad horses! Mad horses!"

Then Colette shouted out, "*Ces chevaux sont fous!*"

The horses smashed through the gates, knocking two guards out of the way. "Sorry, sorry!" she shouted. Colette kept yelling *"Ils sont les chevaux fous!"* The guards were so taken aback that they didn't think to raise their guns.

Octavia turned the horses, and as the guards scattered, she pulled up right in front of Modo. She would have paid a thousand quid for a painting of that moment: his eyes wide, mouth hanging open in shock. She pulled back on the reins and let out a laugh, slowing the horses and turning them so that Modo had time to leap through the open fiacre door. She yanked hard on the reins to circle back toward the gate.

They were heading straight for the fence! The hounds had been released and were nipping at the hooves of the horses, causing them to kick and buck. One gave a hound a good kick and he rolled away; a second hound was soon outdistanced as they began to gallop again. Octavia brought the horses parallel to the gate as she urged them to gallop harder. They were going with such speed that she worried the carriage would shake apart.

Behind them orders were shouted. A bullet hit the back of the driver's seat and split the wood. Octavia laughed. *As mad as the horses*, she thought. Then the fiacre was through the gates and bouncing down the cobblestones. She laughed again when she thought about Modo and Colette rolling around in the cabin; soon they'd be scrambled eggs. She raced down the empty streets, turned sharply left, then right, then left, having no idea where she was going, only wanting to get as far from the bureau as possible.

"You can stop now!" Colette shouted through the window after several more minutes.

Octavia pulled on the reins, but the horses didn't obey. In desperation, she yanked so hard that one rein snapped.

"They've gone wild!" Octavia shouted to Colette. The horses were still frothing, their excited frenzy turning to fear. They wouldn't stop whinnying as they galloped even faster through the night.

"I said stop!" Colette yelled. "Stop!"

"Easier said than done," Octavia shouted back. She yanked on the remaining reins, digging her feet into the driver's box. Another rein snapped and the horses veered to the right. She had lost all control. The carriage was already off the road and bumping along the sidewalk, missing lampposts by inches. They brushed against a wall and a wheel was knocked from the fiacre.

"Jump!" Octavia shouted. "Jump for your lives!" And she leapt, aiming for the straw piled at the edge of the street, landing hard and rolling. She was on her feet again immediately, pleased she hadn't brained herself. The carriage had already careened down the street and was breaking into pieces as the horses dragged it out of sight. Momentarily she thought her companions were still inside, but then she saw something move in the gutter. It was Modo! He was helping Colette to her feet.

"This way," Colette said, gesturing.

Curious men and women, alarmed by the noise, were opening windows and stumbling out of doors, rubbing the sleep from their eyes or shaking the drink from their heads. Colette grabbed Modo and pulled him down an alley, Octavia a few steps behind. They ran, twisting and turning up ever-narrowing alleys, until Octavia felt her heart would burst. Finally Colette led them into an abandoned building and they stopped to rest next to a stinking cistern.

"Remind me never to let you drive again," Modo said.

Octavia laughed. "You should be thanking me. Not that I'm keeping count, but if I were, that would be the fourth time I've saved your life."

"I had the situation under control."

She chortled.

"Well, perhaps I am thankful," he admitted, between panting breaths. "However, you did come within inches of running me down."

"Did you get the documents?" Colette asked.

"I managed to take several, but then I was interrupted by someone: a man named Laroche."

"Laroche? Has he been assigned to your case now?"

"Yes."

"He's a good agent. Very thorough," Colette said.

"Far too thorough; he saw through my disguise. We had a pleasant conversation and a struggle, and then I escaped." He patted his bulging pocket. "I do hope the answers we seek will be found in one of these pages."

Colette smiled with anticipation. "We'll go through them as soon as we reach my apartment."

Modo shook his head. "No. Laroche said they've been watching you for several weeks. We can't go there. We'll need to find some other shelter. Any suggestions?"

"Obviously we can't go to a hotel. Nor would the home of my mother be safe. No, they'll have eyes on all those places within the hour."

"We need a safe spot for just a night," Octavia said. "A place where we can read the documents and sleep."

Colette snapped her fingers. "I know the perfect location to hide."

16

Sanctuary

Modo ducked behind a half-collapsed wall, out of sight of Colette and Octavia, and struggled to change his shape back to the Knight. He was exhausted, and switching to another form was only going to make it worse. But if he walked around Paris with a netting mask on he'd be easily remembered by any passersby or gendarme.

When he was done he joined his companions. They both gave him a long look, as though searching for imperfections. "Good, good," Colette said, but he sensed disappointment in her voice.

She turned on her heel, leading them out of the ruined building and down an alley that opened onto a wide street. Several feet away was a fiacre stand, not much more than a shed painted black; a place for a driver to warm himself.

Colette grabbed Modo by the elbow and marched him up to the stand. She knocked on the side to wake the driver, a white-haired man who sat with a blanket of open newspapers over his legs. He shook the papers off and stood up. Without a word, he climbed into his fiacre.

Colette elbowed Modo and whispered, "Tell him to take us to Notre Dame Cathedral."

"Really?" he asked. "Why?"

"Give the instructions. He will expect them to come from the man."

Modo gruffly told the driver their destination and they climbed inside. It began to rain softly and his heart went out to the driver, though the man had likely been through much worse. The window was fogged and spattered with droplets; it was hard to see the outside world, as though they were traveling underwater.

"Shouldn't we worry about the driver identifying us?" Octavia asked.

"The gendarmes won't post our descriptions until tomorrow," Colette replied. "The afternoon paper may publish them, but we'll be gone by then."

"Why are we going to the cathedral?" Modo asked.

"It is a sanctuary," Colette said.

"We won't find sanctuary from the bureau there," Octavia said.

"I do not expect true sanctuary, but I know the building. There are places to hide if only for a night, and if we need to escape quickly it is easy enough to dive into the river. Let us hope it does not come to that."

"Once we're there, what next?" Octavia asked.

"We will make our decision at the cathedral. You seem to think this is all my fault."

"It was your plan to enter the bureau," snapped Octavia.

"Modo, how do you work with such a viper?" Colette asked.

"Very carefully," Modo said.

They glared at him and he imagined them both slapping his face at the same time. He snickered. A moment later they were laughing too.

"The church will be as safe as anywhere," Modo said finally. "No one would expect us to go there."

The fiacre jostled down the street. When the rain let up, Modo could see that the city planners hadn't been stingy with the gas lamps; the city really was a "city of light." The buildings were just as close together as those in London, but they were more colorful and better kept. The night air certainly wasn't as foggy.

After forty minutes they crossed a stone bridge onto an island on the Seine. The fiacre passed a large building lined with pillars and countless windows. "Is that Notre Dame?" Modo asked.

"*Non*, that is Hôtel-Dieu de Paris, a hospital."

The fiacre stopped and Modo got out, taking Octavia's hand and then Colette's, to help them to the ground. One had to keep up the pretense that they needed help. He gave the shivering driver five francs and bid him goodnight. When the fiacre moved on, Modo found himself standing in a small cobblestone courtyard, and right in front of him, blocking a good number of the evening stars with its massive size, was

Notre Dame de Paris. The red quarter moon lit the stained-glass windows and the stone goblins that crouched along the side of the building.

He had an overwhelming sense that he had stood on this very spot before. It was impossible for him to have any memory of this place; he had been an infant when he had been brought here by his parents. Perhaps it was the French blood in his veins that made him feel this way. Then he recalled how often he had read *The Hunchback of Notre Dame*—far too many times—and imagining that a mere book could make a place seem so familiar, he shook his head and laughed.

"Why do you laugh?" Colette asked.

"No reason," he said, feeling his love of the book was a private matter. "Where exactly shall we hide? I do need to rest. Any moment now I'll collapse from exhaustion."

"Follow me." Colette led them to a side door on the east wall of the church and they quietly crept inside. It was dark, but Colette grabbed Modo's hand and guided him through the pitch black. He in turn held his hand out to Octavia. Hers was warm.

Colette's eyes seemed to adjust much faster than his, for she was leading them past pews, around pillars, and up a set of winding stone stairs that were only dim shapes to him. Their footsteps sounded impossibly loud, as did their breathing. Even the thudding of his heart pounded in his ears, as if the church were amplifying his heartbeat. But the higher they climbed, the more comfortable he felt.

Colette opened an iron grate door and they were hit by the cold. They crossed an open-air walkway lined with gargoyles who vigilantly watched over Paris. The lights of the city were far below, as though the stars and the earth had reversed themselves. They were nearing one of the bell towers! Modo was certain of it, even though the way ahead of them was dark.

Colette pushed open another iron door, into a dark room. It was warmer, at least, but Modo shivered when he heard the fluttering of bat wings above him. Somewhere in that darkness were the bells of the church.

"We're safe here," Colette said, patting Modo's hand before she let it go. "Emmanuel will watch over us."

"Where is here?" Octavia asked. "And who is Emmanuel?" Modo had not yet let go of her hand.

"We are in the southern bell tower," Colette explained, "and Emmanuel is the bell above us."

"How do you know the way so well?" Modo asked.

"As a youth I explored," she said. "It was a game I played, to hide from the priests and my father. He would bring us here every Sunday. I would do my—what do you call it?—*sneaking* during the services."

"So began a lifetime of sneaking," Octavia noted.

Colette clicked on her petite lumière and Octavia let go of Modo's hand as though she'd been caught with hers in a sweet biscuit jar.

"Now, let us have a look at those documents."

Modo pulled the crumpled mess from his jacket and smoothed the papers out on the floor. Colette bent over to examine them, but Modo covered them with his hand. "There were documents about you, Colette."

"Oh," she said. "And what did my kind bureaucratic friends have to say?"

Modo cleared his throat. "There was a report on your mental faculties, including a description of your stay in an asylum."

"Oh, that," Colette said. "Yes, I *rested*, as they like to say." But she wasn't quite able to make it sound inconsequential.

"She was in a madhouse?" Octavia said. "We've been following a madwoman around on a merry chase?"

"The proper term is *sanatorium*," Colette said indignantly. "I was put there against my will. I—I really didn't need it. They wanted my job. My desk. My soul."

"Soul?" Octavia echoed.

"Everything," Colette hissed. "Everything I've fought for! They've taken it all away."

She was shaking. Modo placed his hand on her cheek. "I've been inside those so-called madhouses," he said. "Not everyone there was mad."

"No. Not everyone," Colette agreed, "though the man who believed he was Jesus Christ and Napoleon was certainly unhinged."

"Our debt is paid," Modo said. "Not that I ever thought you owed me."

She shook her head. "It is kind of you to say so, but it is far from paid."

"Well," Octavia huffed. "If you two lovebirds are done we had better read these files or nothing will be solved or paid."

Colette flipped through the pages. "Conjecture upon conjecture. Useless agents! And, wait—" She picked up a page, her eyes flitting back and forth across it. "No, my apologies, there is nothing."

"But there must be *something*," Octavia said. Colette

gathered up the documents and held them out to Octavia, her eyebrows knitted in despair. "I can't read French, you know that."

Modo took them and leafed through, trying to hide his desperation. He used his pocket lucifer to study every page carefully. "I was interrupted," he said. "If I'd had more time, I might've found something of use."

"Then we've come all this distance for nothing," Octavia said.

Colette sniffed. "We cannot stay in Paris, that much we know. Perhaps we should visit Nanterre—we may find others who remember your parents, Modo."

"But that will take days," Modo said. "And the Deuxième Bureau will expect us to go there. They will have eyes everywhere."

"I am aware of that. I suggest we sleep. Perhaps in the morning an answer will come. We will want to leave before sunrise."

Modo sighed and nodded. They gathered what soft things they could find—they were lucky enough to discover a few cloth sacks—and made their beds on the cold stone.

17

More Meat, Please

Lime, his pistol and knives hidden by a greatcoat, strode past the medieval ramparts that surrounded the outskirts of Montreuil-sur-Mer. The hut he was searching for was along the road to Étaples, if the drunks in the town pub could be believed.

The town lay on the banks of the Canche river and Lime hated the place. He had grown up in the squalor of Kuala Lumpur, the son of an Irish merchant. It was a small settlement, made ugly by the tin mines that scarred the muddy rivers and lush countryside. He had embraced that ugliness; things were meant to be scarred. As a consequence he hated anything picturesque and perfect. Montreuil-sur-Mer brought out that loathing. Another perfect French town.

His mute companion slouched a step behind him, eyes dead as ever. *Typhon.* Lime disliked the beast's name. It should have been Grunt or Lump or Dunghead. But it had been named Typhon, and that was the only name the sack of flesh and muscle responded to. Oh, how the Guild Master loved his word games and his Greek mythology. Lime loathed the Greeks.

Lime had spent the first three days in town looking for Monsieur and Madame Hébert. The French townspeople had begun to all look the same. And no one had any memory of potters with the last name Hébert. But there were many potters in Montreuil—half the population. He'd bought their wares, spoken with them, and uncovered nothing. He took pleasure in smashing the bowls and plates in the fireplace of his room at the hotel.

The first potter he visited was the right age to have been Modo's father, but he'd never been married. The second potter and his wife had ten squalid brats running around half naked; the mother was too young to have given birth to Modo.

Every street Lime explored, Typhon slouched behind him. Why the Guild Master had sent the beast with him was obvious. Its brute strength was beyond any Lime had ever witnessed. And as far as he could tell, the thing was indestructible. Mute and dumb as a stone, with the occasional glimmer of intelligent light in its eyes.

They approached the hut and he commanded Typhon to stand a few feet back. The size and extreme ugliness of the monster was helpful for intimidation, but not so helpful when one needed to appear friendly.

The door creaked open and a gray-haired woman poked her head out. "May I help you?" she asked in French.

He guessed her to be fifty-five, a little too old to have had a child fifteen years ago.

"Are you Madame Hébert?" he asked.

She shook her head. "*Non,* Lambert. I do not know an Hébert."

"So you have never met a potter named Hébert?"

"I have not."

Typhon let out a rumbling grunt and the woman looked behind Lime and went pale. Leave it to the monstrous lump of flesh to make a noise now!

"My brother has a simple mind," Lime said, "and he was disfigured at birth."

She continued to stare in fright. "Disfigured at birth? Is he an abomination?" She crossed herself. "Cursed by the devil?"

Lime laughed. "No, only cursed with an abundance of ugliness."

The woman did not smile back. Instead, she crossed herself again. Lime glimpsed a man with reddish-gray hair at the table, his back to them. Then the door closed.

"Thank you," Lime said to the door. Another dead end.

He turned and walked down the edge of the road. The leaves in a tree rustled, a bird chirped. The frost would take care of them soon enough. A moment later he realized that Typhon was missing. The beast's brain was useless gray sludge. He turned to see Typhon standing in the same spot as before. "Follow me, you mud-headed dunderbuss!" he shouted. It had been one of his father's favorite curses. The beast didn't move. "Follow me, Typhon." The monster trudged behind him. Such a literal creature.

They returned to the inn and he asked for three roast hens to be delivered to his room. Once inside, he laid his greatcoat on the wooden chair, knives clicking together, and sat on the bed to gather his thoughts. "Sit beside the hearth, Typhon," he said, and the man sat on the floor and stared straight ahead, shoulders against the wall, legs stretching halfway across the room, his feet bumping a bowl that Lime had been using to water the beast. Lime was impressed by his size. Even his hands were thrice the length and width of a normal man's, except for the tiny pink finger on his right hand. It was so different from the rest of his grayish-green flesh.

Ah, the science that had brought the creature to life, that made it walk and grunt, he did not understand. Dr. Hyde did, of course, and perhaps the Guild Master did too. Lime didn't care how it had been created as long as it obeyed orders.

He was becoming convinced that Modo's parents were not in this town. It had been fifteen years; they could easily have moved anywhere. How many potters could there be in France? He was at a loss as to where to look next. Perhaps he shouldn't have killed that priest. After all, Mauger may have had other documents. Or the midwife. She might have been able to recognize Modo's parents. He'd been too quick to kill. Again. But what was done was done.

There was a tentative knock on the door. Lime unlocked it, letting in a pale, dark-haired chamber boy who carried a large brass platter with three cooked hens surrounded by roasted vegetables. "Set them there." He pointed to the table. The boy did so and left without a word. Lime began eating, meticulously cutting the flesh from the birds with one of his own knives. The birds were still pleasantly steaming. The carrots and potatoes were delicious. At least the French knew how to cook.

He heard a thump behind him. He glanced over his shoulder. Had Typhon moved? The monster was in the same place. Lime finished the first bird, then set the plate of scraps next to the creature. It stared at the food. "Eat, Typhon," he commanded, and Typhon leaned over and began to devour the remains of the hen, bones cracking and crunching between his large teeth. He left the vegetables.

Lime returned to the table and the remaining hens. So where were the Héberts? Had they died? Emigrated? That wasn't beyond possibility. The French were as adventurous as the English. Perhaps they'd moved to India, to Africa, even to America. He banished the thought; he didn't want to spend months sorting through passenger lists.

"More meat," a voice rumbled.

Lime shuddered and looked up from his meal. The monster had spoken and was looking directly at him with those horrible eyes.

"Did you say something?" Lime tried to keep his voice steady.

The monster lifted a foot and stamped once, the floorboards shaking. "More meat," he growled.

So it could speak! Could it think? If so, he couldn't just let it order him around. It needed to know who was in charge.

"Ask nicely," he said.

"More meat . . ." The thing paused, struggling to find the right word. "Please."

Lime carried the last hen over and watched it disappear into the maw of the creature. Then it downed the bowl of water, splashing half of it across its chest, and closed its eyes.

"Yes, you sleep, my pretty one," Lime said quietly, staring at the creature from several feet away.

In time, too much time, he too fell asleep, clutching his gun under his pillow.

18

Eyes That Are Blind

Modo turned his back to Octavia and Colette and let his natural form return. At this stage of his transformation there was little pain; this was where his body was meant to be. When Modo was a child, Mr. Socrates had once given him a hand mirror and let him take his first real look at his own face. He had stared in horror. Mr. Socrates then said, "You are deformed. You are ugly. But remember this day, Modo. It's the day you learned that you've been given an incredible gift. Your unsightly countenance may seem unbearable now, but because of it, the world will always underestimate you." Modo had been five years old.

He was no longer troubled by people underestimating him, nor did he fear the horrified glances of strangers. Who cared about them! No. But the fact that Octavia and Colette couldn't stand to look at him. Ah, that seared.

He had grown more comfortable in his hunchbacked body. Any time he changed into one of his many personae, his skin was itchy. When he had been training, Mrs. Finchley used to slap him lightly with a wooden ruler if he scratched. Habits such as scratching drew attention; spies should not have noticeable habits.

He slipped on his mask so he wouldn't frighten the two women if he rolled over in his sleep. Not that there would be much slumber. They were certainly in a tricky situation. No matter how hard he focused, he couldn't figure out how they would find his parents. By now Lime and his companion would be well ahead of them.

Finally, he stood and slowly wandered around.

"Are you leaving us?" Octavia whispered.

"No," Modo said, "I need to walk out my aches. If I'm not back in half an hour, look for me."

"I'll send the hound," Octavia said, gesturing toward Colette, who seemed to be asleep.

Modo found he could see quite clearly in the dim light. He passed through an open door and into what appeared to be a storage room. There were old pews up here; imagine hauling them up all the stairs. He sat for a few minutes, rubbing his head, then spied an open doorway on the other side of the room.

The next chamber was strangely warm. Modo stood in the center of the small room. It slowly dawned on him just what he was seeing, and he grew numb with shock. He had assumed the shadows along the walls were rectangular crates, but now he could see they were cradles. Wooden rattles sat along the ledge beside each one. He stepped over to the nearest cradle and gasped when he saw eyes peering back.

In a moment he recognized that they were the glass eyes of a ceramic doll. Good Lord, it was a nursery! Way up here? A hearth had been bricked into the exterior wall. This was a place where abandoned infants had been raised.

He touched the blanket, so carefully tucked around the doll. Each cradle held a ceramic child, all neatly tucked in.

Was I once here? thought Modo. Here, up high, away from the eyes of the parishioners.

"Who walks my halls?" a voice whispered in French. "A ghost?"

Modo stood perfectly still. Someone else—a man—was in the room, but he couldn't tell where the voice had come from. "Speak," the man said softly. "Please speak."

His pleading loosened Modo's tongue. "It is no one," he replied in French.

"There are no no ones," the man said.

"A traveler, that is all. I do not want to bother you."

"No bother. No sight. Father is here."

Modo pinpointed the voice. The man was seated in a large chair that faced the hearth. The shadowy figure stood and slowly came around the chair. "This is my home. My hearth. You are welcome."

"Thank you," Modo said.

"I know your voice," the man said.

Was he mad? "You do?"

"Yes. I don't forget a voice. A tone." The man began to hum softly, a very pleasant sound. "One does not hear the bells every day without learning the tones. Please come closer."

Modo could see no harm in doing so. In getting closer Modo could see that the man's eyes glowed eerily white. Cataracts caught the moonlight.

"I hear your small gasp," the man said. "Yes, I am blind. For decades now. I have forgotten what it is to see. Tones! Tones are my eyes, the identity of a person, the expression on a face. Do you hear the children crying?"

Modo had no idea what he meant. "No."

"Come closer, young man. Please."

Modo did so. Before he could react, the old priest had reached out his hands and touched Modo's face. His fingers looked to be knobbed with rheumatism, but they were quick.

"You wear a mask?"

"Yes. To hide a disfigurement."

"Many are afflicted. Some deaf. Some poor. Some rich. God is mysterious."

"Most certainly so."

"May I?" the man asked, and before Modo understood his intention the man had peeled back Modo's mask and let out a sigh as he traced Modo's cheek.

"What is your accent?" the father asked.

"Canadian," Modo lied.

"I know your face." He ran his fingers across Modo's ragged cheeks. "You were the sweetest child."

"You know me? That's impossible."

"All is possible."

"Who are you?"

"I am Father Cambolieu."

His fingers continued to trace the lines of Modo's face. They touched his cheeks, caressed his forehead. It was so gentle and so . . . natural. "You have always had such a strong face. Even stronger now."

"Thank you," Modo said. "Was this the nursery once?"

"Yes, until Father Mauger closed it down. It was too expensive."

"And when was it closed?"

"In 1860."

"Where did all the children go?"

"I was told they went to proper homes and to other churches."

"Wh-who am I?" The father's hands were still on his face.

"You are the boy with the blessed face."

What could that mean? "Did you meet my parents? What were their names?"

"Ah, I am good with names. Monsieur and Madame Hébert." So Modo was indeed an Hébert! The man placed his hands on either side of Modo's head, as if measuring it. "How old are you?"

"Fifteen," Modo replied. "You really and truly knew me as a child?"

"You were here only a short time. Four months. As I recall, you rarely fussed. Then Father Mauger came and took you, said he had found you a home."

"A home?" He had been sold to a traveling freak show. Did that constitute a home? "What do you know of my parents?"

"I wasn't allowed to meet them. In any case, the parents—

or should I say the mothers, for it was often the mothers—rarely showed *us* their faces. Most of the children were abandoned on our doorstep. But your parents had marked you for the church. They were very close to God. Sometimes one can get too close to God."

What did that mean? "I—I am trying to find them. They did not return to Nanterre after leaving me here. Do you know where they were going next?" Modo asked.

"I wanted to know everything about my children," Father Cambolieu said. "I would pester Father Mauger incessantly. Sometimes the abandoned babies had names pinned to their shirts. Others had a doll or a soft blanket. I wanted to understand where they had come from. Why God had sent them to me."

"Yes, yes, but did you know where my parents went?"

"I did. I did. Father Mauger did tell me what he knew of your parents. He said they intended to travel to Montreuil-sur-Mer. I remember it clearly. It is the town where I was born."

The floor creaked behind him and the father seemed to look over Modo's shoulder.

"Ah, we have more visitors. It is a glorious night."

Modo knew Colette and Octavia were in the shadows. He adjusted his mask. "They are my friends. It is time for me to depart. But there is so much I must ask you," Modo said, grasping Father Cambolieu's hands.

"I have told you everything I know, except for my nickname for you. It was Bright Eyes." With that he chuckled. "Bright Eyes. Back then I still had enough vision in my left eye to see that much, at least."

"We must go," Colette said quietly. "The sun is rising."

Modo was reluctant to release the priest's soft hands. He took one and kissed it. "I will return one day and thank you properly."

"I look forward to that day, my son. Go with God. Bless you."

19

A Sudden Revelation

An agitated sleep had left Lime on edge. He awoke to find Typhon sitting in the same spot, like a child who had been scolded by a teacher. He didn't know if the monster ever really slept or even breathed like a human, and he never got close enough to check for a heartbeat. He did know that the creature didn't bleed. When that woman had shot Typhon there were holes in his clothes but there was no blood. For all Lime knew, the bullets were sitting in the creature's chest, rusting to bits.

Lime ordered breakfast. He had already been to the Saint-Saulve church for the third time that week to look at their records, leaving Typhon on a bench near the town's wall. There were no Héberts who had arrived in 1858. He was at a dead end. There were no other paths; there was nothing more he could think of. He would telegraph his master and receive his orders. Perhaps the great mind that was the Guild Master would have an answer.

After breakfast Lime took one last walk, with Typhon a footstep behind. They certainly attracted attention, but the meek little townspeople just watched timidly. He wondered what the reaction would be if he commanded Typhon to start tearing them to pieces. Now, that would be a show! Alas, he was not here for such frolicking.

They walked along the ramparts of the citadel; the stone was falling over in several places. Walls that had been built to keep out the enemy for a thousand years were crumbling to pieces. Lime mulled over what he knew of the Héberts. They had plied their trade at markets in Paris. The father had been relatively unknown in Nanterre.

The church documents had clearly said that the Héberts had intended to move from Nanterre to Montreuil-sur-Mer, but not a single person in their intended destination remembered the Héberts or any other potters arriving fifteen years ago. It was a puzzle. They'd given birth to an abomination and then had handed that child to Notre Dame de Paris, the most revered of all churches in France. Why not their local parish? Instead, they had traveled a small distance to the cathedral, and had left from there to Montreuil.

Were they driven out of Nanterre? Superstitious, fearful people often saw the devil in anyone malformed. More to the point, had the Héberts themselves experienced some sort of religious shame? Had they given birth to a demon? Was the infant's disfigurement a sign of their own great sin? It was possible.

Religious belief had always been a curiosity to Lime. He

worshipped his knives, nothing else. But his mother had been God-fearing and had often talked of spirits and ghosts and demons . . . the demons inhabiting her only son. It wasn't hard to imagine a mother who believed the devil had played a role in creating Modo, a monster-baby. Short of suffocating the infant, which would perhaps have been a sin, why not give it to the church? The priests were the experts in exorcism. Then the Héberts would come to Montreuil and change their names to escape the past.

But he had visited all the potters listed in the Montreuil church records and not one could have been Modo's parents. Only those who lived outside the walls weren't in those records.

That gave him pause.

What had the woman he'd seen yesterday said when she saw Typhon? *Is he an abomination? Cursed by the devil?*

Would a woman who believed such ugliness was a curse of the devil abandon a child? Would she and her husband move to the outskirts of a fortified town to hide from their shame?

"Typhon, you blighted old troll, you've given me the answer," Lime said. The monster said nothing.

"Typhon, return to the inn with me. We have a telegram to send. Then we'll get out of this ugly town."

20

In the Village

Modo watched the French countryside out the window of their private compartment on the train to Calais. After leaving the city in his Doctor form, he had slipped on his netting mask and allowed his shape to return to its natural state. Lately he dreamed of going out with no mask, no shape-shifting to disguise his faults. The Rain People in Australia hadn't seen his disfigurement as a fault. And blind Father Cambolieu had touched his face and pronounced it strong and blessed. But Modo did not want to upset Octavia and Colette, so he put on the mask. They would be at least four hours on the train, so he couldn't yet alter his face. He must save his strength for changing into the Knight face just before they arrived.

He had been born in this land and might have traveled a good part of it in the back of a carriage, so he couldn't stop himself from searching for something recognizable. How foolish! He'd been so young when Mr. Socrates had rescued him. He had no memory of the months traveling with the freak show, but still, maybe he'd been on these very roads before. Then again, maybe he'd never been allowed off the wagon of curiosities. Despite his doubts, it all felt so familiar. The green land, the thick woods. Perhaps some part of his mind did remember, or some part of his soul, if there was such a thing inside him.

Octavia had fallen asleep beside him, her head occasionally resting on his shoulder. Colette sat across from him, staring out the same window. The dark circles under her eyes made him wonder about her time in the sanatorium.

"Please don't judge me," she whispered, so low that Modo didn't know if she'd even spoken. "Don't. Judge. Me."

Modo didn't move, didn't even blink. What to say? He considered closing his eyes and pretending he hadn't heard, but she wouldn't fall for that. "I don't," he whispered. Perhaps she nodded, but if so, it was imperceptible.

When the conductor began to shout the name of their stop, Modo went to the washroom, glad not to encounter any other passengers on the way. He sweated and struggled to change into the Knight. It was the most familiar of his regular personae, and he could maintain the form for at least an hour longer than the others. Perhaps with practice he would be able to wear it for the whole day.

They arrived at Verton and paid passage on a two-horse carriage to Montreuil-sur-Mer. It would take at least an hour. The name of the town was so familiar to Modo, but it wasn't until they saw the ramparts in the distance that it came back to him. "This is Jean Valjean's town!" he exclaimed. "He was mayor of the town!"

"*Who* was the blinking mayor?" Octavia asked.

"Jean Valjean," Modo said, "from *Les Misérables.* He was mayor of this town."

Both women stared at him blankly.

"It's a novel," he said.

"Oh. Well, I don't have time to read novels," Colette said.

"He does this every once in a while," Octavia said, "has little outbursts of literary fancy. I've learned to put up with them."

They shared a small laugh, and Modo snorted and stared out the window. Soon they were passing through the medieval walls that surrounded Montreuil-sur-Mer. He wouldn't have been surprised to see knights and siege engines lining the road. Perhaps there had been battles, but it looked peaceful now. Modo couldn't help gawking at each resident they passed. Could one be his mother? His father?

The carriage drew to a stop in front of a brick coaching inn at the center of town. It was called Le Hôtel de France and was three stories tall with a long slanted roof and three dormer windows on the top floor. It looked like an oversized country house to Modo.

A few people stared at the new arrivals. Modo wondered if visitors were few and far between. "Come," Colette urged. "We shall rent our room, eat, and begin our task."

"I ain't much for little towns," Octavia said in a falsetto. Modo wasn't certain whom she was imitating.

"Do not speak," Colette chided, "unless you can speak in French. We agreed to this."

Octavia saluted. "I shall remain silent, Captain Brunet."

"Stop drawing attention to yourself," Colette said, trying not to smile. "Now follow me. That's an order."

She led them into the Hôtel de France and went straight to the innkeeper at a mahogany desk. "How may I be of service?" the man asked.

While Colette organized their lodging, Modo looked around the room, noting several people waiting on a bench with their luggage. There was a small pub area near the desk. He looked for exits, a habit Tharpa had hammered home.

Before long Colette was handing Modo the key to room 12B. "It's at the top of the stairs," she said as they climbed the spiral staircase. "You'll have a nice view of the courtyard. Very romantic. Which is good since you and Octavia will have to continue your ruse of being married."

"I'll be his simple British wife," Octavia said.

After freshening up in their rooms they met in the pub. It was as dank as any English pub, but the beguiling smell of cooking made Modo's stomach grumble. He ordered roast hen for himself and Octavia; Colette chose lamb stew. He sipped a pale apple cider and their food arrived within minutes. Modo was hungry, but he found it hard to eat. Everywhere he looked he saw potential mothers, fathers. The woman who had served their meal was older, slightly hunched. He couldn't stop staring at her.

"I did ask the innkeeper about the Héberts, but he wasn't familiar with them," Colette said. "That may indicate they don't frequent establishments such as this."

"Of course they don't. They're probably upper class," Modo said, joking, but his own vehemence surprised him. For all he knew they were drunks sitting in the gutter and clutching their bottles.

Colette gave him a peculiar look. "*Oui*, I see. Anyway, it is a small village, we will just have to visit a few of the potters—" She sucked in a breath. "*Mon Dieu!* Don't turn around. Don't even move."

Modo froze. He had never seen such fear on her face. Colette was staring over his shoulder, slouching down in an attempt to hide.

Modo couldn't resist turning his head ever so slightly. A thin, white-haired man was paying at the desk of the inn.

"The Clockwork Guild," Colette said, very low. "The agents I met at Notre Dame are here."

"That shouldn't be surprising," Octavia said. "They did get a head start."

"The one at the desk looks relatively harmless," Modo said.

"That's Lime," Colette said, "the mad poet I told you about. They have their backs to us now. You can look. See the man just behind him?"

Modo turned again and saw a giant whose head was nearly in the rafters. "Zounds!" he whispered.

"A monster with the name Typhon," Colette said. "I shot the brute three times in the chest and he didn't so much as stagger."

Really? Modo wondered. Or was this her madness raising its ugly head? But the man was so immense he hardly seemed human. Lime turned and glanced at Modo. Modo looked down into his cider.

"What are they doing?" Modo asked. "Coming over here?"

"They have left. Let us hope it is for good."

"You shot that hulk?" Modo asked.

"Three weeks ago. It was a small-caliber gun, but still, no man should be left standing."

"You must have missed," Octavia said.

"Three shots found their mark. One bullet went directly through his heart."

"You must have been seeing things. After all, you did spend time in an asylum."

Colette reached for the gun that Modo guessed was hidden in her dress. "Would you like me to use you as target practice?"

Modo thought it best to change the subject. "Well, if they are here, then that's actually good news."

"How so?" Octavia asked.

"They can't have found my parents or they would have already left. So we're not too late. And maybe, if they've located them, and if we're clever enough, they'll lead us where we want to go."

"We will keep our eyes on them. I will poke my nose in a few places." Colette stood up and smoothed her skirt. "You two finish. I have eaten enough."

"You're going to waste away to nothing," Octavia said.

"You sound like my mother," Colette said, and walked out the front door.

Modo continued eating silently.

"You seem nervous," Octavia said.

"I'm not."

"But you keep tapping your fingers on the table. It's a nervous habit of yours."

Modo looked down to see his rebellious hand was doing just that. Octavia knew him too well.

"I am nervous," he admitted. "Now that we're here, so close to where my parents may be living. If they're alive, if they're here, I can't help but wonder what they'll be like. Will they be amazed by what I've become? Or will they turn away—again? I don't know what I'll say to them."

"Perhaps you can ask them why they abandoned you?" She sounded sad.

"Of course. I won't forget that," Modo said.

"As you know, I wouldn't throw my parents a life preserver from a sinking ship. I've become my own woman. You'd do well to remember that you have already cut your own path."

Did I? he wondered. Mr. Socrates had forged his mental faculties, Tharpa had trained his body, Mrs. Finchley had designed his manners and perfected his acting ability. What exactly had he done on his own?

But why was he worrying about the opinions of the people who gave birth to him and then tossed him aside? He was here on an assignment. If they found the Héberts he would warn them of the danger, take them back to Montreal, and hand them over to Mr. Socrates, who would send them someplace safe, and be done with them.

When they were finished with dinner Modo and Octavia went out onto the street, keeping an eye out for the Guild agents. After walking a few feet they heard someone behind them screaming, "*Incendie! Incendie!*" A man came running down the street, his desperate voice echoing in the alleys. Church bells began ringing madly.

"Fire," Modo said. Outside the city walls, he saw a thin plume of smoke, so he ran a few hundred feet to the ramparts and easily leapt onto them, grabbed the scaffolding, and vaulted to the top. "A cottage is on fire!" he yelled to Octavia. "Not far out of town."

By the time he'd climbed down again, Colette had returned. "Commotions certainly seem to follow us," she said.

"I have a feeling we should have trailed Lime immediately," Modo said.

Colette's eyes grew wide. "*Mon Dieu!*"

They ran to the city gates, through crowds. *They must have some kind of fire brigade,* Modo thought. But it was so slow. Most people seemed confused, as if they'd never seen a fire before.

The three spies dashed through the open gate and down the road toward the smoke. Modo quickly outdistanced Octavia and Colette. The small cottage was engulfed in flames; smoke belched from the windows. Two tethered goats strained at their leashes, madly trying to escape the heat. Modo leapt over a dead hound on the front path. The front door of the cottage had been torn off and cast aside. Three farmers stood at the entrance, afraid to go in. Modo jumped a low stone fence, took a deep breath, and threw himself through the doorway.

"Modo, stop!" Colette shouted.

"Modo!" Octavia yelled.

"*Je suis là pour vous aider!*" he shouted, smoke making his eyes water. The conflagration was heaviest near the fireplace, where logs had spilled out onto the floor. A rug and thick curtains danced with flames. He charged through them, into the next room, crouching lower to avoid the smoke. He saw a body, rushed to it, and heaved it up only to have it tear in half. Horrified, he blinked his watering eyes until he could see again. He was holding a sack of grain. Stumbling back, he spotted a man splayed across an urn, smashed pottery and pieces of a chair all around him. A long-barreled shotgun, bent in half, was on the floor.

"Modo!" someone shouted.

He began to cough so hard he thought his lungs would rupture. He nearly blacked out, but bent down and sucked in some of the cleaner air from near the floor. *Get out!* He scooped the man up like a child. He glanced around and saw no more bodies. He crouched as low as possible, gasping as his lungs began to contract again and again. He careered out of the cottage, stumbled several yards, then laid the man on the ground, practically falling on top of him.

As his coughing subsided and his vision cleared, he saw that the man's face was severely bruised. A long cut on his scalp oozed blood. "*Mon Dieu,*" the man rasped.

Modo held his hand. In French he said, "You are safe now. I am here to help you."

"We're all here to help you," Colette added, placing her handkerchief against the wound on the man's scalp. "What is your name?"

"Jean Hébert," the man answered in a daze. Then he blinked. "*Non, non,* Lambert. I was Hébert . . . long ago."

Modo's heart nearly stopped. He sat up and edged closer to the old man. His father? He looked for something in the man's face that would prove it, but who on earth would have features like his own? The man's grayish hair was shot through with spikes of red, though, the same color as Modo's. And there was something familiar about his jawline.

"Are you from Nanterre?" Modo asked, glancing up at Octavia and Colette.

The man nodded. "W-water," he whispered, rubbing his dry lips.

"I'll get it," Colette said, dashing to the well through a gathering crowd. Octavia leaned in to hold the handkerchief against the man's forehead.

"You're kind," he said, "for pulling me out of the fire. You risked—" He coughed. "I thank you."

"It was my duty," Modo said. What a stupid thing to say! But he was at a loss for words and his French was failing him. Hébert was in horrible shape.

"They . . . a thief and a monster . . . they took my wife. I fought. I fought them. . . . I am broken," he said. "That beast."

"You fought well, sir. We will find her," Modo said. "I promise you."

Hébert stared at the sky. Had he died? But then he grabbed Modo by the shoulder. "I wasn't strong enough," the man said. "You're a Good Samaritan. Your kindness will be rewarded." He pulled Modo closer. "There's something familiar in your face. Are you my nephew? Luc, I have not seen you for so long. Years. You've grown." He was coughing more softly now, his breath unsteady.

"I am not your nephew," Modo whispered. The man convulsed and coughed up blood. Colette was quick with the handkerchief. Octavia had taken a blanket from an onlooker to cover his legs.

"Do you have any children?" Modo asked.

The man shook his head. "I . . . no. Well, once we had a child, but he was . . . We gave the boy to God." He paused. "To God," he rasped.

"I . . . I am your son. The one you gave to God." Modo grasped his father's cold hand, cradled his head. "I came to find you. I am your boy. I will take you to a doctor. I am Modo. I am your son."

Colette's hand touched Modo's and he looked up at her.

"He is gone," she said in English.

Modo looked into his father's dull eyes. Then, seeing what was only the truth, he gently closed the man's papery lids and stroked his face.

Modo let out a whimper, then caught himself. Octavia touched his shoulder, but he stood quickly. Something cold and painful was growing in his chest. "Where is his wife?" he hissed. "Where is she?"

"We'll find her," Octavia said. "Please, calm down."

"And what do we do now? Just leave him?"

"We cannot wait," Colette said. "They have a good half-hour lead on us and will be traveling with utmost speed."

She was right. Already a large group of townspeople and farmers had gathered; gendarmes would arrive, and there would be far too much to explain. Modo approached the crowd. "Which of you is the mayor? A priest? Which of you is a leader of any kind?" he asked in French.

Several people gestured toward a man who stepped forward. Modo gave him three gold coins. “Bury my father well. I shall return to ensure it was done properly.”

And then, together with Octavia and Colette, he ran back toward the gates of Montreuil-sur-Mer, rage beating in his heart and coursing through his blood.

21

Four-Wheeled Pursuit

Modo ran to the center of the town, not caring if Octavia or Colette could keep up with him, and skidded to a stop in front of the inn. A carriage had just pulled up and a gentleman was stepping out. Modo yanked the passenger aside, grabbed his luggage from the cab, and tossed it to the ground. He threw a handful of francs at the driver, shouting, "Drive west," in English, then in French. "*Conduisez à l'ouest!*"

"*Non! Non!*" The driver reached for something on his belt. Modo sprang up to the driver's seat and shoved him over the edge, a small club clattering on the cobblestones beside him. Modo snapped the whip and the horses sprang ahead, the carriage lurching behind them. His mother! They had her and they would dissect her, would do whatever it was the Clockwork Guild was doing to create their monsters and nightmare machines. He would not allow it!

"You are not behaving appropriately," a woman's voice said from behind him. He saw a pair of hands grab the lip of the driver's seat. Colette climbed up the side and—rather gracefully, considering the circumstances—sat beside him.

"This is appropriate behavior," he shouted. He snapped the reins again. "Faster! Faster!"

It was only after he caught his breath and some of his wits that he asked, "Is Octavia aboard?"

"She is. Though whether she will survive your driving is another question. You cannot even keep the horses on the road. Here!" Colette grabbed the reins. "Hold them like this."

"I was doing well enough," Modo said. "Where does this road take us?"

"Back to Étaples. This is the only road to the coast and they will not be racing like we are."

The small window between the cab and the driver's seat slid to one side. A pair of eyes looked out.

"Oh, the French girl is steering," Octavia said. "No wonder we're in such a hullabaloo."

"This carriage is not designed for such speeds," Colette yelled back.

"Well, you two seem to have everything well in hand," Octavia said, "I'm going to get forty winks."

"You can sleep now?" Colette asked, incredulous.

"No worse than a quiet day in a St. Giles pub." Octavia slid the window shut.

Colette gave the reins another snap and the horses sped up. Farmers pulling carts of vegetables rushed to get out of their way. Colette shouted at an old woman with a blood-stained poultry sack slung over her shoulder. The grizzled woman stepped off the road a moment before she would have been trampled by the horses, and gave them several rude gestures.

"The horses will tire soon," Colette said. They were already slick with sweat, their manes drenched.

"Then we'll steal others!" Modo stared hard at the horizon, as if he could will the enemy to show themselves. He assumed Lime had a carriage. If they were on horseback they would travel faster, but it would be difficult to hold a struggling prisoner on horseback. Unless, of course, they had taken measures to stop her from struggling. It was also possible that they had taken one of the many side roads.

Ten minutes passed. Then twenty. The horses' breathing was ragged. Just as Modo was beginning to lose hope, he caught sight of a distant carriage. "There! There!"

"I see it!" Colette flicked the whip and the horses whinnied angrily but sped up. The driver of the other carriage was coming into focus: a thin, tall man. "That is Lime, I am certain," Colette said.

"Then hand me the reins," Modo said, grabbing at them.

At first she wouldn't give them up. "Why?"

"Only men drive carriages here. Besides, Lime will recognize you. Get down, into the cabin."

"You do not give the orders, Modo. This is a partnership!" she said, relinquishing the reins. "At least hold them correctly. You must feel the horses' mouth from this distance. So, do you have a plan?"

"To smash right into them and knock Lime off his perch."

"Will your mother survive the collision?"

Modo had no response. Colette had caught him off guard.

"Your plan will fail. The horses will not charge directly into another wagon and besides, they are exhausted. Better to approach from behind slowly and not let them know who we are. We should wake Octavia."

Modo heaved a sigh, pulled on the reins, and pounded on the roof until the window slid aside. "Yes, what's all the pounding for?" Octavia shouted.

"They are just ahead of us," he said.

"Do you have a plan?" she asked.

"What is it with you two?" he snapped. "Of course I have a plan! We are going to catch up with them. Slowly. From there we'll have to adjust as the situation develops."

"Ah, we're winging it, then," Octavia said.

Before Modo could protest, Colette said, "If you pull up alongside them I will jump across to the back of their carriage, get your mother out of that monster's clutches, and, if possible, get her back into our wagon. Lime won't even see me."

"You won't go alone," Octavia said. "I'll help steal the poor woman from under their noses. Let's hope your driving skills are up to it, Modo."

"Then that is our plan," he agreed. It seemed impossible to pull off, but he couldn't think of a better idea.

Colette climbed along the side of the carriage, her dress flapping in the breeze. Octavia opened the door and followed her until both were hanging off the back. Having these two on his side was like having ten good men. Modo felt a surge of hope. Lime and his partner wouldn't know what hit them.

He brushed sweat from his brow. His features were slipping back to ugliness; exertion had sped up the process. What did he care? He'd frighten Lime half to death, then break him like a twig. *Do not let anger drive your decisions,* Tharpa had told him many times. Well then, he'd use it to overpower his enemies instead.

Modo eased the carriage closer and closer, until it was only twenty feet behind Lime's. They were now traveling on a winding road toward a town. Étaples, Colette had called it. Modo could see a port in the distance.

Lime lifted a pistol and Modo prepared to swerve out of the way if he turned to shoot. Lime aimed the weapon straight up and fired, sending a flare arcing through the darkening sky.

A few seconds later an answering flare lit the sky. It had come from a large steamship anchored near the coast. Lime was much more prepared than Modo had expected; there'd be swarms of Guild soldiers on that ship.

He urged the sweating horses to a gallop and within a minute he was side by side with his enemy. He wanted to leap into the other carriage. The curtains were drawn and that behemoth of a man was in there with his mother. It was all he could do not to jump.

Remember the plan! He slowed the horses, trying to match the other carriage's speed, hoping to make it easier for Colette and Octavia to leap onto the back of Lime's carriage.

"*Nous sommes pressés!*" he spat out. He'd nearly shouted "in a hurry" in English. "*Passagers importants!*"

Lime turned and glared. His skin was so pale it was almost luminescent now that dusk was upon them. "Fools rush in," the man replied, "where angels fear to tread. Nay, fly to Altars; there they'll talk you dead."

Colette had been right. He thought himself a poet and was quoting Alexander Pope, of all people, and not even accurately! Modo pointed at his ear and shrugged as if to say he didn't hear. He edged his carriage as close to Lime's as possible, so close that his horses nearly rubbed sweaty shoulders with Lime's horses. Then he felt a lift in the weight of the carriage as Octavia and Colette leapt off.

"*Passagers importants!*" Modo said, jerking his thumb over his shoulder at his cargo. That was when he realized that their plan could be adjusted. It was too difficult to pull his mother into a moving carriage. Modo could more easily hop across and knock the poetic teeth out of Lime's head, along with his consciousness. Then he'd yank on the reins and bring the carriage to a stop. But how to stop Typhon from hurting his mother?

"Why, dear lass, are you taking so long to pass?" Lime shouted.

Modo shrugged. "*Je ne parle pas anglais.*"

"How do you know I'm speaking English?"

"*Je ne parle pas anglais!*" Modo repeated.

Lime chuckled. "The little mockingbird doth sing." Had Lime seen through his ruse? Modo gave the reins another snap; then, once he was a few yards ahead of the other wagon, he yanked the reins to the left, forcing his horses to cut across the path of the other carriage. At the same time he cracked his whip at Lime, hoping to knock him off his perch.

As if it were a well-rehearsed feat, Lime caught the end of the whip and pulled so sharply that it flew out of Modo's hand. Lime used his own whip to attack Modo, the leather flying with such precision that it caught Modo below the eye.

Modo raised both his hands to protect his eyes, but the whip laid open the flesh on his cheek. He screamed with rage, but even through that he could hear Lime's high-pitched cackle. "'Better to reign in Hell than to serve in Heaven!'" the man yelled. Another crack and Modo's left ear was stinging with pain. Modo released the reins and leapt, hoping he was soaring toward Lime.

A shot rang out.

22

A Hole in Your Skull

It had unraveled far more quickly than Colette had imagined possible—*A poor plan falls apart like a house of cards,* her father had drilled into her. She'd leapt across to the back of the other carriage and swung around the far side, all without Lime noticing. Octavia was only a few handholds behind her. Colette gave her a smile and Octavia grinned back.

After a signal to Octavia, Colette pushed aside the window, revealing red plush curtains. A stench like dead meat assailed her nostrils.

She moved the curtain back slightly and peeked in. The side of the monster's head was inches away. She moved the curtain a little farther. He was staring down at Madame Hébert. Her bonnet was in disarray, her face ghostly pale, and eyes downcast, as if she did not dare look at her captor.

Colette noted Typhon's matted, dark hair, the greenish

ear stitched into place on the monster's skull. It was as if this man were not born of a woman but sewn together by a tailor. Was it possible? Was that why she couldn't kill him with bullets? He might not have had a heart, but whatever his making, she was certain he had a brain, and most men preferred to keep their brains within their skulls. With one hand gripping the wagon, she brought her derringer up, used the barrel to thrust the curtain aside, and then placed it against the side of Typhon's head, whispering, "Don't move or I'll blast a hole in your head." She nodded to Octavia, who had to crawl over Colette to get to the carriage door.

The hulking thing made no reply. Was he deaf? Colette dug her derringer harder into his temple. That would get his attention. He turned his head ever so slightly, the pale skin wrinkling, his dull eyes measuring her. They held no intelligence. No pity. Nothing human.

"Do not move," she repeated.

Octavia opened the door and climbed in, scrambled over the monster's legs, and rammed open the opposite door. It would be a short leap to the other carriage. She then turned her attention to Madame Hébert, grabbing her arm and trying to yank her out of the prison on wheels. But the woman wouldn't budge or even open her eyes. She might have been drugged.

"Madame Hébert! We are here to help you," Colette whispered in French.

Before Colette could react, Typhon smashed his fist through the thin carriage wall and grabbed her wrist, squeezing her arm so tightly that she felt as if bones would break. She pulled the trigger, her derringer fired, and at the same moment the wagon lurched to one side. The monstrous man was still squeezing her arm. Had she missed his head? How was that possible? He was less than an inch away from the barrel of her gun! She pulled the hammer back again, with her teeth. She wouldn't miss a second time!

Before she could finger the trigger she was yanked into the cabin through the window, glass breaking around her, and landed on the floor beside Madame Hébert. The wagons crashed together, tearing off the door of Lime's. Octavia fell out, nearly pulling Madame Hébert with her.

"Octavia!" Colette shouted. Had she survived? Colette saw a flapping dress—Octavia had found a handhold on their carriage and was pulling herself inside. Colette grabbed Madame Hébert's hand, intending to pull her across.

"Woman stay," Typhon grunted. He yanked Madame Hébert out of Colette's grip and sat her, almost gently, across from him. He turned to Colette, who was reaching for her stiletto. "Woman go."

She raised her arms, but he smacked her so hard that she flew out the opposite door, and, at the last moment, Octavia caught her and dragged her into the other carriage.

"Anything broken?" Octavia asked.

"No." Colette wasn't certain. "We need an elephant gun to kill that thing. A cannon."

Then there was a great crash and the carriage disintegrated around them.

23

A Moment of Beauty

Modo was wrestling with a human eel. Every time he thought he had a firm grip, Lime slipped out of his hands and landed another blow. And all the while Lime was laughing and shouting, "Tra la la!" He was absolutely cracked. Modo did manage to knock a knife from the man's hand, but he was rewarded with a fist right to his throat.

They had reached the outskirts of Étaples when the carriage veered off the road and struck a post and then the side of an inn. Modo was thrown face-first to the ground and then scrambled to his feet.

Both horses had broken free and were charging madly down the road, dragging their harnesses behind them. All the carriage windows were smashed, and it had landed with the front jammed into the ground, the back wheels still spinning in the air. A moment of silence passed, enough time for

Modo to see that his carriage was on its side a hundred yards behind him, the two horses trying to pull themselves out of their harnesses.

The door to Lime's carriage smashed open and Typhon leapt out, clutching Madame Hébert. She was flopped over, so Modo couldn't see her face.

But this was Modo's first good look at the giant. Nearly twice as tall as Modo, legs like the trunks of trees. Modo felt for a weapon, but his stiletto had fallen out of its sheath. He had no gun, but Colette had said that bullets were useless, and now Modo believed her. Typhon hadn't moved, but he was looking around, for Lime, perhaps.

And now, more horrible than this monster, rising in the air over Typhon's shoulder, was what Modo first took for a dark cloud. Then he realized that an airship was approaching, scudding earthward. It had probably taken off from the deck of the steamship. It was steel-plated and would be heavily armed. Typhon began lumbering toward the dock.

Modo ran and jumped, aiming squarely for the monster's back, but in midair a whip wrapped around his throat. He was jerked backward and flipped hard onto his spine, the breath knocked from his lungs. He grabbed the whip and pulled. Lime came tumbling off the roof of the carriage. Modo hit him with a palm strike, knocking him to the side. Modo ripped the coils of the whip from around his neck, charged toward Typhon, and head-butted him in the spine. Typhon kept going, the woman now draped across both his arms. Modo struck him again and this time the giant turned, gently set the woman down, and faced Modo. The airship was getting closer.

For such a massive creature, Typhon moved with great speed. Modo dodged his first blow and came in under his arms, planning to execute a body throw, but the thing countered quickly and locked hands with him. Modo had never met a man stronger than himself; he had lifted wagons, even an airship's boiler with his bare hands, but he couldn't budge Typhon. He was hefted like a sack and held in the air. The man's eyes were empty, his face a map of scars and stitches.

"Woman to skyship," Typhon grunted. "Must get her."

"Don't talk him to death," Lime shouted. He walked underneath the struggling Modo, rubbing blood from his nose. "Break the bastard's spine, Typhon," Lime spat, grabbing Madame Hébert's arms and dragging her to the ropes that dangled from the airship.

Modo was lifted higher, and had a clear view of the airship. No sign of Miss Hakkandottir, though a black Clockwork Guild flag flapped at the bottom of the aircraft. Along its side was the name *Erebus.* Six soldiers in gray uniforms were rappelling to the ground—Guild soldiers.

"Let me go!" Modo shouted.

"Break spine." Typhon lifted Modo even higher and maneuvered him so that he was hanging over a stone fountain next to the inn. Then the monster let out a small huff of air and Modo fell to the cobblestones.

"Leave him alone!"

Colette was between them now, her stiletto buried deep in the center of the creature's chest. Typhon yanked the stiletto out and stared at the black sludge clinging to it. Colette swung a piece of the carriage, but it broke on Typhon's arm. He dropped the knife, grabbed her by the shoulder and legs, lifted and spun her as one might a child in a playful game. Wildly, Typhon released her. She flew several yards through the air, out of Modo's line of sight. A moment later there was a crash and a groan.

Typhon lumbered back and glared down at Modo.

Modo could only raise his arms, like some upturned insect flailing on its back. Was his spine broken? Typhon leaned over and stared directly into Modo's eyes. It had a hideously ugly face. There were stitches across its cheeks, and its eyes were two different colors.

Modo tried to shift his own face, to go back to his own ugliness. Perhaps that would shock the creature.

Typhon held his massive hand a few feet above Modo's chest. Oddly, it had a disproportionately small pinkie finger. Modo was briefly mesmerized by that finger, and his own suddenly itched.

Typhon poked him hard in the chest. Modo groaned.

"You broken," Typhon announced, then lumbered toward the airship.

For several moments Modo couldn't move. He heard the *pop pop* of pistol fire. He gritted his teeth and forced himself to roll onto his side. Octavia was crouching behind a statue of a man on horseback and firing her derringer at the airship. Modo still couldn't catch his breath, couldn't get up. He turned his head to see the airship beginning to rise, the soldiers aiming rifles at them. A bullet struck the cobblestone near Modo's head, spraying him with stinging chips of stone.

A bell rang in a nearby church. Modo blacked out, for how long he couldn't say. When he opened his eyes again, his head was in Octavia's lap. "Modo! Modo! Wake up! Wake up!"

With great effort, and her help, he was able to slowly sit up. "Don't move too quickly," Octavia said. "You look like hell. Your face has some rather wicked gashes."

Modo nodded. Townspeople had gathered, and he could hear the buzz of their whispering. "Where's my mother?" he asked.

"I'm sorry, Modo. I tried to stop Lime, but he's got her."

"And Colette?"

"She's . . ." Octavia averted her eyes. "She's over there. She's not doing well." Octavia helped him to his feet and he limped to where Colette had been thrown.

"It's really bad," Octavia warned him.

And it was. Colette had struck her head and was bleeding from several scalp wounds; a trickle of blood leaked from her nose. Her body was crumpled on the cobblestones, her left arm obviously broken. Her eyes were open.

They crouched over her.

"Colette," Modo said.

She raised a hand as if to wave. "Did you . . . did you save your mother?"

"No."

She squeezed her eyes shut. "Ah, I am so sorry, Modo. This is what happens when you do not have a proper plan." She gritted her teeth. "I—I am not long. . . ."

"I won't hear of it," Octavia said. "Someone's gone for the doctor." She squeezed Colette's hand and tears came to her eyes. "We still have too much to argue about."

Colette managed a smile. Modo dabbed a handkerchief at the blood on her face.

"Tavia—may I call you that?"

"Please."

"May I"—she coughed, but her voice remained weak—"have t-time alone with Modo?"

"Of course." Octavia left and Modo could hear her trying to keep the townspeople back, saying, "*Non! Non!*" The total of her French vocabulary.

"Modo," Colette said in a faltering voice. "I have failed you."

"No, you haven't." But to himself he said: *We failed. We failed, failed, failed.*

"I ask—" She took a sharp breath and it was several moments before she sucked in another. "Will you show me your face? Just once more."

"No."

"Please, Modo. Don't deny me this. I must see it."

It was easy to shift his shape as he was completely exhausted. He let his features slide, his face blossom back into ugliness. A few moments later it was as deformed as it had been at birth. His hair began to fall out in clumps. Modo prepared for her reaction.

She looked up with red-veined eyes, blinked. "It is beautiful," she whispered, so sincerely that he wondered if she were delirious. "*Merci*, my *bonne chance* friend." She closed her eyes and breathed one last broken breath.

He brushed her dark hair back behind her ear and began to sob. She was, despite her wounds, still so perfectly elegant. So much lost. His sob turned to a low howl, his body shaking.

After several moments he felt Octavia's hands on his shoulder, pulling him away. "We have to go, Modo. Gendarmes will soon be here."

He stood and turned around to see that a very large, noisy crowd had now gathered. A few braver townspeople explored the wreckage, perhaps looking for more victims; the warier ones had gathered at the edge of the debris. Some backed away from Modo when they saw his face.

"She was Colette Brunet!" Modo shouted. "She served your country well. Her name was Colette Brunet."

And then Octavia led him away.

24

The Boy with the Iron Shoulders

A young man named Oppie slept restlessly on a cot in a military tent he shared with several other soldiers. He dreamed of his home far, far away in London.

More than a year earlier he had been inside a giant that walked across London and swung its metal fists at the Parliament buildings. He was one of many children chained to the giant to make it work, and he remembered only blurred images of those events. If he didn't know better he would've said that none of it had happened. A nightmare, a horrible flight of fancy. But he had bolts sticking out from his shoulders that proved differently, and memories of a redheaded witch with a metal hand and an evil white-haired doctor who had poked and prodded and made him drink potions that changed him. When he closed his eyes at night he saw the hideous pair lurking in the darkness, so he rarely slept well.

He had been removed from the broken body of the giant, set on the ground, and given chocolate. He did recall talking to Mr. W, a detective type who'd had a room at the Red Boar, Oppie's place of employment. Then Oppie had been taken away in a carriage to be poked and prodded and questioned by men in black uniforms and an old, gruff man named Mr. Sockrats, or something like that. And later still, Oppie was poked and prodded by other, friendlier doctors. Within a week they had cut the ends off his bolts, patched him up, and sent him home to his mum.

He enjoyed six weeks of bliss and joy and magic. His mum suddenly didn't have to work because of something she called "shush money." So she stayed home and Oppie went to school—actually went to school—the place Mr. W had said he should attend. He'd started to read his first words. And the best part was that his father was growing stronger each day. He'd been yellow with some sickness that had crawled down his throat, but his mother could now buy medicines and pay a doctor. Within a week his dad got up and walked and laughed and rubbed Oppie's head and said, "My boy, my boy." And Mum had told Oppie that he had a brother or sister who would be delivered by a stork. A stork, of all things! He didn't understand exactly where the stork was from, but his mum kept rubbing her tummy.

One night his dad went to sleep. The next morning his mum was shouting for the doctor, but his dad was already cold and yellow and dead. Then Oppie got sick too. His shoulders grew bulkier. His feet and his hands outgrew the rest of his body. Then the rest of his body began to catch up. Sometimes he'd grow an inch in height overnight! And his temper grew too. He wouldn't remember his tantrums, but would wake up to broken chairs or dishes or pots lying all around him, his mum huddled in a corner like a frightened bird.

The men in black uniforms returned, along with Mr. Sockrats, who told Mum that Oppie was changing because of the potion Britain's enemies had given him. It was affecting his body and his mind. Making him age. He didn't understand, but he had to go with the men to a secret fortress. His mum hugged him and said she'd see him again when he was all better.

Then they put him in the back of a carriage, and thus began a journey that would take him away, far, far over the ocean.

25

Valuable Cargo Arrives

Miss Hakkandottir was the first to see the airship *Erebos* descend from the heavens. She was standing on a rocky plateau looking over the cliffs when she spotted the dark oval in the sky.

She marched to the dock as the *Erebos* lowered to the ground. A squadron of Guild soldiers had been on guard there all morning, piquing her curiosity. She knew the airship had been on a mission in France, and judging by the torn straps and the trailing smoke, it had returned at full speed. Its armor was frosted, a sign that it had been traveling dangerously high in the atmosphere and catching strong air currents. The outer balloon looked worn.

Soldiers caught the landing ropes and the ship descended gracefully until it was floating only a few feet from the sandy ground. The squadron flanked the airship and the side gates opened. First to step haughtily down the gangplank was Lime, a triumphant light in his eyes, a buffalo coat wrapped around his thin frame. Behind him trudged Typhon. The monster still amazed her. She had watched as Dr. Hyde had brought it back from the dead. She wondered if the doctor would ever do the same to her one day.

She had hoped to see one of the Association's spies—Mr. Socrates or Modo—all trussed up and stumbling down the gangplank, so she was disappointed when a frightened woman, who kept crossing herself, was led down by soldiers instead. She was short, haggard, several years older than Miss Hakkandottir, her hair protruding wildly from under a torn bonnet. She had the strong-shouldered build of a peasant, of someone who worked with the earth. And so plain! Lime gave Miss Hakkandottir a leering smile, then followed the soldiers and the woman to the Crystal Palace.

What had she just witnessed? Who could be so important? She stood watching until they had entered the palace gates. The woman matched no one in Miss Hakkandottir's files.

Only an hour later, sitting alone at a table in the mess tent eating rabbit stew, did she put it together. She dropped her spoon with a clatter and immediately went to the doctor's cave.

She found Dr. Hyde arranging his collection of needles. "I would like to see her," she said gently.

He shuddered and turned. "Ah, Ingrid, you know that is not possible. She has just arrived. We need her to be in perfect condition for our tests. She must rest."

"Did the Guild Master expressly forbid me from visiting her?"

Dr. Hyde paused to think that through. Perhaps because his brain was steeped in formulas and calculations, Miss Hakkandottir found him easy to manipulate.

"I would never harm her," she promised. She put her metal hand on his shoulder. "I am only curious."

She did have some affection for him, or something resembling affection. He had, after all, constructed her metal hand. She would never want her weak flesh-and-bone hand back again; the metal one was perfect. It struck fear in the hearts of her enemies and it never wore down.

He stroked her metal hand. "Perhaps your hand needs adjusting. Though it did not rust with the altitude and humidity of your airship adventures."

He was trying to change the subject. He found a small lever in his pocket and used it to adjust her index finger. "Ah." He tightened it. "Better?"

"Yes, much. Could you one day replace my arms? My legs? My body?"

His eyes widened, magnified by his odd glasses. "If required. I would turn you into a goddess."

"*More* of a goddess," she corrected with a hard laugh. "We would rule the world."

He laughed too, and she knew that he was picturing them side by side. Perhaps he too would have his own gleaming metal body.

"Please, Cornelius, let me see her."

"I—I suppose there is no harm in it." He paused. "She will be extremely valuable to us."

He led Miss Hakkandottir to a stone door, which he opened with a key from his pocket. The room was one of the many recent additions on the island. She followed him inside. He turned another key and an electric light buzzed to life. A perfectly clear quartz wall cut the chamber in half. On the other side of the wall was the woman, sitting on a stone slab, gazing at the floor. She looked as though she had just awakened, terrified. Hakkandottir stared at her. How tiresome and weak some humans were. But from this woman had come such a powerful child.

"She can hear me clearly?" she asked.

"Yes." He gestured at holes drilled into the quartz. "But please don't upset her. I need her to be as relaxed as possible for my tests. Fear and anger may alter her blood chemistry."

The woman looked up, and Miss Hakkandottir was taken aback by her proud eyes, the way she fixed them on her and did not turn away. There was a bandage on her arm, but there were no bruises. A Bible sat on a stone table. Perhaps the Guild Master had given it to her. To what end, Miss Hakkandottir couldn't guess.

"So you are the mother of Modo," Miss Hakkandottir said in French.

The woman shook her head.

"But indeed you are. Lime is an unerring fox and he sniffed you out. You are the mother of a most interesting creature."

"I have no children."

"You had one. Of that we are certain."

"No. I have none. I would not have willingly given birth to that abomination."

That term made Hakkandottir smile. "Yes, an abomination. You did give birth to one. And perhaps you will be the birth mother of even more."

"Please, Ingrid," Dr. Hyde remonstrated. "We are not to upset her."

"I am nearly done, my dear," Miss Hakkandottir said, without moving her gaze from Modo's mother. She didn't know exactly why she wanted to see the woman writhe. Was it because Modo had bested her? Modo had battled Fuhr, her friend, and dragged him to his death in the Thames. Modo had been in the submarine *Ictíneo* when it stabbed her ship from below, sinking the unsinkable *Wyvern*. And he had turned his horrific face upon her at the Egyptian temple in Queensland and she had been forced to flee. Three times he had defeated her. Defeated the Guild.

Was she just here then to taunt Modo's mother? She shrugged. Or maybe there was something she could learn about such a powerful adversary. Was the Guild Master using the mother as bait, hoping to lure Modo here?

"I shall tear your son into pieces and feed him to my hound," Miss Hakkandottir said. The woman met her eyes, then picked up her Bible and began reading aloud.

"We must leave her," Dr. Hyde said. "Please."

"I have seen enough. Words will not save you," she said over her shoulder as Dr. Hyde pulled the door closed behind them.

26

A Better Woman Than I

The return voyage to Canada was not one Octavia would ever want to repeat. They had reported by telegram to Mr. Socrates; within hours they received commands to return home, home now being Montreal, of course. She and Modo sailed first to Liverpool, stopping so tantalizingly close to London. She wanted to flee to the rugged and ragged streets of Seven Dials where she had grown up. She'd be safe in any of those ratholes they called pubs. Even the Clockwork Guild wouldn't poke their noses in there. Instead, she and Modo booked a second-class cabin on the SS *Montreal*, playing husband and wife for the third time.

Modo was a dark and quiet stone sitting at the end of his deck chair, or, more often, he could be found in their cabin staring out the porthole with that blasted netting mask covering his face, and his emotions. The bruises and cuts on his face were healing quickly; inside his heart, though, she doubted things were going as well. Octavia did not pry.

Besides, she was not in much of a mood to talk. She had spent less than three days with Colette and had quarreled with her, yet her death was like losing a close friend, a mate. Such a blow. She was an equal. *No,* Octavia had to admit, *she was a better woman than I.* Colette could speak several languages, had risen to the top of her ranks despite fellow agents trying to undermine her because she was a woman and half Japanese. Even half mad, she had been formidable.

Colette had been broken by that bull, Typhon, as though she'd been a doll. The sight and sound of that would haunt Octavia. There'd been nothing she could do to prevent it. She'd been crawling from the wreckage of their carriage when Typhon lifted Colette over his head.

"It looks like it'll be another boring day," she said, pouring her tea. "But only four more to go before we're back in Canada."

She could only imagine how all of this was affecting Modo; he had given her little more than two-word sentences since their departure. She so missed the Modo she'd once known.

"Yes," Modo answered, "same as the last."

"What do you suppose Mr. Socrates has in store for us?"

"It doesn't matter."

"What do you mean?"

"With or without him I'll find my mother and save her from those . . ." He shook his head as though he couldn't find the words to describe the Clockwork Guild.

"Just like that?"

"I'll find the hiding place of the Guild and I'll break them." He was bending his teaspoon in his wrath.

"Modo, the best way to do that is to work with Mr. Socrates." She was surprised by her own words, and yet she knew they were the truth. "You know it too. After all, you're on a ship returning to him."

"It was the only course I could take." He sighed. "I'm confused, Tavia. I am French. I am English. I was orphaned. I have parents. One is dead and the other doesn't know me. They abandoned me and yet I must save my mother. And Colette is dead. Dead. Dead. My mind bounces from one dark moment to another. It's all too much."

"Nothing is too much for you, Modo."

He looked up at her. Was this another gibe? But she returned his gaze.

"Why are you being so kind?" he asked.

"I cared for Colette too."

"You did?"

"She was a beautiful, remarkable young woman. Truly heroic. I've come to think of her as a sister."

"A sister?"

"Yes. She was an incredibly annoying and strong-willed she-devil. I would've been honored to call her sister."

"She was strong. I am heartsick," he admitted. He shook his head and smiled, looking out at the sea. "She would be laughing now if she could hear us."

"We'll go back to Montreal, Modo. You never know what ol' Mr. S will have up his sleeve."

"I hope you're right."

"I'm always right," she said. What was she doing? She was

thankful to Mr. Socrates for taking her from a life of pickpocketing, but he often got on her nerves and always put the needs of Britain before the needs of his spies. Now she was actually talking him up to Modo. To Modo! This was how bad things had become. "And if he doesn't have a plan for us, Modo, one that involves rescuing your mother, I'll go with you. If she is that important to you, then she is that important to me. We'll make certain Colette did not sacrifice her life for nothing. Come hell or high water, together we'll find your mother."

He stared at her for a long time. He was so hard to read with that mask on, but she thought she saw disbelief in his eyes. Or bewilderment.

"We will," she added. "I swear this to you."

He nodded. "Then the Clockwork Guild and whoever else stands in our way had better be ready to run."

27

Stepping Out of the Trenches

Mr. Socrates had been part of the great siege of Sevastopol during the Crimean War. He remembered the back-breaking labor of digging trenches on one side of the Russian port city while their comrades, the French, dug trenches on the opposite side. Summer passed; fall, winter, spring. Then another summer, fall, and winter. The harsh weather and the long months had been horrible for morale. And then, when they felt Sevastopol had been truly weakened by shelling and starvation, they rose up from their trenches and charged the city.

Now it was time to rise again. Hiding in Montreal had been necessary, but it was time to act, to step out of the trench he had dug around himself and charge into the unknown.

He was beginning to feel at home in Montreal: the food,

the newness of the buildings, the energy of a colony. He could comfortably spend his last years here, away from the hurly-burly of London. But being comfortable was wrong. He had to live with the heart of a soldier, moving from camp to camp, and be ready to charge the enemy at a moment's notice.

Above all, it was time to follow his instinct.

And so he sent several telegrams, packed a kit bag and luggage, and had Tharpa order a carriage to the docks. He left Mrs. Finchley to keep Montreal House in good order. "Guard it with your life," he said. "You're the last bastion of our part of the Association."

She nodded and smiled sardonically. "I shall fight the cobwebs and the mice until my final breath." They looked at each other, smiling grimly. How many years had he known her? Twenty? Then she said, almost defiantly, "You give Modo and Octavia my love."

"I most certainly will not," he said. "They are agents, not our children. Your children."

Her smile was curious. "They belong to us, either way. And you know that."

He stomped away from her. Women! He could not fathom the pathways of their minds. A minute later he and Tharpa were in their carriage, rolling toward the docks.

He took the wireless telegraph and folders of reports with him. He had received updates from Cook and Footman, and the latest was the most exciting: a telegram saying that they'd discovered a mysterious hidden shipyard on the coast of China. It flew no flags of any country and most of the workers were European. It was most likely a Clockwork Guild shipyard.

But how to deliver the Guild a hammer blow? He did have one ace in his deck, an experiment that, from all reports, was coming to fruition. It was waiting on Vancouver Island on a patch of land deeded to the Association by a retired general. It had been part of Mr. Socrates' long plan.

Intuition told him he was making the right decision. This new weapon—these new weapons—would be a saber through the heart of the Guild.

He thought again of the siege of Sevastopol. Of how he and his regiment had charged those walls under harrowing cannon and rifle fire. It had been a failure on the British side, he remembered with a bitter laugh, but the French broke through on the other side, and by nightfall they were all in the quarters of a dead Russian general, drinking his vodka.

28

Westward Ho!

Modo was so impatient to get his feet on land that he stood by the gangplank with their luggage long before they had docked in Montreal, next to several tall-masted ships. Octavia stood beside him, using her umbrella as shade from the sun. It was colder here in Canada: the early October wind chilled Modo. Or was he shivering with nervousness? He had assumed the Doctor persona again. The moment the sailors lowered the gangplank Modo scurried down it. He and Octavia were the first to have their papers stamped at Customs House. He strode up a ramp to the street.

"Wait, Modo! I'm not a gazelle!" Octavia blurted. He slowed down, and once she had caught up, she hissed, "You should try running in a dress. It's abominable!"

"I'll leave that to my imagination."

He was just about to wave down a calèche when he saw

Tharpa standing outside an ornate carriage, beckoning them over. Modo placed the luggage in the carrier on the back and shook Tharpa's hand. He wanted to hug his weapons master. He hadn't done that since he was a child, but he needed it now. Instead, he held on to Tharpa's hand longer than usual.

"You have returned, young sahib, and young Miss Milkweed," Tharpa said, slapping Modo's back. "Old sahib awaits you inside, as you have likely surmised."

"I have. It's good to see you, Tharpa," Modo said. A well of emotion was rising up in him, so he bit the inside of his cheek.

"Mrs. Finchley sends her regards to both of you," Tharpa said.

Modo nodded, a little confused. Wouldn't he be seeing her in a few minutes? He reached for the carriage door.

"Modo! You help the lady in first!" Octavia reminded him.

"My apologies." He bowed to her, then opened the door with a flourish, took her hand, and helped her step into the compartment. He followed, sitting across from Mr. Socrates, who wore a long coat trimmed with fur. Modo was surprised at how happy he was to see his master again. How he wished he could lay all of his problems at Mr. Socrates' feet and have them solved.

"Welcome to your home away from home, both of you," Mr. Socrates said as the carriage began to roll down the street. Tharpa was riding with the driver. "I hope you rested well on your journey." He leaned back in his seat, his walking stick across his legs. "We're about to travel west by train, all the way to the coast."

"We won't be stopping at Montreal House?" Octavia asked. "I need a bath. And my clothing needs a wash."

"There's no time. We'll have the clothing and you laundered along the way."

Octavia frowned and turned to stare out the window with a huff.

"And what of Mrs. Finchley?" Modo asked.

"She's in charge of Montreal House." Mr. Socrates raised an eyebrow. "You'll see her when this next phase of our battle is over, Modo. If that is your worry."

It was. He had wanted to tell her about what he'd seen, to be held in the safety and comfort of her arms like a child. Of all his teachers, she would be the one to understand his pain. There was no point in mentioning this to Mr. Socrates. Perhaps, Modo decided, he could write to her.

He felt time pressing on him. Thirteen days had already passed since his mother's capture. She could very well be dead. He couldn't help imagining how she must have cowered in the car of the airship.

"Where are we going?" he asked.

"First, Modo, I need to hear in your own words what happened in France. Every detail. Of course, I'll want your version too, Octavia."

Reporting was a skill Modo had perfected during his years of childhood training at Ravenscroft, so he spoke calmly from that place in his mind where he remembered every pertinent detail. He didn't even tear up as he described Colette's death and his mother being hauled away. Octavia followed with her own observations.

"I've read files on this Lime," Mr. Socrates said. "Several agents have fallen to his blade. Typhon is someone new."

"Larger than any man I have seen," Octavia said. "And he smelled."

"Smelled?"

"I was in the carriage with him. He stank like rotting flesh and formaldehyde. And he had stitches along his neck and face and arms."

"From wounds?"

"No. The pattern was more like a surgeon had, well, stitched him together."

"Curious," Mr. Socrates said.

"He was impressively strong too," Modo added, "but he was cold, sir."

"Cold?"

"His flesh was like ice. And he was impervious to bullets and Colette's blade, which struck his heart."

"You are certain she hit him there?"

"Yes." Modo remembered it so perfectly. Colette, his savior, standing between him and the monster. She had paused in disbelief when he didn't fall.

"Do you know the origin of the name Typhon, Modo?"

"I . . . I hadn't thought about it, sir."

"Come now. You know the Guild has a penchant for Greek names. Who was Typhon?"

Because Mr. Socrates' teachings had centered on military tactics and history, Modo had not spent much time on various mythologies, though he had memorized every tale he'd read. The Greek and Norse stories of how gods and Titans had once walked the earth were too fanciful for Mr. Socrates.

But Modo was pleased to be able to dredge up the answer from memory.

"Typhon was the father of all monsters in Greek mythology," he said. "His hands reached east and west. He had a hundred dragon heads, and massive snake coils for legs. He had wings, and fire flashed from his eyes. Even Zeus feared him."

"Your brain is a great big book, ain't it, Modo?" Octavia said. "If we cracked open your skull we'd just find pages and pages of words."

"I'm glad I impressed you."

"Oh, I didn't say that." But he could tell that he had.

"The Guild picks certain names for a reason," Mr. Socrates said, "and in those names perhaps we'll discover something about their plans. Why this name for this man? You said he had stitches."

"And a very tiny little finger on his right hand," Modo added, almost forgetting the detail. His own finger tingled when he spoke of it. "It was pink, like normal flesh."

"What kind of man survives so many wounds? So many surgeries? Who knows what they've done to make him this resilient, this powerful. They must see the man as being very important. Any sign of his cerebration?"

"His what?" Octavia asked.

"How smart he is," Modo explained. Octavia stuck her tongue out at him and he nearly laughed—how he needed a good laugh. "He spoke in short sentences. Very gruff. He seemed to do whatever Lime asked of him. But there was one order he didn't obey. He was told to break me and could have easily snapped my spine. But he only dropped me."

“Very curious,” Mr. Socrates said. He took his walking stick and leaned forward. “But we haven’t asked the important questions. Why do you think the Clockwork Guild wants Madame Hébert? And what do you suppose they will do with her?”

“I . . . I can’t.”

“Don’t hold back, Modo. This is of the utmost importance.”

“It has been a long journey, Mr. Socrates,” Octavia said. Modo gritted his teeth; he didn’t need her to defend him.

“I don’t even want to imagine what they want with her, sir,” he snapped. “Don’t you think I haven’t been running through a hundred horrific scenarios? How can you ask me to speak of this? You know what the Guild is capable of. Your guess is as good as mine. Don’t make me speak of my mother this way.”

“Don’t be weak—weakness will be used by the enemy to break you.” That sharp tone! After years of hearing it, Modo involuntarily straightened.

Modo thought hard and finally drew in a deep breath. “Okay, I can think of two reasons. One, they want to get to me. They would dearly like to capture me. So this suggests they are using her to draw me to them.”

“A doubtful scenario,” Mr. Socrates said. “They would have to communicate with you again in order to give you the location to which they want to lead you.”

“Exactly, sir. My second conclusion is that there’s something in her, in her biology or her . . . her body . . . her blood . . . something they can use. In the past they’ve employed drugs and metal enhancements to modify and strengthen hounds and children. What monsters they dream up! For what exact purpose they'll use my mother, I do not know."

"We must look into the abyss, Modo," Mr. Socrates said. "It's the only way to defeat such blackguards. It is becoming obvious to me that they intend to bring at least one more Typhon into the world."

"That makes sense," Modo whispered.

"Then what is the connection between Typhon and Modo's mother?" Octavia asked.

"There isn't one," Modo said. "There can't be."

"No, Octavia has a very valid point," Mr. Socrates said. "Excellent rational thinking. If this Typhon has been somehow strengthened by . . . by stitching parts of other men together, then he would be well served by the ability to regenerate. And, Modo, no one is stronger nor heals more quickly than you. And your finger grew back."

"No. The Guild can't be aware of my regenerative abilities. We didn't even know ourselves until Miss Hakkandottir cut off my finger." He stared at his hand. She had sliced the little finger off while he was hanging from her airship and he'd fallen to Earth, leaving his finger behind.

Mr. Socrates tapped Modo's hand with his walking stick. Modo drew it back. "It would not be beyond Miss Hakkandottir to keep a trophy of her battle with you. And, once that trophy was in their lab, for Dr. Hyde to experiment with it."

"It can't be." Modo recoiled in shock. Octavia gasped. But his finger had itched when he'd seen Typhon's little finger. As though his body recognized the truth. "Typhon did have a disproportionately small pinkie finger," Modo said. He shuddered, though he knew it was better to face facts without emotion, as Mr. Socrates had always taught him.

"Then it is possible that there's a connection between you and Typhon as well. Ah, we have learned a lot in a short while. We'll have plenty of time to think upon these riddles and others as we travel."

The carriage stopped in front of Bonaventure Station, a grand stone building that reminded Modo a little of Notre Dame. There were rows of carriages waiting out front, loading and unloading passengers. Modo was the last to get out, and Mr. Socrates pulled him aside and said quietly, "I'm sorry about Monsieur Hébert and the girl. Come along."

Modo paused. His master had actually sensed that Modo was feeling some pain. *Perhaps the old man has grown a heart.* It was curious, he noted, that Mr. Socrates referred to his parents by their last name only. Not as *your mother and father.*

Tharpa tossed half the luggage to Modo and carried the rest himself. Modo followed Tharpa into the train station, almost running across the intricate marble floors. Within minutes they were on a westbound train leaving the island of Montreal.

"Where are we going?" Modo asked.

"Westward ho!" Mr. Socrates said jauntily. "We're traveling through Ontario, then taking the Grand Trunk line. We'll follow the North Pacific route through the United States, since the laggardly Canadian government has not yet figured out how to build its own national rail line. This band of metal that crosses the United States is quite the accomplishment. And all done without the British. I guess the old colony is growing up."

"I'm sure they'd be pleased to know they have your approval," Octavia said.

"Indeed they would," Mr. Socrates said. Modo wasn't certain if he was joking or not.

"Is the Clockwork Guild located in the American West?" Modo asked. "How soon will we lock horns with them?"

"No, no," Mr. Socrates said. "The West is not that wild. The Guild is somewhere in the Pacific Ocean, I am certain. I'm following my intuition on this one."

"You mean we may be going through all this trouble and ending up in the middle of nowhere?" Modo asked.

"Be assured, I know their general whereabouts. The real difficulty will be discovering their base."

"And what will our assignments be?" Octavia asked.

"To deal with events as they unfold. Enough about work. Let us enjoy our trip."

Modo and Octavia exchanged a glance. No plan? His intuition? Who was this man?

The hours passed. The car didn't have the first-class cabins Modo had come to admire in England and France. Instead, there were two rows of seats on either side of the train. They did have beautiful wide windows and above them, in the curve of the ceiling, were elaborate stained-glass windows. Dressing rooms and lavatories were at the far end of the car.

The lack of cabins would make for an uncomfortable trip. Modo wouldn't be able to hide his disfigurement as easily, but for some reason, he found he didn't care. His mask would have to be enough to protect the other passengers from seeing his face. And if they were put off by the mask, too bad.

He and Octavia were delighted to discover saloon cars,

balcony cars, dining cars, and refreshment cars. Modo bought a copy of *The Moonstone,* by Wilkie Collins, from a boy with a basket of books for sale. He loved a good detective story.

They had taken seats at the front of their car so they could not be so easily gawked at. Modo sat nearest the window. They passed into Ontario and through Toronto and crossed at Sarnia into Michigan. At eight o'clock a steward announced, "It's bedtime, folks." In the space of a few minutes the seats were lowered; beds and red curtains gave everyone privacy. Tharpa was across the aisle from Modo and Mr. Socrates, sharing with a stranger. Octavia had a seat to herself.

Modo had never slept in the same room with Mr. Socrates, never mind inches away from him. "Good night, Modo," he said, pulling his nightcap on tight. Mr. Socrates fell asleep almost instantly, but Modo's mind was still aching from all that had happened. Unbidden, Colette's face filled his mind. She had asked to see his brutal features before she died, had actually wanted his face to be the last image she saw. His face!

There had been other deaths in his life, but not someone he . . . he . . . loved. That was it. He had loved her. Not in the same way as he did Octavia, but under different circumstances they might have spent a lifetime together. She had tried to save him from the monstrous Typhon and had given him a gift by looking at his face. Of saying he was beautiful. Would a dying woman lie?

Such were his thoughts for a very long time, before he finally drifted off to the rhythm of a train chugging westward.

29

Experiencing Elocution

Typhon was sitting on a stone, gazing in wonder at the Pacific Ocean. They had named him Typhon, but he didn't feel as though the name truly belonged to him. He wasn't Typhon; he was several people at once. There were voices in his head, bubbling like a brew, but this voice, the one that was thinking at this moment, was his own. Wasn't it?

His thoughts had returned slowly, as though he were waking from a deep sleep. For so long the only other voices he heard were those of his masters; their commands would rattle around in his skull until he obeyed them. As time passed, more of his own thoughts sprouted up between those commands. Occasionally, he would even have memories. They were dark names and feelings. A mother. Yes, he remembered a mother who had held him as a child. And the feeling of coarse, itchy rope around his neck. Then darkness. Did the memories belong to him or to someone else? And he remembered too the emotions of those moments. The comfort, the uncertainty.

They had tried to turn him into a laborer, but someone had to constantly give him instructions. So they let him wander the island. They fed him when he was hungry, but the soldiers and even the mechanical hounds kept their distance.

Every night he would visit Dr. Hyde to be examined. Sometimes there was a stitch that had broken and needed mending. "Your flesh will eventually grow together," the doctor said, "like the regeneration of a lizard's tail. A very exciting scientific discovery, Typhon."

The monster nodded.

"And Lime tells me you've learned more words. You speak well, at times."

"I speak well."

"Yes, yes, I've heard you speak before. But it's great news that you've retained those faculties. Communicating will be much easier."

"I experience elocution."

"Ah." The doctor stared at him dumbfounded, his eyes behind his gold-rimmed glasses so big they were comical. Typhon nearly laughed. "You use such complicated words."

"Yes. I can . . . I am cognizant of that."

"Marvelous, simply marvelous," the doctor said.

Perhaps, Typhon mused, he would crush the doctor's skull. This was the man who had brought him to life; the first face he had seen when his eyes opened. This old, tiny, frail-boned man. Typhon lifted his hands, then lowered them. He chose not to commit the act. It would be an interesting experience, but he had a curious affection for the old man.

"I am very proud of you," the doctor said. "So very proud."

Typhon nodded. "Who was I?"

"Who were you?" the doctor said. "Oh, I see. You have some questions that all children ask: Who am I? Why am I here? Very interesting. I didn't expect that. Do you have memories of, how shall I put it, another time? Another you?"

"Sometimes, yes."

"Oh, now, that is *very* interesting. You see, you were not one person, but several. Your brain is amalgamated from the gray matter of a man named William Middleton. He was a prospector and a murderer. And from that of a man named Duncan McTavish. He was a writer and a murderer. Other brains were required, though I only used smaller portions of those. Do these names mean anything to you?"

"They sound familiar." But he couldn't picture either man.

"Well, do tell me if you experience any more memories. Curious that they can live on after the electric charge of life has been snuffed out and reignited. I have more good news, Typhon." The doctor gestured to the walls with a palsied hand. "Soon you won't be alone."

Typhon looked around the room at the others, frozen in coffins of ice. Would they be his brothers? His sisters? His friends? Or his enemies? He should destroy the bodies now. Then he wouldn't have to risk being destroyed by his enemies.

"You are dismissed, Typhon," Dr. Hyde said.

He walked out of the cave and along the wet, stony

ground. There were always soldiers around, and sometimes that woman with the red hair. And he had once stood before someone called the Guild Master. A tiny man with a powerful voice. He could not find any older memories of such people inside his head. He did have memories, though, of a wife with a reedy voice. Had he been married? Had he children?

Sometimes he would see Lime. The man with the metal teeth had barked at him and treated him like a dog. He would snuff him out for that. He imagined the event, the glee he would feel. He could do it now, but the hounds and the soldiers would tear him apart. It would not be wise to kill Lime at this juncture. He would wait.

Besides, Typhon was beginning to understand how small Lime really was. He had not built a palace on this island. He had not given the orders that created Typhon.

He walked where the seagulls flew along the edge of the island. He watched other, little birds flit through the air. So pretty. He sat under a palm tree and held out his hand.

He held it perfectly still for three hours, breath shallow and quiet. Finally a bird with pretty yellow wings landed on it. He watched the bird. It watched him. He couldn't think of the name of the bird. He should know that.

Then, with a quick squeeze, he crushed it.

"Canary," he said.

30

An Old but Young Friend

Though the trip across the American West was one beautiful landscape after another—each could be a giant painting like those in the National Gallery at Trafalgar Square—Modo wished the train would chug faster. He'd shovel the coal himself if it'd help. Their travels took them from Wisconsin to Minnesota and on. Sometimes the station was the only sign of civilization. This was a country that had survived a massive and horrible civil war; he'd read about tragic battles, desperate charges, countercharges, and hand-to-hand combat. This was also the land of adventure, according to the penny dreadfuls; six-gun shooters, sheriffs, and gangs of unruly cattle thieves. And savage Indians too.

No, *savage* was the wrong word. He remembered the Rain People of Australia. In the short time he'd spent with them, they'd been far from savage. He'd long since decided it was best to judge who was savage by their actions.

Every second stop was a fort: outposts surrounded by nothingness as far as he could tell. There was little to do but wander from car to car. Read. Wait. Mr. Socrates had predicted that it would take four nights and four days. Impossible to imagine crossing such a large continent in such a short time, but he knew an airship would cross it at twice the speed.

The close quarters of the train made it particularly hard to hide his deformity, and only by acting the invalid were they allowed to keep his bed down and the curtains closed. Invalid? He could outwrestle any man on the train, except perhaps Tharpa. But being an invalid gave him time to read.

When he did change into the Doctor, he would dress and stroll up and down the aisle or play chess against Tharpa.

"You've tramped this train from beginning to end at least a hundred times," Octavia said. They were in the observation car watching the green hills of Montana pass by.

"I have to do something. I'm clamped in, trapped, and angry."

"Anything else? A sore toe, perhaps?" She clapped his shoulder. "Ah, Modo, we are all trapped. Though Mr. Socrates seems to have a light in his eyes. He's enjoying this."

"The man has no plan."

"Then no one can predict his actions."

Modo shook his head. "You sound like him. I had no plan when we attacked Lime's wagon and Colette died."

"Do not carry her death on your shoulders, Modo. All three of us accepted the risks, and we came up with the best plan possible in such a short time. You didn't ask her to stand toe to toe with that monster. She chose to."

"You're right. But I'd feel better if our master was plotting everything out carefully."

"He hasn't led us astray before. Perhaps we're better off without a plan this time. And at least we're on the move. We could be stifled in Montreal House reading Plato to each other."

"Now, don't you poke fun at Plato." He put his hand against the window. "I—I keep wishing I had said something more to my father. I don't even know if he heard me. Who was he, Tavia?"

"Maybe when we have more time you could . . . we could return to Montreuil and ask some questions."

She wanted to go there with him! He couldn't help smiling.

"I have to confess something to you, Modo," she said.

"You do?"

"I once said I didn't care about my parents. Didn't want to meet them. It's a lie. I . . . I'd like to set eyes on them once. To see what they look like. I know it sounds odd, but I now envy you that you saw your father. My dad was likely strung up by the hangman or is sleeping in Davy Jones's locker."

"I hadn't thought of that, Tavia. I'm sorry."

"Oh, don't be sorry. Once I got over the first glance I'd tear a strip off 'em. After all, how dare those louts abandon me?"

"I feel the same way," Modo said, "but it's harder to be angry now that I've seen them."

"Well, we'll rescue your mother. And you can jabber with her till your tongue falls out."

"It seems impossible," Modo said. "There are just four of us. Against the Clockwork Guild. What are we thinking?"

"Like I said before, perhaps Mr. Socrates has a trick up his sleeve, or hidden in his walking stick."

"I sure hope he does." They took in the view for a while, until Modo said, "I just don't understand exactly who I am. What country I belong to."

"You're Modo," Octavia said, as though it explained everything. "We don't belong to countries, Modo. We belong to friends."

"I belong to you?" he asked.

"Well . . . yes, of course. You're my mate." She gave him a friendly punch in the arm. "And you're such a bore when you're a sourpuss. Don't trouble yourself about what'll happen. I live in the moment."

"That's one of your many wonderful traits."

"It's the only way, Modo. I told you about Garret once, didn't I? My mate who was hanged for stealing a watch. He's the one who taught me to live by the day, the hour, the moment." She paused. "It's best not to think about him. Gets me teared up."

The vast mountains of Montana and Idaho—the Rockies—were stunning. And someone had cut a path through all that rock so this band of steel could wind through the mountains. How much dynamite had been used? The whistle blew as they passed a town called Hellgate.

"They do have particularly clever names for their towns," Octavia said.

The final stop of the train was a small station near the coast. Modo leapt into the fresh air, clutching his and Octavia's luggage. The four agents loaded everything into a canvas-covered wagon with a driver who was, to Modo's great disappointment, wearing a conductor's cap. He'd expected a cowboy hat. They began rolling toward Seattle. He was glad for the canvas as clouds scudded over them, thunder sounded, and just like that, it began to pour. The horses snorted and struggled, kicking up mud as they dragged them down sludgy First Avenue past square wooden buildings that looked as though a good wind would knock them over. Every second building was a saloon.

"This really is the wild west," Octavia said. She had opened her umbrella and was hiding underneath it since water was soaking through the canvas. "They don't even have cobblestone streets." They slogged their way to the port and, after Mr. Socrates had paid for tickets, loaded their soaked selves onto a stern-wheel steamboat named *Alexandra*. It was not the largest Modo had ever seen, but it fit thirty passengers comfortably and chugged across the Strait of Juan de Fuca to Victoria. How many cities, rivers, lakes, and mountains had been named after the Queen? They passed an island and docked near what looked to be government buildings, small by comparison to the Parliament buildings of London, but still impressive.

"This is the farthest edge of the British Empire in North America," Mr. Socrates explained after they'd debarked the paddleboat.

The city's newness and size reminded Modo of Sydney. The familiar buildings and bridges were British in style. Civilization! He nearly sighed. Within minutes Mr. Socrates had summoned a small black carriage. The ride took them through the streets and under a vined archway with the sign "God Save the Queen." They passed the Bank of British Columbia; beside it was the Victoria Boot and Shoe Manufactory.

"It's all so very quaint," Octavia said. "It's like they've made a tiny copy of everything in England. Which reminds me, my boots need mending."

"There's no time," Mr. Socrates said. "We're less than an hour from our destination."

Soon they were pulling up to a military establishment. "Esquimalt, the headquarters of the British Pacific Fleet," Mr. Socrates said. Seeing the ships and marines, Modo hoped his master had formed a plan as they were traveling. A marine opened the carriage door and Mr. Socrates produced papers from his pocket. The marine squinted at the passengers, his eyes on Octavia so long that Modo felt like giving him a bop on the nose. The marine nodded and said, gruffly, "Your transportation will be here soon enough." He motioned to the driver. "The civilian is not allowed any farther."

They got out and pulled their luggage down. An uncovered wagon, the box stained with some black substance—blood?—pulled up. They threw their luggage on and climbed into their seats. Their driver was another marine. With a flick of the reins the horses began to trot down the main road of the naval base.

"Ah, they added more docks," Mr. Socrates said. "Good. Good."

There were docks, of course, and sailors standing outside wooden barracks. "I was invalided here during the Crimean escapade." Mr. Socrates looked at the barracks. "Fir trees and coal make this a valuable area. And it's within easy striking distance of the United States, if need be."

"Are we going to war with them?" Octavia said. "Did they dump our tea in the sea again! Outrageous."

"One must prepare for all possible outcomes," Mr. Socrates said. "You can trust an individual, but never trust the country."

"And does that include England?" Modo asked.

"Especially not England," he replied with a smile. "Empires are not created by accident."

The HMS *Shah*—an iron-hulled, wooden-sheathed frigate—waited in the dock, metal glistening in the dull sunlight. Three masts towered above the deck and two steam funnels puffed smoke. The warship looked brand-new. It was a sword, Modo decided, sharp and powerful. Meant to cut through the ocean and the ships of the enemy.

They were soon past the docks and encountering fewer buildings, though there were massive stores of coal. Several men were shooting at a practice target and charging straw dummies. *Ah, the life of a marine,* Modo thought. It would be so simple.

They arrived at a guard post and were stopped by men in black uniforms. Modo recognized the uniform—members of Mr. Socrates' Permanent Association. The exact position of these soldiers in the hierarchy of the British army had never been made clear to Modo. It was likely that they weren't accounted for on any records.

Their driver climbed down, saluted, then began walking

back to the naval base. "It's good to see you again, sir," an Association soldier said. "I'll take you the rest of the way." He climbed into the driver's seat.

"Where are we going?" Modo asked Octavia.

"The outback, I guess," she said. "Mr. Socrates really is unpredictable. Or he's lost his faculties."

"I haven't lost my hearing, Octavia," Mr. Socrates said.

They drove through two more checkpoints. Modo was intrigued: what secret were they about to see that needed three separate security checks? Even the marines weren't allowed beyond the gate. They entered a camp around which stood a ten-foot-tall "thorny" fence. A secret within a secret on a distant military base.

They passed through a copse of pine trees that opened up into a large clearing. Before them stood at least twenty white tents circling a tall pole flying a British flag. The wagon lurched to a stop before the largest tent. "First we dine," Mr. Socrates said.

"I can only imagine what we'll be dining on," Octavia whispered.

Mr. Socrates led them into a mess tent with wooden tables set with metal plates. It stank of smoke and burnt food. "Sit, sit," Mr. Socrates commanded, and as they did, two cooks scooped piles of an unrecognizable goulash onto their plates.

"What's this?" Octavia asked.

A grizzled cook waved his spoon at her. "Food. Plain and simple."

Plain and gray was more like it, glued together by a gravy dotted with globules of fat. Modo poked at what he believed were white potatoes. He began to eat. The gruel tasted peppery, with the slightest hint of lime. He couldn't identify the stringy meat he was chewing on. Venison? Beef?

"It has everything you need in it," Mr. Socrates said.

"Oh. Is this pleasant loblolly your recipe?" Octavia asked. Even Tharpa was looking at it twice.

"No. I am good at making tea, but little else in the kitchen. I approved it. It's made our soldiers strong."

Another experiment? Modo wondered. He finished the food on his plate.

"Ah, you were all hungry," Mr. Socrates said, looking satisfied. "I'm glad you enjoyed that; you'll be getting your fill of it here. Now come along. I have a squadron of soldiers I'd like you to meet."

He knew his way around the camp. He led them past a series of empty tents, each with five cots.

"So where are we?" Modo asked.

"Welcome to Camp Cobra, a base for the Permanent Association," Mr. Socrates replied. "This is where we train and plan and, when the time is right, strike."

Beyond the tents was a field littered with straw dummies that had been torn in half. It looked like a battlefield. "But who are you training? Association soldiers?" said Octavia.

Mr. Socrates's eyes twinkled. "Your question will be answered momentarily. Listen."

As if on cue, a low rumble emanated from the north. At first Modo thought it was thunder, but the ground began to shake under his feet like an earthquake. Mr. Socrates gave the slightest hint of a smile. He was enjoying this! The rumbling grew to a pounding, and Modo's heart pounded in response. Then came a deep, monstrous roaring. He met Octavia's eyes;

she looked a little nervous. Tharpa was as calm as ever, and it occurred to Modo that he'd been here before.

The roaring was closer. Was it bison? He'd read about how large they were. He fully expected to see a herd stampede over the rise and trample them.

To Modo's great shock a giant charged over the rise, followed by another and another—twelve-foot-tall metal creatures with massive, gleaming helmeted heads, and arms and legs that hissed. A dozen pounded along in formation, holding what looked to be multi-chambered elephant guns. The armor on their chests was dented yet glittering. They yelled in unison and Modo nearly wet his britches.

Right behind them was an Association soldier, holding a speaking trumpet. He gave a command and the giants split into two groups, drew massive wooden clubs from their backs and began fighting each other.

Octavia's mouth was hanging open. Mr. Socrates grinned ear to ear, obviously pleased and proud. "These men are the most elite fighting unit in all the world."

"There are men inside all that metal?" Modo asked.

"Of course," Mr. Socrates answered. "Very large men standing on steam-powered legs and strapped and bolted into their armored torso. See how smoothly they move?"

The dragoons continued to battle, arms hissing with steam. After several minutes of exchanging blows they were given a sharp order and they retreated back into formation. They stood motionless as the Association soldier shouted at the top of his lungs about their laziness.

When the diatribe was over, Mr. Socrates commanded, "Sergeant Beatty, send me Trooper Entwistle!"

The sergeant barked another order and one of the giants turned, saluted with a huge metal hand, and lumbered across the field.

"You are about to get a good, close look at a secret weapon about which neither the prime minister nor the Queen is aware," Mr. Socrates said. "A member of our Seventh Dragoons regiment, or the Lucky Sevens, as we call them."

Modo remembered that dragoons were part of the cavalry, trained in lance and rifle warfare. These men were riding metal machines instead of horses. When the giant stopped a few feet from them, Modo strained his neck to look up at its face. Behind the slit in the visor were two glowing eyes.

"Remove your helmet," Mr. Socrates commanded.

"Yes, sir, Mr. Socrates," the man replied. He unlocked the golden helmet, which was adorned with a small image of the crown and topped with a horsehair plume. Modo had expected to see some grizzled veteran inside, but the soldier was young. His eyes were confident; his face tanned by hours of outdoor training. There was a familiar cut to his jaw. And he was freckled.

Recognition struck Modo. He hadn't seen this face for over a year. He had once peered at it through a keyhole in a London inn. The face had been much younger then.

"Oppie," Modo said incredulously, "is that really you?"

31

Bolts of Anger

The boy was much larger and older, and scarred, but Modo knew him. Oppie had been ten years old the last time Modo had seen him, just a year and a half ago. Yet today he looked sixteen, if not twenty. By what little Modo could see of his body in all that metal, he guessed Oppie was at least six feet tall.

"Do I know you, sir?" the dragoon asked. Such politeness seemed odd coming out of something so large and powerful.

"Oppie, it's me," Modo said, then nearly smacked himself for being such a dunderhead. Modo had been wearing a mask the only time they'd met face to face, after the Association had brought down the Clockwork Guild's giant constructed of children. Before that, Modo had rented a room at the Red Boar and Oppie had brought his meals to his door. Modo had not wanted to show his face, so he had entertained the boy by reading to him through the keyhole. What name had he been using back then? Ah, yes! "It's Mr. Wellington," Modo said. "I'm Mr. Wellington! But my real name is Modo."

The man was silent, measuring. "I've never seen your face before, sir."

"I wouldn't pull your leg, Oppie. You brought me pork buttons and ale every night. Don't you remember?"

"I think I recognize your voice. It's a pleasure to see you, sir."

His lower-class accent was gone. He'd changed so very much in such a short time.

"I—I don't understand . . . ," Modo said to Mr. Socrates.

"Oppie is a dragoon now," he said. "You may return to your duties, Trooper Entwistle."

"Thank you, sir." With a clanking of gears, he saluted, clicked his helmet into place, then strode smoothly away, his metal suit hissing. His back was protected by several plates.

"We added to the Guild design," Mr. Socrates explained, "stealing the pattern from their giant. We also dredged up Fuhr's body from the Thames. There wasn't much left of his flesh after the fish had had their way, but his coal-fired arms and legs were intact—a true marvel."

"It really is astonishing," Modo said.

"The dragoons can travel absolutely silently for short periods using their electric batteries. But once their steam engines are fired up they can burst through brick walls or scale the highest cliffs. They are bolted to the structure using the shoulder bolts Dr. Hyde had already inserted into the children. We had to extend them again, of course."

"You extended the bolts?" Modo echoed. "I thought you'd found a way to cut them off."

"For the others we did, but not the dragoons. It was the only logical thing to do."

"Good Lord," Octavia said, "is that Ester?" One of the cavalry soldiers had removed her helmet to reveal short red hair. Octavia had known one of the children in the Clockwork Guild's giant too.

"Yes," Mr. Socrates said. "Lance Corporal Ester McGravin."

"I thought you were going to return them to their parents!" Modo said.

"We did." Mr. Socrates leaned on his walking stick. "At least, to those parents we could find. And when we couldn't find parents, some of the children became robust enough that they could work on farms in Canada or Australia. They are doing well. Others died within a few months. Failed livers and such. We discovered the causes through autopsies. There were fifty-seven children who made up the giant. Twelve of them were altered permanently by the tincture they'd been given and could not adapt to civilian life."

Modo watched the dragoons march in formation, their metal feet shaking the ground.

"Altered in what way?" Octavia asked.

"It accelerated their growth and their aging. Each of those soldiers is over six feet tall. They're all aging before their time. A week is the equivalent of a month for them."

"So how long before they die of old age?" Modo asked.

Mr. Socrates sighed. "We don't know. They also have some deep behavioral problems. They are unpredictable and possibly dangerous. Oppie, for example, twice attacked his mother. They need constant supervision and extremely focused goals. It became clear that only the Association could care for Oppie and the others."

"This is caring for them?" Modo asked. "You've turned them into—into war machines!"

"I don't like your tone, Modo. Each of them chose to come here."

"How long have they been at this camp?" Octavia asked.

"Eight months. We couldn't keep them in England; there are too many prying eyes and squeamish hearts. And this is absolutely top-secret. Even those soldiers in Esquimalt are not allowed on this base."

"And why are you showing them to us?" Modo asked.

"Because they will strike the blow that shatters the Clockwork Guild."

Of course. So Mr. Socrates did have a plan. But what a plan! Modo's mind could not believe what his eyes were seeing.

Mr. Socrates led them back to the tents. Had the child soldiers stayed here through the winter? Modo wondered. The tents contained little more than cots and a brazier. He could only imagine how harsh the winters would be here; it seemed almost cruel. As cruel as Ravenscroft.

"These will be our lodgings for the remainder of October and likely November, too," Mr. Socrates said, pointing at four separate tents.

"We're going to just sit here?" Modo demanded.

"Do you have a better suggestion?" Mr. Socrates asked. "Shall we jump on a raft and paddle off in search of the

Clockwork Guild? Have you any idea exactly how big the Pacific is?"

"You said you aren't certain that they're even in the Pacific."

Mr. Socrates grabbed Modo by his lapels and pulled him into a tent.

"Your insubordination is becoming rather tiring," he said quietly. "I did not raise you to be a thorn in my side."

"Mrs. Finchley raised me."

"Modo." There was sadness in his master's eyes. "I am not your father. I know you want to find your mother, and perhaps you seek to avenge that French girl's death. But believe me, anger only leads to rash decisions. I learned that the hard way. Allow me to do my job and you will be able to do yours."

"Yes, sir."

Mr. Socrates let go of Modo's lapels. "And, Modo, don't feel you have to hide your face here. The soldiers have been prepared. No one will stare at you. You are to feel at home and conserve your energy. Very soon we will be going to war."

32

A Statue Stands

Several weeks earlier Footman and Cook had crossed the United States by train and taken a steamship to Hong Kong. There the real work had begun. It'd taken several bribes and days of scouting before they discovered the entrance to the secret shipyard along China's coast on the Yellow Sea. And now they sat on the green mountainside above it, squirreled away behind a cypress tree, drinking cold tea and eating hardtack and dried rice. Footman surveyed the scene below with a spyglass, his eyes still unbelieving.

It was a massive shipyard in a perfectly protected cove. Hundreds of workers, mostly European, were laboring with hammers, hauling coal, or tending to various other duties while heavy cranes moved giant beams of steel and metal plates into position. It was ingeniously hidden; from the ocean it was almost impossible to spot the entrance because of the way it fit into the folds of the mountains. Moreover, the Guild had disguised the access with a wooden flotilla that looked like rocks from a distance.

There were at least a thousand men working on a multitude of projects. Three enormous warships were in various states of construction: the *Hydra*, the *Gorgon*, and the *Medusa*. The first two were nearly ready to launch; the third looked like the skeleton of a giant whale that had been beached. It was months, if not a good year, away from completion. Footman couldn't help watching in wonder as smaller boats raced at impossible speeds through the waters.

"Stunning ain't it, mate." Cook chewed a dried plum. "A whopping big operation. You see the little boats? Tritons, they're called. I've never seen anything go that fast on the water."

"Yes, they are impressive."

"They take them out in groups of two, but they're going straight out into the Pacific. Not hugging the shore. Wherever those little ships go, that's where our mutual enemy resides."

"So we must steal a boat," Footman said. "And follow them."

"I like the way you think, Footman. The question is how?"

"I have a plan."

"I'm all ears," Cook said.

Footman led him back toward the entrance to the bay. It was guarded by sentries in an old pagoda-style tower that perhaps had once been home to monks. It took Footman and Cook two hours to make their way down there. The door to the pagoda was closed, and Footman had no idea how many soldiers would be inside.

"I go, you wait," he said. "You're clumsy."

"All too true, Footie. Just shout if you need help."

Footman stole through a line of shrubs and up to the door. It was unlocked. So they weren't expecting an attacker. He opened the door slowly and crept up the stone stairs. The lookout guards were at the top, and judging by their voices, there were at least two. Soldiers, even the well-trained ones, could not always be focused after hours of staring and waiting. And it was very likely that no one had ever trespassed here. Footman padded to the top floor and peeked in the door. One soldier was staring over the water. The second played solitaire on a table.

He struck the first in the temple with his palm; the second received a kick to the side of the skull. They both fell, unconscious.

"Shall I come up now?" Cook asked from the bottom of the pagoda.

"Yes."

Cook was not exactly quiet coming up the stairs, and he clapped his hands when he saw Footman's handiwork. "Bravo! Wasn't sure if you needed my help or not. They sounded like a bit of trouble."

"No trouble." Footman had already undressed the shorter man and was pulling on the soldier's gray uniform.

Cook changed too, and then they waited, briefly debating how long the shifts might be. First one hour passed, then another. "Cards?" Cook asked. Footman shook his head.

"What's your real name?" Cook said.

"Footman," he answered.

"No, your Chinese one. Singsongy, innit?"

"I am Footman; that is all."

"Funny thing, Footie. My real name's Cook. Albert Cook. And I became a cook. Destiny, eh?"

Footman shrugged. "Names are never who you are."

Soon after he'd arrived in London, he noticed that the higher class in England often called their servants by their occupation, not their name, so he took the name Footman. Mr. Socrates had not disagreed, for they knew others would make assumptions about him if that was his name. Assumptions could always be used against the people who made them.

Footman had worked for Mr. Socrates for more than twenty years. He'd first met his employer in Shanghai and had been hired at the age of eighteen. Then his name had been Gong Le, and he'd trained under the Shaolin masters, warrior monks. He'd completed his years of chi kung, of long runs and armed and unarmed combat, by carrying a red-hot cauldron down a long alley, balancing the great pot on his forearms. Seals on the cauldron burned a tiger on one arm and a dragon on the other. They still sat there, symbols of his time, his training and beliefs. He had wanted to see the world, so he turned his back on the monks. Mr. Socrates opened up the world for him.

Footman jumped to attention when two of the boats sped toward the exit of the bay. Earlier, they'd seen the lookout soldiers run out and open a section of the camouflaged flotilla, so Footman and Cook knew they should do that too.

They scurried down and let the first boat pass. It was large enough for ten men and was steered using a round wheel with two handholds. *Triton XII* was painted on its side.

When the second boat arrived, Cook put out his hand and signaled: stop. The boat, *Triton XIII*, pulled up to the small dock. There were two Guild soldiers inside, both wearing goggles.

"You want me to handle them?" Cook whispered. Footman nodded.

"What are you stopping us for?" the driver asked.

"Paperwork," Cook said. "Got it right here." He stepped onto the boat and gave the first soldier a punch to the skull that dropped him. The second swung, making contact with Cook's shoulder, then he was knocked out by Cook's left hand. He stripped the men of their goggles, then casually tossed their bodies onto the dock. "That was a little sloppy," Cook admitted. "But we haven't all been trained in a Shaolin temple, now have we?"

Footman shrugged and jumped onboard.

"I'll take the wheel," Cook said. He needed a few moments of experimentation to familiarize himself with the controls of the boat and then they were out on the water, keeping the first boat within sight. Their speed was amazing. It seemed faster than a train as it jumped over each wave. They put on the goggles to protect their eyes from the spray.

Footman pointed at the pack of food and bottles of water. There were several boxes of coal next to the firebox, but the coal had been compressed and, he guessed, would last a long time.

"They were expecting a long trip," Cook said. "Not certain I like taking such a small craft out on such a great big ocean, good as its engine is, but I guess we have no choice."

"We don't," Footman agreed.

Cook spun the wheel like he'd piloted the boat his whole life.

As the sun set, the lead boat drew farther and farther ahead until it was out of sight. They kept a straight course, following the compass next to the wheel.

"We'll keep following these bearings," Cook said. "They were going straight, and there's enough coal and food for a few days."

They had a wireless telegraph, but since there were no telegraph cables in the Pacific, it was useless. The only way to get a message to their master would be to take it to him themselves. They had received one last communication giving them coordinates for where they could flee to, if necessary.

After four hours of traveling in the dark, a slight glow appeared on the horizon and grew brighter. "There she be, mate," Cook said. In another half hour they were close enough to see an island with a large central building that appeared to be made of glass. Footman had seen the Crystal Palace in London and recognized this replica. Cook slowed the engine.

"We know the coordinates of the enemy now," Footman said. "We should leave."

"We could take a closer look," Cook answered. "This boat's got an anchor. How's your swimming these days?"

"I swim well," Footman said, "but I think we should get back to Mr. Socrates."

"I'm the senior officer."

"Leadership was not delineated."

"Delineated?" Cook laughed. "Where'd you learn such fancy words?"

Cook pushed the anchor over the side, tied his shoes together, hung them around his neck, and jumped into the water. Footman sighed. Cook had been in the house for the past five years; perhaps he had grown tired of boiling carrots for Mr. Socrates. He knew that the boat wouldn't be easy to find, so Footman followed him moments later.

He easily caught up with Cook and passed him. The island had a beach and docks that were well lit and well guarded, so they swam around to the north, where rocky crags grew out of the water. They swam for half an hour. The cold water was beginning to get into Footman's bones, but the tiger and the dragon on his arms would keep him warm. Cook was huffing and puffing; he should have been training more often.

Footman led Cook to a protruding rock and they clung to it to rest. The tide was at its lowest, the moon bright, showing that the rock walls were almost as smooth as glass. Perhaps they'd been blasted to make them so smooth. They would be impossible to climb with bare hands.

"Looks like we'll have to go back to the boat," Cook said. "Too bad."

"Wait!" Footman pointed at a dark spot on the wall. "I think there is a cave over there."

They swam several yards until they were just below the mouth of the cave, then climbed up and into it. They had to crouch and crawl to make their way inside. It had been pure luck that they'd seen it, Footman realized. An hour later and the tide would have covered the entrance. He turned on his pocket-watch lucifer and followed the cave thirty or so feet into the island. It gradually sloped up, where it became drier. In time they came upon a man-made tunnel.

"We will not be able to leave this way when the tide rises," Footman said, wringing the last of the salt water from his shirttails.

"Then let's not dillydally, mate." Cook was shaking with cold.

Footman climbed a ladder to another tunnel, which led to several more tunnels. They chose one, and with each step it stank more of decay, and of vinegar.

But they continued to work their way toward the surface, covering their noses with their hands. At the end of one tunnel Cook found a trapdoor and pushed it up. "Land ho," he whispered, poking his head up. Then, after a quick glance around, he crawled out. Footman followed, and they both sucked in fresh air, suppressing coughs. What was that stench?

They were near the cliffs, looking down the island at a massive dock, a line of cannons pointed to the sea. "They are sixteen-pounders at least," Cook said. "Twelve of them. It would take an armada to storm this place."

The glass building at the center of the island glowed red, as though it were a living thing. Soldiers were walking to and fro in front of the gates, several of them pulling wagons filled with wood and brick. Even in the dead of night there was work to be done.

Footman spotted several huge hounds and guessed that these were the half-mechanical hounds Mr. Socrates had spoken about. One sniff of his or Cook's scent and the hounds would be on them, but the breeze was working in their favor and they were far enough away to be safe.

"Quite the setup," Cook whispered. "Guns, hounds, I've counted at least a hundred soldiers. If that's the night shift, then it must be like an anthill when the sun rises."

"You talk too much," Footman said.

"I'll keep me smackers closed."

As they explored the island they stayed close to the huge rocks, and were hidden by the surrounding shrubbery. They were about to step around a large rock formation when Footman noticed there was a cave mouth that emitted light. He put his arm back to stop Cook, and peeked around the edge. Not far away, a white-haired man stood at a table, his back to Footman, measuring liquids into several flasks.

Footman knew immediately that this was Dr. Hyde; he'd been briefed on all the enemies that they might encounter. The doctor stood next to a long operating table. And was that an arm lying on it? And a torso? What horror was this?

He poked his head farther around the rock and gasped. Along the back wall hung half-finished men who'd been stitched together. Tall, strong men, their eyes closed. A green fog gathered around them, a gas hissing from several pipes. Footman pulled Cook in front of him so he could see.

"Good Lord," Cook whispered, "let's get the seven hells out of here."

They slowly worked their way back toward the trapdoor. As they crept along, Footman took a measure of the place. The glass building was at least a hundred feet tall and two thousand feet long. The logistics of transporting the materials to create it were mind-boggling. The massive dock, with its cranes and airship tower, could resupply the largest of warships. The entire island slanted down toward the dock on the east side so that all armaments could be fired toward the enemy. The cliffs protected the operation from the west.

Cook led them around the central mountain of rocks. Just as they approached the trapdoor, he stopped. A huge man was sitting on a stone, staring up at the moon. He turned his gaze to Footman and Cook.

"I saw you climb out of this hole," he said. His voice was ragged. "I waited for you to return."

The monster was expressionless, as though his face had frozen. His eyes glimmered with moonlight, but not much else. Footman had never been superstitious, but standing here under the moon he believed he was looking at the undead. "You are intruders," the thing said.

"Intruders?" Cook said. "We're delivering coal, mate. That's all. We're lost."

The man stood. It was like watching a stone statue move. "No. You are too clever to be one of the soldiers. They all drink of some pacifying tincture. And they wouldn't say 'mate.' Therefore, you are from off-island and an enemy. If you run, the hounds will shred you to pieces. I haven't told anyone you're here. Just get past me and you'll be free."

"So it's a game for you, is it?" Cook asked.

The man nodded. "A momentary entertainment."

Cook gave Footman a glance and raised his eyebrows.

"Do not try—" Footman began when he saw the glint of daring in his friend's eyes. Cook charged. He lowered his head and butted the man squarely in the chest, a move he had used in perhaps a hundred brawls. The monster lifted him with a huge hand, flipped him over, and smashed him headfirst against a boulder.

He was clearly dead. Footman would never have dreamed a man as strong as Cook could be swatted down like a fly.

"You are smaller," the creature said. "Perhaps not easier to kill. Please prove entertaining."

Footman had a knife in his pant leg, but knew it would be useless. He reached inside his shirt and let out a small battle cry as he dashed toward his enemy. The man opened his arms as though to embrace him. At the last second, Footman flipped open the pocket-watch lucifer, blinding the giant. At the same time, he leapt to one side and tried to race past. But he wasn't fast enough, and the monster struck him in the ribs, a glancing blow that threw Footman several feet. He rolled along the stones, which cut into his skin, but he leapt up, ignoring the pain. Trapdoor ahead! He measured the distance with his eyes.

The monster pursued him with a bull-like speed. No time to think. He'd be crushed. So he ran past the trapdoor, toward the sound of the crashing waves, the rocks under his feet slick from the mist. He glanced back to see the monster at his heels. His own death at his heels.

Footman ran straight off the edge of the cliffs and dove into the Pacific.

33

Over the Falls

"I'm not going to have to rescue you from drowning, am I?" Octavia asked. They were north of their camp, staring down the edge of a small cliff at a river below. There was a waterfall, and she would have thought it rather beautiful if she wasn't dreading the next step.

This was their first day of what Mr. Socrates had suggested would be weeks of training. Working as a team, they were to cut their way through rough bush using a compass. A prize was waiting at the end of the "map" Mr. Socrates had given them. He hadn't said what it would be.

"I'm a much better swimmer than I used to be," Modo said. "Are you just worried about your hair?"

Hair? That was the last thing Octavia was concerned about. She'd tied it back with black ribbon to keep it out of her eyes and hadn't worn a dress since her arrival two days ago, only black military fatigues. A slimming color, she noted, making her look all the more boyish. Good! She wasn't one of those overdressed plump ladies who spent their life lounging on velvet chairs. Her accessories were a utilitarian brown belt and a razor-sharp saber that Tharpa was teaching her how to use.

After a week on a boat and days on a train, it was glorious to be active again, even if it meant tramping through the bush. She preferred city streets, of course.

They had crawled, run, and cut their way to this location, only to find the river blocking their path. Going around it might take days, and the idea of spending the night out here didn't appeal to her.

"One of us should see if it's deep enough," she said. "I nominate you."

"Ladies first," he said.

"But you're the gentleman."

"You're more a gentleman than me."

"What's that supposed to mean?" It was the closest thing to a joke she'd heard from Modo in weeks. "Ah, Modo, if I stick around you're going to talk me to death." With that she stood, began to run, and jumped into the air, aiming close to the waterfall. She hoped the water had carved a deep enough well that she wouldn't break her legs! It must be all right—after all, Mr. Socrates wouldn't have sent them here unless it was possible. Halfway down she wondered if she'd made a mistake; maybe they were supposed to use their rope to cross.

The water was shockingly cold and she sank much deeper than she'd expected to; at any moment her legs would strike the bottom and snap like twigs. Instead, she came to a stop and began kicking, climbing for the surface, and was soon splashing in the open water.

"It's toasty warm," she shouted, then swam for the opposite shore, as Modo, doing his best impression of a cannonball, struck the water nearby; not the smoothest dive she'd seen. But Modo had only recently learned how to swim.

"You splash around like a mad dog," she said. "You'll scare the beavers, the ducks, and the whatnot for miles around." She had taken to swimming in the Thames when she was a street child, but had never enjoyed taking a bath. It wasn't until she'd become an agent and had her first hot bath that she understood why the aristocrats spent half their lives in bathhouses.

"At least I can float." His wet netting mask clung to his face, showing his deformities and making him look like a sea monster. Despite wishing it could be otherwise, she still shuddered. But she had sworn to herself that she wouldn't show any weakness.

They climbed onto the bank.

"The compass still works," he said.

They made their way up the ravine, following the coordinates Mr. Socrates had provided. Soon they were tramping through the bush again.

"Maybe that was our toughest test," she said.

"Not so loud," Modo replied, "you're snapping every twig."

"I'm going to snap you." But he was right. She could move quietly in the street, but in the forest she wasn't certain where to step. Modo, on the other hand, moved as though born in the forest. He was a peasant's son, after all. Maybe that was it.

"What do you think the point of all this is?" Octavia asked.

"I don't know. Maybe Mr. Socrates just wants us out of his hair. He— Wait . . ." Modo grabbed her shoulder and yanked her back a step. He pointed at the ground. "A trap." He lifted a leafy branch. Below it was a hole.

"How did you see that?"

"Fresh leaves on the forest floor alerted me."

"Since when did you become Robin Hood?" she asked.

"Are you Maid Marian?"

"No. I'm always Richard the Lionheart. But I see Mr. Socrates doesn't want this to be just a gallivant around the forest. At least there aren't as many insects and snakes here as in Australia."

They took another compass reading and Modo checked his watch. "We're about an hour behind," he said. "We've maybe traveled two miles."

It was the first time they'd been alone in two days, so Octavia decided to bring up a question she'd wanted to ask the day before. "I'm curious, Modo," she began, "how do you feel about the dragoons?"

He shrugged. "I don't completely trust Mr. Socrates' motives. I can't help wondering if there was something else that could have been done besides turning them into soldiers."

"I talked to Ester. She's very happy with her position; says she was made for it, in fact! And she's eager to stick a poker in the eye of the rotters who tortured her."

"But they've been turned into weapons. Again. Oppie wanted to read and become a detective. That's all he wanted when I met him."

“Do you think Mr. Socrates gave them more of the potion?” Saying it made Octavia go cold. The birds seemed to grow quiet. Modo was taking a long time to answer.

“No,” he said finally. “I—I think he’s made some hard choices for Queen and Country, but he wouldn’t do that.”

“How can you be sure?”

“Because if he had, he’d have kept every one of the children, not just a dozen of them. Can you imagine fifty dragoons?”

She didn’t want to point out that maybe there were other bases where dragoons were being trained. No, she told herself, Mr. Socrates sometimes had a chunk of ice for a heart, but he wouldn’t go that far.

“The dragoons want to hit back at the Clockwork Guild, I have no doubt of that,” Modo said. “And they seem to be mature enough to make their own decisions. And . . . Wait.” He stopped next to a tree. “I hear something. It’s like—”

Men in gray uniforms thudded from the trees around them.

Guild soldiers! How’d they find us? Modo blocked a blow, then twisted and threw one soldier against another. Octavia ducked under the club of yet another soldier and struck the man in his midsection.

Well, lower than the midsection. He collapsed and she smiled to herself. They never expected a lady to do that. Octavia was never a lady.

When all of the men were unconscious, Octavia said, “How did they find us?” Modo peeled away the uniform of one man to discover a black shirt beneath it.

“Our men! Why, they were just posing as Guild soldiers!

I wondered why they had no pistols. This is another part of our training, I see."

"What'll we do with them?"

"Just leave them," Modo replied. "They'll be up and around soon enough."

Then, following the coordinates, they broke through the forest. Sitting on a stump of a pine tree in the middle of a clearing was an envelope. Octavia snapped it up. Inside were a pair of tickets. Each said: *This ticket good for one hot bath at the officers' tent.*

"So the old man has a sense of humor after all," Modo said, and they burst out laughing.

34

Contentment Under Adverse Circumstances

For Modo, a hot bath seemed an indulgence he could not afford—after all, he needed every moment to perfect his martial skills. But after Octavia said that he smelled like an old dead dog, he found himself in a steam-filled tent, sitting comfortably in a claw-foot tub that looked far too fancy to be out in the middle of the bush. It had probably been used by officers for several years, maybe even Mr. Socrates himself. He relaxed, letting his face return to its natural shape and his hump protrude. It was his first rest and first proper bath since he'd departed for Paris, a trip that felt as if it were years ago. When *was* the last time he'd had a hot bath? A year ago, at least. Certainly not on the submarine *Ictíneo.* Or in the jungles of Australia, or on any ships or airships he'd been on. Even in Montreal House, hot water was intermittent.

On a shelf in the bath tent he found a red-covered book

called *Roughing It in the Bush.* He flipped through it. It was an account of a woman in the bushland of eastern Canada. He stopped when he read: "IT IS DELIGHTFUL to observe a feeling of contentment under adverse circumstances." He read the sentence several times. It was a delight to be in this bath in the middle of Camp Cobra. But should he be partaking of delight?

That was the problem with rest. Anytime he stopped to take a breath, thoughts rose up like Macbeth's ghosts. Colette's broken body, her look of joy as she gazed upon his face. Had she been delirious with death? Then he thought of his father, crushed by the same monster. He must avenge their deaths, but Typhon had spared his life.

He remembered the creature's odd look as it showed its pinky finger to him. As though it were a secret signal. His own little finger had tingled. Had a part of his body really brought that monster to life?

He was out of the bath before the water was cold. He dried his tufts of red hair and stared in the mirror for several moments. He hadn't looked in a mirror for ages. He examined his face, tracing the sunken nose and lopsided features. It wasn't as ugly as he'd remembered. In fact, he thought he saw a hint of distinction. He laughed at himself and slipped the mask on. Distinguished or not, it'd scare the living daylights out of the soldiers. Despite Mr. Socrates' promise that he could walk around unmasked here, he didn't want to test it.

He dressed and walked back to his tent in the center of Camp Cobra. He presumed the name was a reference to a trained cobra coming out of a basket. It was curious how military men chose the toughest, most frightening names for their ships and their camps, but often named their guns after girls.

The battle cry of the dragoons startled him. He walked over the hill, to where he could see that a training course had been set up overnight, complete with coils of thorny wire, mudholes, and a fifty-foot-tall wooden climbing wall. The dragoons stood in formation across from the wall, about to conduct their first charge.

"Boys and their toys," Octavia said.

She'd sneaked up on him! He needed to be more alert.

"A tough course," he told her, hoping his voice hadn't given away his surprise. "I'm curious how they'll do."

The dragoons began to clank ahead, forcing their way through the wire, strands snapping. One stepped into a mudhole and struggled to extricate himself, but the others charged on, yelling in unison. The cacophony made Modo stiffen, even though they were charging away from him. There was something about the noise that reminded him of the horrible potions the children had ingested. He shuddered to recall how they'd looked strapped to the iron giant attacking the Parliament buildings. Absolutely monstrous.

"I just know Mr. S is going to want us to run through all that muck too," Octavia said. "He enjoys seeing me suffer."

"If he really wants you to suffer he'll make you wear a dress while you do it." Modo found it difficult to keep his eyes off her when she was wearing the Permanent Association uniform. When she caught him staring, he glanced away and said, "The wall will be the real test for them."

As the squadron moved on, their arrowhead formation remained intact. The first dragoon climbed the wall, using iron fingers to grip the wooden slats. Holes had been cut into the wall and Association soldiers were shoving large posts through them, slamming them into the armored man. He clung to the wall, continuing his ascent. A second dragoon climbed; a third followed, with the rest firing above their heads. Live rounds! They were practicing covering fire, blowing the heads off dummies at the top of the wall.

"This is what Odysseus must have felt first looking upon the Cyclops Polyphemus," Modo said.

"Good Lord, you are so full of fantastical bosh sometimes. Stop quoting mythology as if it were real life."

"It was an observation. This is a quote: 'He was a horrid creature, not like a human being at all, but resembling rather some crag that stands out boldly against the sky on the top of a high mountain.' That's the first description of the Cyclops."

She put her hands on her hips. "It's a good thing Mr. Socrates raised you in the country. You'd have been pummeled senseless at my orphanage."

He was searching for a retort when the engine on a dragoon, who was near the top of the wall, made a loud bang. The dragoon fell forty feet into the mud and began to sink. Association soldiers swarmed around him within seconds, but they couldn't pull him up.

Modo dashed to the dragoon's side. The man was struggling, face sunk into the mud, and would soon drown. Modo grabbed a metal-encased arm and, grunting hard, pulled the dragoon to a sitting position. The man's nose and mouth were plugged up with sludge and straw, but he couldn't use his metal hands to clear them. He began flailing his metal arms in panic.

"Stay calm!" the sergeant shouted. He ducked under the dragoon's arms and pulled soil and mud from his nose and mouth. The dragoon sucked in a breath. Then he took another and another, wheezing and coughing repeatedly. He continued to breath wildly. "Now, now, calm down." The sergeant patted the man's back.

Modo realized it wasn't even a man, but Ester. Her face was hardened and chiseled like a man's from the effects of the tincture. Tears ran down her cheeks.

"Now, now," the sergeant repeated, his voice soothing, and he actually patted her cheek. "Calm down, Lance Corporal McGravin. Calm down. That's an order."

"I—I will, Sergeant," she promised between gritted teeth.

"Are you injured?"

"Yes, Sergeant." She nodded down toward her right arm.

He delicately removed a steel plate and they could clearly see that her arm was broken.

"It's not so bad, Lance Corporal," Sergeant Beatty said. "We'll fix you up. Now get on your feet, unless your legs are hurt."

"They aren't, Sergeant." She slowly stood. Everyone took a few steps back as she wobbled on her feet.

"Report to Blighty tent. Sawbones will put you back together."

She lumbered away, carrying her helmet in the crook of her good arm.

"Form ranks!" the sergeant shouted, nearly rupturing Modo's eardrums. "Resume your positions!"

Modo ran back up the hill to Octavia. "Will Ester be all right?" she asked.

Modo nodded. "She's certainly tough as nails."

He and Octavia watched the drill for another hour until lunch was served. Modo was famished. He made his way to the mess tent; it was already crowded with the enormous dragoons, each with special sections cut out of their uniforms for their shoulder bolts. They were talking jovially. Even Ester was already at a table, a metal brace on her arm. Modo wondered if the tincture made them more immune to pain. Did they heal faster too?

He stood in line and received the same gray food they'd had for breakfast, lunch, and dinner. Modo took a seat beside Oppie.

"Mr. W," he said. "Pleasure to have your company."

"Please, just Modo. I don't have a surname."

"One name is all you need?" Oppie was eating the food quickly. "You travel light."

"I guess you could say that." Modo's eyes strayed to Oppie's nearest shoulder bolt. He tried not to stare at it.

"I've learned to read, a bit," Oppie said. "I remember you telling me to learn. Sergeant Beatty reads to us at night. He teaches us the words."

"He sounds like a good man. What do you read?"

"Oh, I can't read much on me—my own," he admitted. "Just fairy tales and some of *Alice's Adventures in Wonderland*."

"Good!" Modo rubbed his hands together. "I love that book!" And then he began to quote: " 'I almost wish I hadn't gone down that rabbit hole—and yet—and yet—it's rather curious, you know, this sort of life! I do wonder what *can* have happened to me! When I used to read fairy tales, I fancied that kind of thing never happened, and now here I am in the middle of one!'" Modo laughed, a little embarrassed for having let his performance get away from him.

"Yes, that's it!" Oppie said, excited. "You know it by heart!"

"Just that speech and a few others. I'm extremely fond of the book."

"Sergeant Beatty will be reading the last chapter to us tonight. It's good for us to learn to read. It helps with tactics and the manuals they give us."

Modo creased an eyebrow. They were being read to like children at bedtime, then trained to kill in the morning. They really had gone down the rabbit hole. "How do you feel about your training?" he asked quietly. "About being here?"

Oppie's eyes narrowed. "It's a good place. I love being part of the Seventh Dragoons. We're the Lucky Sevens! They feed us. And if I get a chance to strike back at the Guild I'll be happy."

"Is that all this is about?" Modo asked.

Oppie turned to look at him. His eyes were fierce. It was hard for Modo to remember the child Oppie had been only a year earlier.

"Have you had your flesh cut into, your childhood plucked out?" Oppie asked. Modo nearly answered that he had. "Where else do I go? The army has given me a home, companions, and a purpose. I'll destroy the ones who created me. Destroy them." He jabbed the fork in the table. A few dragoons glanced their way.

Perhaps Oppie hadn't completely grown up, Modo thought. "Did you ever see your parents again?"

"Yes." At this, Oppie's eyes grew gentle again. "My dad

died. My mum, she tried to care for me, but she didn't know what to do. I wasn't 'Little Oppie' anymore. I broke things. And outgrew my clothes so quickly. She was given money."

"Money?"

"Yes. For her to live and to look after my sister, or my brother, I don't know which the stork brought."

"I see," Modo said. "Was she paid for her silence?"

"Paid to tell others I'd run away. Paid to compensate for the loss of my wages. I understand. Me being here keeps my family in bread and a roof over their heads." He looked down at Modo. "Your questions . . . bother me. You think I'm the boy that you once knew. I am. But I'm not. I have grown up. I've found a place where I belong."

"I'm happy for you, Oppie," Modo said. Was that the truth?

It was complicated. Part of Modo felt that what these children had been twisted into was horrible. And yet, without these monstrous men, there was no chance of defeating the Clockwork Guild, not to mention rescuing his mother.

My mother, Modo thought. *My. Mother.*

Perhaps he too had gone down the rabbit hole.

35

A Peculiar Boat with Peculiar Cargo

It was a dark, cold, and stupid night, according to Sergeant Booker. Stupid, he thought, because he had lost his day patrol shift in a card game and was now in the observation tower on Macaulay Point, swinging the port light back and forth across the empty waters, shivering and staring out at the Pacific. The perfect, natural harbor of Esquimalt stretched before him.

It wasn't like anyone would attack the home base of the British Navy's Pacific Fleet. They had enough six-pounder guns to ward off the Russians, if they had a fleet worth considering. And the Chinese were in Stone Age junks. Laughable, really. In any case, Britain already controlled the Chinese. The Americans, now, they might make noise. He had been face to face with the Americans during the San Juan Islands

Pig War, but they hadn't shown any sign of aggression for twenty years now.

It began to spit rain, so it was now a useless, stupid, *wet* night. No one would be entering their harbor tonight.

Which was why he was stunned to see a motored boat enter the bay and begin to circle in the open water. It was a type of craft he hadn't seen before—there was no captain at the helm! Booker rang the warning bell and seven marines appeared within a minute.

"Glouster, you take the light. Keep it on the boat," he commanded. "The rest of you come with me. Let's see who our visitor is."

They climbed into a rowboat and Booker stood at the stern as four marines rowed and two pointed their rifles at the target. The mysterious boat circled slower and slower and the motor gurgled as though it would die at any moment.

"Ahoy, there!" Booker shouted. "Stop your engines! Ahoy!"

The craft continued on. It took some hard rowing, but they were soon able to pull up to it, close enough to jump. Booker was the first over. The fumes were strong, thanks to the coal that burned in the smallest steam engine he'd ever seen.

Lying across the bottom of the boat was a Chinese man, clearly dehydrated, his breathing labored. He opened his eyes and said, "T-take me sock rates."

"What?" Booker said. "Speak English, man! What was that?"

"Mr. Socrates," the man said. "Take me to him. I am his footman."

36

Element of Surprise

Octavia awoke and looked at the clock in her tent. A quarter of six exactly. After two days of heavy training her muscles ached. Tonight she would turn in her ticket and take her bath, an hour of heaven that would keep her going through another day of saber fights, body throws, calisthenics, and long runs.

A soldier stepped into her tent without knocking. "Report to Mr. Socrates' tent at zero six hundred hours." He turned and marched out.

"Good morning to you too, bufflehead," she said. It wasn't shocking to have him enter unannounced. She was considered a regular member of the Association forces and the soldiers knocked only if a tent belonged to a commissioned officer, so she'd learned to dress quickly. She'd been sleeping in her uniform for the past few days, to save time. She dropped to the ground and did twenty-five push-ups, and when she was done her brain was fully awake. All the hand-to-hand combat training with Tharpa had sharpened her skills; several times she'd taken down Association soldiers, to their great surprise and embarrassment.

"I'm a real prizefighter," she told herself. "A slasher, no less."

At a minute before 0600 hours she crossed to her master's tent. It was four times the size of her own and bright with oil lamps. Mr. Socrates sat at a table, maps spread out across it. Tharpa was there too, with Modo sitting across from him in his own Association uniform and his black mask. Anticipation shone in his eyes.

Then she recognized the man sitting beside Mr. Socrates: Footman! She had only ever seen him answering the door or serving food at the many Association safe houses, but here he was at Camp Cobra! All this time that he'd been fetching tea and answering the door, he'd actually been one of Mr. Socrates' agents. Footman's arm was in a sling, his face was bruised, and he looked like he hadn't eaten for days. Tharpa set a cup of tea in front of him.

"So, last to the table, Octavia," Mr. Socrates said.

"Fashionably late, sir," she said. "It's a woman's prerogative."

"But not a soldier's. Please have a seat." He waited until she had done so. "As you can see, Footman has returned. He's brought valuable intelligence about the Clockwork Guild. He and Cook even managed to steal one of their Triton boats."

So Cook was an agent too? How could someone so good

with pastry and beef also be an agent? What next? Mrs. Finchley proclaimed as the true master of the Permanent Association? "Where is Cook?" Octavia asked.

"He's dead," Mr. Socrates said matter-of-factly. "We'll get to the events that led to his death in a moment."

Octavia felt her chest tighten and she exchanged glances with Modo. With his mask on it was hard to read his reaction. She had been so fond of Cook.

"Footman has provided us with the exact location of the Clockwork Guild's island." Mr. Socrates tapped the center of a map with his finger, indicating what looked like open water in the Pacific. Octavia noted that it was northwest of Hawaii, the only islands she recognized on the map. "They've been hiding there all this time, building up their armaments. They have even assembled a replica of the Crystal Palace and use it as the center of their operations."

"Why the Crystal Palace?" Modo asked. "They hate all things British."

"There must be some symbolic message for us in that choice, but it doesn't matter. What does matter is that we've discovered that the Guild is very close to completing three massive warships, even larger than the *Wyvern.* With those ships manned and armed, the Guild would become very difficult to defeat. Footman also discovered that they are working on what I can only describe as a horrible cadaver project; our fears about another Typhon were correct. Please tell them what you saw."

Footman nodded. "Bodies. We discovered a laboratory with many bodies. And Dr. Hyde was sewing them together."

"You mean dissecting them, don't you?" Modo asked.

"No. Reconstructing them. Later on we had to fight one of those dead men. He killed Cook and broke my ribs and arm."

"What Footman is describing is an encounter with Typhon or another creature," Mr. Socrates said. "They have either animated the dead or are using new tinctures to make the living act with all the feeling of the dead. Neither Footman nor Cook could injure their opponent. The Clockwork Guild's science in this realm is well beyond our own. If they're creating more Typhons, that would be a powerful advantage in any battle. Imagine ten Typhons leading an infantry charge." He let this image sink in. "Remember, Modo, what his name means? Typhon was the father of all monsters in Greek mythology. This is a message to us from the Guild."

Mr. Socrates stopped to sip his tea. His hand was steady as he set the cup down. Octavia thought he even looked younger—he loved this part of his life! "We must strike now, before those ships arrive." He looked around the table, gauging everyone's reaction. Octavia remained solemn and unreadable. She liked sneaking in and out of houses or alleys, but full-force attacks on enemy islands were not on her list of enjoyable activities.

"Footman's keen eye has taken a measure of their island," Mr. Socrates said. "During the night I designed a map with details of their defenses." He unfolded a small map, drawn in ink. It looked rather messy to Octavia. "Here is the palace. Below it, the port, well guarded by guns. There is an observation tower, here, along with an airship dock. Tall cliffs on the three other sides of the island make it unassailable from those directions. But Footman discovered water caves in the cliffs that took them to the surface. They may even lead into the fortress."

"The dragoons are too big for the tunnels," Footman pointed out.

"Yes. They're designed for a frontal assault. The number of guns will make that a very difficult task."

"With the full strength of the British Navy behind us," Modo said, "it shouldn't be so difficult."

"We'll not have the full force of the navy," Mr. Socrates said. "We are a small but elite force. And we'll have the element of surprise on our side."

"I do hope that we'll have more than surprise," Octavia said. "Maybe a few howitzers. Just a suggestion."

"We'll have plenty enough military muscle," Mr. Socrates said. "Trust me when I say that a full-frontal assault with the navy would require months of planning, requisition forms, and convincing certain implacable admirals. Ah, if only Lord Nelson were still with us. *There* was a man who could make quick decisions." He paused and pointed at the map. "If we strike now we can destroy them with one blow. If we wait they could get wind of our plans, pack up their island, and slither away."

"But what is the plan?" Modo asked.

"It will be unveiled the night of the invasion. Until then, only I will know what it is."

"And when will the invasion begin?" Octavia asked.

"We leave tomorrow night."

So soon! she wanted to shout. How could they possibly organize troops and armaments and supplies?

She looked at Modo to see how he was taking all this. His eyes glittered with excitement.

37

Aboard the HMS *Shah*

Early-morning fog stretched its tendrils across the docks of Esquimalt, seemed to reach right inside Modo, through his clothes, under his mask, making him shiver. He and Octavia were the last in line to board the HMS *Shah*. Ahead of them on the gangplank were the twelve dragoons in their green uniforms, their hair cut short, kit bags hanging from their arms. They were led by their sergeant and followed by twenty Association soldiers, bayoneted rifles slung across their backs. Not a bugle nor a drum was heard. In fact, the base seemed deserted. Everyone but the necessary seamen and soldiers had been ordered to their quarters. It was, after all, a secret mission.

Mr. Socrates was on deck beside the captain, watching the arrival of his troops. The armored suits were being hauled up by crane and placed on the deck under the instruction of

Tharpa. And there were marines already onboard, lined up to silently welcome their comrades-in-arms. Modo guessed that Mr. Socrates needed some extra muscle and marksmanship. Several marines looked stunned at the size of the dragoons.

"There are fifty of us," Octavia said.

Modo counted quickly. "You're right. Plus the sailors, of course. Fifty against, what? Three hundred Guild soldiers? How many mechanical hounds?"

"Ten at least," she said. "And there's Typhon, and it sounds like there are more creatures just like him."

"They'll have airships and Triton boats. Imagine those with cannons."

"It's quite a list. Are you nervous?" Octavia asked.

"No," he lied, "I'm eager." That was the truth. He desperately wanted to get there. His mother could be long dead by now; Colette and his father certainly were. He must strike back at the Guild, rescue his mother. And if it was too late, exact revenge.

They were given officers' cabins. The HMS *Shah* began to shudder, a whale awaking from slumber, as they unpacked.

They traveled without stopping, four days and nights of steaming southwest, the air growing hotter and more humid, so that by the third day Modo wished he were dressed in tropical khaki, not the damnably hot black uniform.

They trained on the deck every day, soldiers running back and forth, doing their best to march and drill, and three times a day they ate the gray gruel. And still Mr. Socrates gave no hint of his plans. Modo began to wonder if there was any sort of strategy at all, other than a full-frontal assault. How many of them would live through that?

On the fourth evening a command was shouted along the deck and lights were put out. Not even a cigarette could be seen. All was silent, except for the clanking and creaking of the ship. The thudding of the steam engines far below echoed like war drums.

Modo met Octavia at the bow, and they stood staring into the dark. The breeze was cooling, and he wished he could lift his mask to feel it full upon his face. It was far warmer than London at this time of year. Several sailors were manning the guns. He braced himself for flares, cannon fire, and explosions to light up the sky.

But nothing happened, and an hour passed with him and Octavia staring forward at the dark ocean and their dubious future. At some point he realized she was holding his hand. He didn't remember when she had taken it, but he held tight and wished for this moment to never end.

"Do you think we'll still be alive tomorrow?" she asked quietly, with more seriousness than he'd ever heard in her voice.

"Yes," Modo said, trying to sound as confident as possible.

"How can you be certain?"

"I guess you won't get to tell me that I was wrong." He let out a forced laugh.

"I feel as though I've known you my whole life, Modo," Octavia whispered. "Somehow I was meant to know you. We are supposed to be standing here together, right now. Do you believe that?"

"I don't know. Fate is . . . it's not rational."

"Well, feelings aren't rational. So what! It's a feeling I

happen to have. That I was meant to know you. To be your friend."

"Friend?" he asked.

"We are more than friends, Modo. You know what I mean."

No, he didn't, actually. Once again she was speaking in riddles. He looked away from her. "Don't talk as if we're about to die. It's bad luck."

"You don't believe in luck, Modo."

"I don't. Nor do I want to think about our deaths or about life beyond tomorrow. I want to think only about our duty."

"And what is our duty? To Queen and Country?"

"To Colette's memory. To my mother. To put an end to this Guild once and for all."

Her hand tightened on his. "But what's the point if we don't succeed?"

"We have to."

The engine rumbled, then stopped, but the *Shah* was still moving. The masts creaked above them.

"We've switched to sails," Modo said. He took a deep breath in an effort to calm his now racing heart.

"We are closing in on our destination," Mr. Socrates said from behind them. Modo quickly released Octavia's hand. "Come and receive your orders."

They followed him to a cabin, passing the dragoons, who were getting into their armor with the help of the Association soldiers. The soldiers looked like black ants scurrying around wasps.

It was a small cabin lit by a single lamp. The porthole

was covered with black cloth. "Quick, the door," Mr. Socrates said. Modo shut it.

Their master handed them two maps: one of the island, the other of a series of tunnels. "Memorize these," he said. After they had both studied the images he took the maps back. "You two will have tasks that best suit your skill sets," he explained, pointing at the tunnel map. "While the dragoons attack you'll be entering the sea cave. By my calculations the tides will be at a sufficiently low level by four a.m., an hour from now. If possible, you'll first free Madame Hébert. Given how valuable she is to the Guild's experiments, my best guess is that she's in the cave near the center of the island. Hand her over to the protection of the Association soldiers."

"And what's the other assignment?" Modo asked.

"To capture the master of the Guild. It will be a tricky job, since a full-out battle will be under way."

"Assuming we can find him, that is."

"Assuming he's a man," Octavia pointed out. "He could be a woman."

"Perhaps," Mr. Socrates said, "but doubtful. If it's unworkable for you to take him prisoner, then I expect you to eliminate him."

"Kill him?"

"This isn't a game, Modo. This is how our business is done. If he escapes, then many more Britons will die, perhaps thousands." The ship shuddered to a stop. "The *Shah* has orders to begin shelling the island at sunrise, which will be six a.m., or earlier, if targets become clearly visible. You'll have to work fast. We have arrived. Prepare yourselves."

He flicked off the light and opened the door to the dark.

38

Sounding the Alarm

It was only chance and sleeplessness that had taken Miss Hakkandottir to the docks so late that night. She had traversed the island and was now standing at the end of the pier looking out at the Pacific. She had just visited Dr. Hyde, who was hard at work on his creations. They were ugly creatures; it was an ugly business, but necessary. She still did not understand the intentions of the Guild Master, but she felt better when she walked. And her presence kept the soldiers alert. She'd caught one guard sleeping and dealt him such a blow with her metal hand that he was now in the medical tent. That would keep the rest of them on their toes.

She missed the *Wyvern* and how strong she'd felt standing on the deck of such an incredible warship. It had been a part of her, and when it went down, she felt that part of her sink into the ocean too. The airship *Hera* was another part of her, almost like her metal hand. She had failed far too many times.

The Crystal Palace glowed dimly behind her. The Guild Master would still be working. It was nighttime here, but it would be daytime in other countries. He had a multitude of agents around the world who reported to him.

She stroked Grace's large skull. The mechanical hound was silent since she had no vocal cords, a design of the good Dr. Hyde. Grace had been a valuable companion for years now. The dog made the familiar clicking sound from the back of her throat that meant she was happy. "Yes, you always stand with me," Miss Hakkandottir said.

She stared at the dark horizon. How much of her life had been spent as a pirate on those waters? That had been her first introduction to the Guild Master. Even then he'd had no name. She would work hard to get into his good graces again. Then she laughed. "Good graces?" she said. "And you are my good Grace."

The dog clicked in agreement, then lifted her ears and looked toward the west. She made a rasping sound, as close to a bark as she could get.

"What do you hear, Grace?"

A moment later Miss Hakkandottir heard something too, a sound like the buzzing of giant insects. It was not familiar, though sometimes she discerned a mechanical whine. There were no shipments that she knew of arriving at this hour.

She saw the bow of a craft glinting in the moonlight a fair distance away. Behind it were two other boats. She squinted. They were square-shaped boats with gates at the front. British flags flapped in the moonlight.

"Sound the alarm!" she shouted, and sprinted back across the dock, Grace pounding the boards beside her. "Now! Sound the alarm!"

Sirens began to scream. Guild soldiers took their positions, and orders were shouted as bright electric lights came to life, pointing out to sea. Miss Hakkandottir raced up the circular stairs to the top of the observation tower and watched the boats draw closer. The clear outline of helmeted heads. Soldiers! Rifles on their shoulders.

"Fire!" she hollered. "Fire, now!"

The field guns let loose their first volley—*boom, boom, boom!* The sound shook the very tower itself, but it was not easy to bring the big fourteen-pounders to bear on moving targets, and the shots landed well past the boats. The enemy gained speed as they approached, engines buzzing like wasps. The first craft hit the shore and skidded several feet onto the beach. Someone jumped off the back and began swimming out to sea.

Then the gate of the boat dropped open. The Guild soldiers, who had gathered along their trenches, fired. The enemy was standing in the boat, guns at the ready but not charging the men. No matter how many shots they fired, the enemy didn't fall, just rocked back and forth, taking hits here and there. Helmets flew off and still they just stood in the harrowing fire.

Then it dawned on her. They were dummies! At that same moment the second boat struck next to a stanchion on the pier. The third landed near the base of the observation tower. The gates flipped open and more dummies were revealed.

"Cease fire!" she shouted. "Cease fire!"

It took a full minute before her orders were relayed. When the soldiers finally stopped firing all she could hear was the ringing in her ears from the booming of the big guns. The dummies continued to sway, many of them torn in two by rifle fire. What did all this mean?

"Board the vessels!" she commanded. A group of six Guild soldiers approached the first of the landing craft.

The boat exploded, sending a cloud of shrapnel through the approaching soldiers and knocking them to the sand. Then the second boat blew up. She watched in disbelief as the pillar on the pier was smashed to pieces. The third boat, which had beached itself directly below the observation tower, burst into flames like a giant Roman candle.

The tower she stood on began to sway gently, and then, as though it were tired, it gave way.

39

The Island Assault

Modo sat in a boat that was cutting silently through the waves. He shivered when he heard the cannon fire begin. They were approaching the opposite, rocky cliffs of the island. Octavia put her hand on his shoulder; it was comforting to feel her touch at that moment. Each boom seemed to shake the island; it certainly shook his confidence. He'd heard smaller cannons before, but these ones sounded like hammers of the gods.

The operation was under way and there was no turning back. To his left and right were six other boats, each transporting Association soldiers and the fully armored dragoons, metal glinting in the moonlight. He was thankful for his mask: none of the soldiers or Octavia would know how frightened he was. As for them, their grim faces seemed carved in stone. The soldiers were silent but for the occasional hissed command. The boats were surprisingly quiet, magically gliding along thanks to their electric engines. "A trick we stole from your friends in the *Ictíneo*," Mr. Socrates had explained. "Electric boats provide a swift, inaudible attack."

With all the rifle fire and cannons going off at the docks, no one would hear the slight humming sound of the boats from such a distance. As they approached, no alarms sounded on this side of the island. It seemed deserted above them. Had the attack on the docks drawn all the sentries to the battle? One could only hope.

At this moment his master would be back on the deck of the HMS *Shah*, watching the mission unfold through his spyglass. Tharpa would be at his side. Modo wished Tharpa were going into battle alongside him. Maybe he'd feel more confident. He patted himself to be sure his Colt pocket revolver was in its holster and his knife in its sheath.

They glided right up to the rocky cliffs, fully a hundred feet tall, slick with spray, unassailable by ordinary men. Even Modo, an expert and natural climber, wouldn't risk it. But given what he'd seen of the dragoons, he was fairly certain they could ascend the rocks with little difficulty.

"Do you see any caves?" Octavia whispered. "Footman said they'd be on this side."

"It's a big island."

He squinted, wishing for a bit more moonlight. No cave that he could see. It was so dark it'd be difficult to find it.

"The entrance is here somewhere," he said. "We just have to keep searching."

Modo watched as the dragoons stood in their boats, reached up and found holds with their metal hands, then, one by one, began to scale the cliffs. They climbed like insects. It was a glorious sight, seeing them move in perfect unison. Mr. Socrates had long ago spoken theoretically about soldiers in mechanized suits of armor, and now here they were as promised, and about to strike the Clockwork Guild.

Several stones hit the water, and the group looked up to see a dragoon hanging by one arm, scrambling for another handhold. Moments later he plummeted and, without so much as a squawk, splashed into the ocean and sank.

There was no rescue attempt, not even a pause in the operation. "Could it be Ester?" Octavia said. "Or Oppie?"

"We won't know until later," Modo said, surprised at how steady his voice sounded.

The lead dragoons were already reaching the summit. Modo expected them to be pushed back, but the last of them reached the top without incident. The cannons went on booming. Ropes were lowered and Sergeant Beatty and the remaining Association soldiers climbed up.

"I do wish we were going with them," Modo said. "I don't much like crawling into holes."

"I'm part sewer rat!" Octavia said. "We'd better find this cave quickly!" She flicked on her pocket lucifer.

"Put that out!" Modo hissed.

"If no one saw the dragoons, no one'll notice us."

Modo took out his own light and shone the beam on the rock walls. After a few minutes, he spotted a hole, barely large enough for a grown man. "There it is!"

"You first, since you're part monkey," Octavia said. He directed the sailor to maneuver the boat closer, then jumped up, grabbing at the lip of the cave. It took some effort, but he climbed in and lowered a short rope. Octavia was soon beside him and they pulled out their compasses.

They crouched and crab-walked their way deeper into the cave. At times Modo had to squeeze his shoulders together to shove himself through narrower passages. Thankfully, the tunnel eventually widened. He slipped and splashed into a deep pool of water. He kicked and found the floor, and carried on, pushing against the water, holding his pocket-watch lucifer high. "It's deep," he said. "Be careful."

"Yes, sir," Octavia answered, splashing in behind him. He could see the edge of the pool ahead.

It wasn't long before the map they'd memorized became useless. There were several fresh tunnels, which only confused them both. In time they found themselves in a small chamber surrounded by numerous openings. A smidgen of light could be seen at the end of a few of the tunnels.

"This way," Octavia whispered, pointing at one of the partially lit openings.

"Are you certain?"

"Yes."

They followed the tunnel to a dead end where a ladder was fastened to the stone. The light source was somewhere above them. Modo climbed up first. Footman had warned them of the stench, but it was beyond anything Modo had imagined: a mix of carcasses and sulfur and other foul odors. The higher he climbed, the worse it stank. He was close to retching, so when he reached the top he covered his nose and mouth with one hand and helped Octavia up with the other. When she emerged she took a deep breath as if she needed a gulp of fresh air. Modo wrinkled his nose in disgust.

"How can you stand the stench?" he asked.

"Oh, no worse than the cabbage soup the headmistress used to feed us every day," Octavia joked, but she looked pale.

There was a sputtering lamp overhead. The tunnel in front of them was partially collapsed, but Modo's lucifer revealed enough room for them to squeeze through.

Octavia glanced at her compass. "That tunnel goes west, toward the beach. The cave that we're supposed to be entering is in that direction."

"Then let's take it, but we'll have to do so in the dark," Modo said. They both put out their lights. After a minute, Octavia flicked hers back on.

"This is madness, Modo. We could fall into a pit or be sucked into slime. I won't look good dead."

"That's for certain," he said glibly, and then an image of Colette flashed through his mind, how she'd looked after her death. He didn't want to so much as imagine losing Octavia that way.

He flicked on his light and led the way. With each step it grew colder, as though they were walking into winter. The stink subsided. When they reached a chamber lit by gaslight, he peeked around the corner. No one was there, but along the wall were stacks of neatly labeled crates. Modo and Octavia crept into the room, shivering. Big square chunks of ice were sticking out of a blanket of straw. The crates were labeled with Roman numerals. "Do we dare look inside?" Octavia asked.

"What would they keep at such a blood-numbing temperature?" he wondered aloud as he reached to lift the lid on a smaller crate. The wood creaked as Modo worked the lid back and forth till it finally popped off. They gasped and

Octavia clutched her chest. There, looking up at them, were about fifty eyeballs, each neatly tucked into felt holders like they were eggs. They could only be human eyes, plucked out and waiting for . . . for what? He quickly closed the lid.

"Well," he said. "I certainly don't intend to look in any more crates."

"I'm with you," Octavia said, her own eyes wide and uncertain.

They crept out of the chamber and along another tunnel. Once again a putrid smell assaulted their noses. He paused at the entrance of the next chamber and motioned Octavia to stay still. He could hear shuffling, and when he peeked around the rock he saw men in white coats setting down a crate. Then they got into a lift; one pressed a button and they ascended silently.

Modo cautiously entered the chamber. The room was humid and he began to sweat, drops running down into his mask, his eyes burning. In the center were two vast brass cauldrons boiling over a coal fire. Glass tubes led from one to the other, a bloodred substance inside them. He peeked over the edge of a cauldron and saw a bubbling red liquid with pinkish streaks. It smelled horrible.

"That's worse than boiled cabbage," Octavia said.

"I can't imagine its purpose."

"Best not to."

A grating noise came from behind them. They turned to see that the lift was on its way down, and quickly hid behind a stack of barrels along the walls.

A man stepped out of the lift, his back to them, and began to pick ice from the top of a barrel, crunching it in his mouth.

Modo signaled his intention to Octavia, counted to three using his fingers, then leapt. She jumped at the same time.

But as Modo flew through the air, the man pivoted and gave a glittering smile as he darted out of the way. Lime!

He stopped some distance away and turned. "Ah, a couple of Alices have tumbled down the rabbit hole." He drew long knives and waved them. "I came down here to escape the booming booms. *Boom boom boom.* I'm not much of a military man. A little too noisy for my taste."

"You're hiding, you mean," Modo said.

"I'm being selectively brave. And thank you for making an appearance. I'm happy to have you entertain me."

Modo triumphantly drew his pistol and was pleased to see Lime stop smiling. Aiming to wound, he pulled the trigger. All he got in reply was a click of the hammer. He pulled it again and again. The gun was dripping water.

"Ah, so grievously sad," Lime said, taking a step toward them, twirling his blades. "'One, two! One, two! And through and through, the vorpal blade went snicker-snack.'"

40

Applauding the Designer

By the time Oppie and the other dragoons had crested the top of the cliffs, there were only eleven of them and a small team of regular soldiers. The noise of their ascent had been covered by the gun battle on the beaches, but now the guns had stopped firing.

"Form ranks!" Sergeant Beatty commanded, and they split into two groups. At that moment Oppie knew for certain that Edmund had been the one who'd drowned, as he'd always been on Oppie's left in their squadron. A horrible way to go. He'd miss Edmund; they'd played with toys together in those first months at a place called Ravenscroft. Later, when they'd been shipped to Esquimalt, they'd played with guns and axes.

"Squadron A, take the point! Full speed!" Beatty commanded. Ester's squadron chugged forward, the dragoons' mechanized arms and legs hissing. Oppie was in the second group of five, bringing up the rear. He pushed all thoughts of Edmund from his mind.

This was what he had trained for! The crimes of Oppie's enemies had grown and festered in his heart since the day they'd kidnapped him as a boy. How he had been longing for this moment and now that it was here, oddly, he found himself thinking of his mother. Her face loomed before him.

Such thoughts would only cloud his mind. He banished them.

"Squadron B! Forward! March!" Oppie's troop pounded down the path toward the beach, hundreds of yards away. The beach was lit in such a way that he could clearly see a redheaded woman waving her arms, directing the Guild soldiers. Miss Hakkandottir! He had seen her when he was a child. Her face was burned in his memory.

Silencing the massive field guns was their first objective. Ester's troop had almost reached them. The Guild soldiers tried to hold their position, but their lines were split in two by the giant dragoons.

His squadron began their charge, but Oppie slowed as they passed the glowing mouth of a cave. Inside, an old man with stringy, long white hair was watching the unfolding battle. Ah, yes, Dr. Hyde.

"Sergeant Beatty!" Oppie yelled, but he was at the rear of the squadron and his sergeant was out of earshot. Oppie brought himself to a stop, motors burning, steam hissing, his chest heaving, as there was more than a little exertion required on his part to keep his armor in motion. One of his squadron's objectives was to capture the doctor. He'd do his best not to kill him in the process.

The doctor was much smaller and older than Oppie remembered. He'd been a child when this man had forced his tinctures on him. He didn't give his fellow soldiers a backward glance; they would be able to take the beach.

Dr. Hyde met his gaze and then his eyes took in the spectacle of Oppie's armor. "You are beautiful," the old man said. "You are so very beautiful."

It had been a lifetime since this man had administered the potion and promised Oppie he'd become something extraordinary. "You don't recognize me?" he said, flipping back a section of armor protecting his shoulder.

The doctor looked at the bolt that protruded from Oppie's shoulder. "Your bolt. Shoulder bolts! I . . . remember . . . you are mine."

"Yes," Oppie said. "I am yours. Your creation. And I have come for you."

One blow and he could crush the old sawbones into pieces. How easy and satisfying—destroy the old man as he had destroyed Oppie. But his orders had been to capture, not kill.

"Come with me," he said.

"Young man," replied Dr. Hyde, "I cannot leave my work. It is the most important work of all. And it is very nearly done."

"I have orders. I must follow them."

He grabbed the doctor's shoulder with his iron hand, which moved as though it were his real hand. He had worked so hard to perfect it, had practiced picking up eggs without breaking them. The doctor looked at Oppie's metal hand, examining all the gears. "Marvelous work," he said. "I can see how it can be improved, but still I applaud your designer."

"You'll meet him soon enough."

"I cannot leave. My creations wait for me. They are close to life. It has been so very good to see you again."

"You will—"

Then, without warning, Oppie found himself flying to the side, the doctor slipping from his hand. He rolled, the armor protecting him from breaking his back on the stones. He stood, pistons whining, and turned to face his enemy.

A massive man stood before him as the doctor limped slowly back into the cave.

"My master requested your departure," Typhon grunted. They had been warned about this man too. But he was larger than Oppie had imagined—nearly as big as Oppie. His skin had a mottled greenish pallor that seemed to glow in the moonlight. Their orders had been to destroy him.

Oppie unsnapped the ax from his back and charged.

41

One More Die to Cast

The Guild Master watched from the observation deck of the Crystal Palace. He heard the sirens first, tearing him away from his work with telegrams and calculations. He strode to the eastern windows, where much of the island was visible to him, and looked down. There was a light in Dr. Hyde's cave. Flares filled the air around the docks. And the gunners were firing at targets—boats—in the dark ocean. Then a great explosion, then a second, a third. The destruction of the observation tower and the crashing of the flaming airship into the ground had been particularly bothersome. The metal shell had protected it from rifle fire but not from an explosion of that magnitude. A design flaw?

Defending from a raid had not been a major part of his calculations. There was only a small chance they'd ever find him, so he'd only dug a few trenches and put up barricades.

This was a well planned attack. How had they discovered the island? There was that one small Triton ship that had been stolen. He had assumed the thieves had fled with it. Maybe not.

No matter, the enemy was here, had hunted down his Guild. No need for panic. It wasn't as though this scenario hadn't occurred to him. It was part of the risk. He just hadn't foreseen the metal juggernaut soldiers that were currently routing his own troops. Had the British advanced so much in such a short time?

Ah, but they had come at a time when his forces were weaker. He'd lost so many men when the *Wyvern* had gone down. They had recruited more, but they weren't yet as well trained.

What was Britain's ambition? Kill or capture?

How to make either more difficult was the question. He had often thought of himself as a tortoise, slowly making his plans for the world. What did a tortoise do when attacked? Withdraw into itself.

He would be the tortoise, and he had one more die to cast.

42

Cauldron Boils

Octavia watched Modo throw his useless revolver at Lime. The man ducked and gave them another broad smile as he clashed his knives together.

"'Beware the Jabberwock, my son!'" Lime taunted. "'The jaws that bite, the claws that catch!'"

"'Jabberwocky'?" Modo said, drawing his own knife. "Quoting poetry at me?"

If that was poetry, Octavia wanted no part of it. Modo's knife was much smaller than Lime's, and, though Modo was strong, he hadn't grown up in Seven Dials to fine-tune his knife-fighting technique. Octavia drew her saber, brushed by Modo, and rushed Lime. When he raised his knives, intent on slicing her from gullet to belly, she dropped to the floor and blocked them both with her own blade in a move Tharpa had taught her. She struck Lime directly in the knee with her foot.

He let out a shout and tripped backward, and she gave him another good kick. He reached for her foot but too late, and he was upended into one of the boiling cauldrons. It was almost comical, except that something very strange happened. He let out a muffled scream as he seemed to be pulled into the cauldron, the hot, smelly pink substance wrapping around him. He kicked his legs.

"I suppose we should drag him out," Modo said. They yanked on his boots, now still, and he was surprisingly light as they pulled him to the floor.

"My Lord!" squeaked Octavia.

All that remained of Lime was a skeleton, which quickly fell to pieces. His metal teeth rattled across the rocks toward Modo, who booted them away.

"Acid," Octavia said, taking a few steps back. The sight of Lime's bones was enough to make Octavia want to vomit. The acid sloshed around on the floor, as though it had a mind of its own.

"Let's get out of here," Modo said.

They ran into the lift. Modo pressed a button and they rose thirty or forty feet, passing other tunnels. Octavia caught a glimpse of more crates and containers. "Should we stop?" she asked, but Modo shook his head.

"To the top. Dr. Hyde's cave must be above us somewhere."

With a clunk they reached the highest floor. It was made of smooth stone that led down a long tunnel to the south. It gradually grew wider and opened into three tunnels.

"Ah, Modo, we are cursed by tunnels."

"At least it's not London's sewers, eh?"

They took the middle tunnel, and for the first time found themselves at an actual door. The lock was no problem for Modo. He simply pulled on it hard and it snapped. Octavia had always been impressed by his strength.

Beyond the door the room was brightly lit by several gas lamps hung from the ceiling. A small bench sat just inside the entrance. Modo stopped in the center of the room, putting his hands on a wall of glass. A step later, Octavia saw what had captured his attention.

"Mother," he said softly.

43

A Horrible Whistling

It took all of Oppie's concentration to deflect blow after powerful blow. His countless hours of training, of swinging clubs and fists against the other dragoons, made each move natural. But how could his monstrous opponent, who was just flesh and blood, unleash such staggering hits? Oppie had even used an ax to deflect Typhon, but the handle broke in half like a toothpick.

The sun was rising, its light showing how ugly his opponent was. He punched Typhon in the temple, a wallop that would have taken off another man's head, but the monster didn't even blink.

"You are a worthy combatant," Typhon said.

"Such fancy words." Oppie had wanted to say something clever, but failed. He struggled, pushing his body and his mechanical armor to its limit. His anger made him stronger.

He landed a kick in the center of Typhon's chest, knocking him into a barricade strewn with wires. It broke into pieces. The creature was up again in a heartbeat, smiling lopsidedly. "Very impressive."

Typhon lifted a stray beam and swung, taking Oppie out at the legs. As the dragoon pushed himself onto his knees, Typhon hit his head. Oppie's helmet broke in two and flew off, exposing his skull.

The monster was toying with him! But Oppie rose up, shoving the beast ten yards back. There was a great boom in the distance.

"Let's have at it, as they say," Typhon grunted.

A horrible whistling began to fill Oppie's ears. He thought Typhon's punch had done something to his hearing, but the screeching grew louder. Even Typhon paused.

Then a shell landed several feet away, blasting Oppie against a bin, which collapsed and dumped coal on him. Could he drown in coal? He was suffocating under the weight of it. He kicked and dug his way to the surface, coughing up dust and chunks of coal. The world was completely silent. This time he knew his ears had been damaged.

He got to his feet, his armor-plated legs steady, his vision clouded with smoke. As it cleared, he saw Typhon lying on his back. Oppie limped over to him. The monster was fully intact, despite how close he had been to the shell blast. He wore a peaceful expression, though he looked quite dead.

A small movement caught Oppie's eye. The strangest thing: the monster's little finger was curling and uncurling, as if inviting Oppie to come closer.

44

Shelling at Sunrise

Mr. Socrates stood on the deck of the HMS *Shah* and watched through his spyglass. Darkness and smoke made it hard to make sense of the morning's events, but he'd known early on that the explosive boats and the feint for the beaches had worked. The three perfectly timed explosions had caught the enemy unaware and brought down the dock and the observation tower. He had been particularly happy to see the airship burst into a satisfactory series of flames. It had lit up the beach, making the assault that much easier to observe.

They'd been able to rescue two of the three soldiers who had piloted the dummy boats and set the charges. The third might still be somewhere in the water.

The official sunrise was half past six, but a full hour earlier the sky grew light enough that their targets became visible, so they began pressing them with fire.

The dragoons drove the Guild soldiers back. It was like watching Titans battle humans. Then they had ripped the firing pins from the enemy's field guns, so the HMS *Shah* was now safe from the long-range guns and the beaches were open for the third phase of the attack.

He counted. He had lost three of the dragoons. From this distance it was impossible to tell which ones, only that two lay immobile on the beaches. Perhaps they were not past medical attention.

At Mr. Socrates' command the ship's guns began to fire again, smashing the trenches where the enemy was trapped. Then, satisfied that the volley of shells had weakened their targets, he and Tharpa climbed down a rope ladder and led a flotilla of electric boats jammed with marines and sailors toward the shore.

Five minutes later he was striding up the beach toward the front line.

45

Bed of Stone

Modo's mother lay on a stone bed covered with a thin mattress. Her red hair had been combed, but clumps had fallen out. She was gaunt and her skin so unnaturally pale that her veins made a spiderweb pattern across her arms and neck. Her forearms were freckled with needle marks. Clearly they had been stealing from her, blood and perhaps more. She was not a beautiful woman, and Modo found himself surprised by that. He had imagined her to be handsome, though he, of all people, should not have expected to have an attractive mother.

The quartz that separated them was clear as glass. He pounded on it, slamming his fists again and again. She stirred but didn't awaken.

"We must get her out of there!" he shouted, and pounded even harder.

"Yes. Yes," Octavia said. "Calm down. There must be another way."

"Yes, there must be. We . . ." His voice trailed off. His mother had opened her eyes and was looking at him for the first time since she and his father had left him at Notre Dame. Of course, there was no sign of recognition on her face—after all, he was wearing a mask—but surely she must realize that he and Octavia were not part of the Guild.

The woman blinked, looking drowsy.

"We're here to take you home," Modo said in French. He had no idea if she could hear him. "We are friends."

She didn't speak. What incredible pain had she already endured? What torture at the hands of this horrid Guild? He placed his open palm against the quartz, a sign of peace. Of love, perhaps.

Then a section of the floor inside her chamber slid aside. A nearly bald man rose up through the hole on a lift. He paused, not quite startled, and stared at Modo and Octavia. He rubbed his chin for a moment.

"Dr. Hyde," Octavia said.

He was only a few inches taller than Modo. The doctor examined him through the glass without any hint of fear. Then he nodded, turned, and lifted Modo's mother from the slab of stone.

"Where are you taking her?" Modo shouted. "Where?"

The man didn't respond as he carried her to the lift, then disappeared through the floor, leaving the room empty.

Modo slammed his fists against the quartz.

"Come," Octavia said, pulling him back toward the door, "we'll find another way."

A bullet struck the wall and the room echoed with the shot. A Guild soldier blocked the doorway, pulling back the hammer on his rifle. Modo lifted the wood bench and threw it, knocking him to the floor with such force that he didn't get up again.

"Let's go!" Modo said, leading Octavia through the door. "We will find her. We will!"

46

The Power Vested in Me

When the barrage arrived, Miss Hakkandottir watched it cut through her ranks and she screamed with rage as the Guild soldiers scattered. The tincture that had been used to bind them also weakened their brains, sometimes in unpredictable ways. Despite the training, they were now like mice fleeing from some discovered hidey-hole.

"Form ranks!" she shouted, to no avail. She instructed Grace to herd the soldiers like cattle, so the dog snapped at their heels. "Form ranks!"

Miss Hakkandottir began to chase them and pull them into formation, smacking several with her metal hand. The moment she let one go, he ran. Panic set in. She didn't have time to execute each and every one of them.

A hasty retreat was her only option. She leapt from the trench and ran from the oncoming enemy, Grace at her heels.

Wagons and barricades had been blown to pieces by the attack, and the farther she went, the thicker the smoke. Guns fired behind her, a good sign; she was at least going in the right direction.

She jumped over a dead horse and landed in an open crater. It had been created by a shell that had blasted everything away when it landed. Something large was moving in front of her, and when the wind blew the smoke away, she saw one of the giant metal soldiers looking down at the body of Typhon.

He had bested Typhon! The man's helmet was off, and she was shocked to see his face, so childlike on the body of an adult, enclosed in a giant metal hornet. Seeing her, he raised his head.

"You," he said. "I know you! I remember you!" He pointed his metal finger at her as though he'd caught a mischievous child. "Miss Hakkandottir, by the power vested in me, I declare you under arrest!"

It was the oddest thing she'd heard all day. The boy-thing actually recognized her and he was . . . arresting her? She laughed, almost uncontrollably, then drew her pistol and fired. The bullet ricocheted off his shoulder. She fired again. Another ricochet. "Put down your weapon!" he commanded. He lumbered toward her, gaining speed.

"Get him, Grace," she hissed. Her hound leapt, but he swatted the dog aside with his metal arm.

"Grace!" Miss Hakkandottir screamed, but the hound hit the rocky ground hard and didn't move again. She nearly charged the soldier but drew up short. There was only one way out. She fled. Straight for the Crystal Palace.

47

A Game Well Played

Mr. Socrates watched from the beach with a sense of pleasure and confidence as the HMS *Shah* sent a barrage of shells toward the Crystal Palace. The first phase had unfolded with relative ease. And the second phase had gone equally well. The ship's doctor had assured him that the two wounded dragoons would live, but five Association soldiers and three marines were dead. In exchange the enemy forces had been scattered and a collection of prisoners had been taken on a boat back to the HMS *Shah* for questioning. The enemy's guns and airships had been destroyed. Typhon, the odd, monstrous creature, was dead; Mr. Socrates had inspected the corpse himself. Impressive, that one. He had not seen Modo and Octavia yet, but he was convinced they'd soon emerge from the tunnels.

The only detail that irked him was the Crystal Palace itself. From a distance it had looked like one shot from the *Shah*'s nine-inch muzzle-loaders would shatter it, but apparently not. So it couldn't be glass. It was some sort of impenetrable material, thick enough to withstand their heaviest guns. Through his spyglass he could see that they'd succeeded in breaking off a few chips, but it appeared structurally sound. An astounding architectural feat!

They had scored one direct hit at the top of the building, shearing off the airship landing tower. At least they could be sure their enemies wouldn't be fleeing that way.

In short order his snipers silenced the last of the rifle fire. Now the enemy could only retreat to the palace. They'd be trapped in their shell.

How to bust the shell open was the problem. He hadn't counted on a siege. He had enough supplies for a week, but there might be months of supplies stored away inside those walls. A siege would require that he get a message back to Esquimalt. It would be weeks before reinforcements arrived.

He raised his hand, sending a signal to one of his lieutenants, who in turn made a sign to a flagman on the beach, who waved *cease fire*. The *Shah*'s guns fell silent.

Mr. Socrates stepped out from his cover. Only a gifted marksman could hit him at this distance from the palace; it was worth the risk. He raised his speaking trumpet and shouted, "*Clockwork Guild agents! It would be best for all concerned if you were to surrender now.*"

The Crystal Palace was quiet. The quartz was clear, but he couldn't actually see inside. Tharpa stood a few yards behind him, his rifle trained on possible sniper nests.

"*It would be best for all concerned if* you *surrendered*," a woman answered, using an even louder speaking trumpet. There was no way to detect her actual location, other than the general direction of the palace. He knew her voice, of course. Miss Hakkandottir. He'd hoped a shell or a bullet had removed her from this earth, but, alas, no such luck.

"Ah, Ingrid, how lovely to hear your voice again." His trumpet made him feel as though he could blow their walls down by merely speaking. *"Your Swedish accent is a joy to my ears."*

"Ha! Intelligence has failed you. This is what comes of mediocre agents," she retorted. *"I'm Icelandic."*

He was amused. Had his sources actually been so far off? *"Are we to settle this with swords again?"* he asked.

"It would be less than gentlemanly of me to duel with such a doddering old fool."

"Enough!" he snapped. *"I will address your master."*

"I am the master of all you see," she replied.

"No," Mr. Socrates said. *"You're not capable of such visionary thinking. Send him out. Ingrid, I'm growing tired of this charade. It's such a lovely palace—do not force us to destroy it and all who remain inside."*

He expected her to shout a defiant answer, or take a shot at him. Instead, a male voice whispered into the speaking trumpet.

"You have done well, Alan Reeve. I salute you. A clever plan executed with great precision."

"With whom am I speaking?"

"You may call me Prometheus." His tone was flat. Disinterested. He'd named himself after a Titan. Was the man mad? Of course, Mr. Socrates had himself taken on a last name of

distinction, but that was only to hide his past. This man, on the other hand, might well believe himself to be a Titan.

"Well, Prometheus, I also salute you. Let us chat, shall we? Face to face, over tea and sweet biscuits. On the deck of my ship."

"I have analyzed our situation and there is no other choice for us but surrender. It was a game well played. I shall open the gates for you conquering heroes."

Immediately, the main doors at the front of the palace began to slide apart. The dragoons raised their elephant guns, the soldiers and marines raised their rifles. It was still dark inside the palace, but something large was sliding out.

"It is an offering of surrender," the invisible speaker said, a smile now in his voice.

About a dozen Guild soldiers were heaving against a giant wooden crate, rolling it across wooden poles toward them. What odd sort of gesture was this? How was this a surrender? It slowly descended the paved road from the palace. The crate had air holes and was so large that it could easily contain at least twenty horses.

Horses! The Trojan horse! "Fire! Fire at the crate!" he commanded, and his men obeyed. The Guild soldiers stopped and fled back into the palace, and the gates slammed shut after them.

The box collapsed, revealing five monstrous hulking men, eyes dead. They were much larger than Typhon, and they had been redesigned more than Mr. Socrates had dreamed possible. One had four arms; another had large horns; a third had ten-foot-long tentacles. The final creature was part metal and part human, plate armor fastened like scales to his flesh. His arms were clearly steam-powered, ending in huge crablike claws. The machines of war, the cannons and Maxim guns that tore men apart, were civilized compared with these creatures. Their appearance shook him to the core.

There was something else. A small wave of silver was running across the ground in front of the monsters. Mr. Socrates squinted. Metal spiders.

He retreated behind their barricade and took stock of his soldiers. The helmeted dragoons were hard to read, but helmetless Trooper Entwistle was staring, wide-eyed. The Association soldiers and the marines fired automatically, but Mr. Socrates knew they had to be unnerved. They'd faced cavalry charges and cannon fire, but none had seen an enemy as terrible as this. It was too late to call down a barrage; it would hit his own men too. That could only be a final option. One of the flagmen ran screaming onto the beach and into the water.

Mr. Socrates thought of Sun Tzu and his *Art of War*: *He who knows when he can fight and when he cannot will be victorious.* Was it time to flee? They could be off this beach and back in the boats in minutes, leaving only a few to cover their retreat. Those men would die, undoubtedly. No. They had not sacrificed this much only to be driven back. This was what the Guild had created, what they ultimately wanted to unleash upon Britain. Their new ships would make the invasion possible, by carrying these beasts across the Pacific.

Sun Tzu had also said: *Look on them as your own beloved sons, and they will stand by you even unto death.* "Hold your positions," Mr. Socrates commanded. "I'm right here, men. Standing beside you."

The monsters began lumbering toward them, but first, a hundred little spiders scurried over the lip of the Association's trenches, and up the soldiers' arms. Most shook them off, but one marine screamed after being bitten, then fell over. After a few short convulsions he was dead. Poison! The other soldiers were quick to smash at the spiders with the butts of their guns, but one ran up a dragoon's leg, found flesh, and the dragoon fell over, waving his arms and thrashing around.

Four sailors fled into the water. Mr. Socrates couldn't blame them. They might have held their position if they'd been on a ship, but not here, faced with something so outside their understanding. He too felt an overpowering revulsion at the melding of human and animal parts, sewn through with metal and gears.

It took a full minute of stomping and crushing to kill the spiders. By then the monstrous squadron was nearly upon them. The elephant guns only slowed the beasts down; nothing could stop them. And they wouldn't die. They just would not die.

They were already dead.

48

A Timely Burst of Anger

It was clear to Octavia that they were very lost. They'd climbed back down into the tunnels hoping to find the route Dr. Hyde had taken, but the tunnels underneath the cave went off in every direction, except back toward anything that might be below the quartz prison room. And the longer it took, the more intensely she could feel Modo's growing anger.

When he slammed his fist into a beam she said, "You are a trained agent. Calm yourself!" Part of her wanted to laugh; she sounded just like old Mr. Socrates. But Modo was becoming unhinged with rage.

"I am calm!" Modo spat, but when they came upon three white-coated men, he chased them down and began throwing them around. It was like watching a hound tear into cornered rabbits.

"Stop!" she shouted. Within seconds the men were all unconscious.

"Take a moment and think!" Octavia said, pushing Modo into a corner. "We could've questioned them."

"What am I doing?" He looked at his fists. "How do we find Hyde?"

"Maybe these tunnels don't join up with any routes below the cave. We could go back to the surface and look for another entrance."

"But I'm certain we're close!" He pulled out his compass and stared at it. "This is west. The tunnel led west. We must be right next to it." He jammed the compass back into his pocket and slammed his fists against the wall. "No!" he said, bashing at it again and again. He had lost all discipline.

Octavia grabbed him by his shoulder and hissed, "Modo! Modo! We're doing the best that we can," as earth and stone fell around them. "Getting all brutish won't help."

"I'm sorry, Tavia. I'm just so tired of holding back. All these thoughts running around in my head." He let out what might have been a sob or a sigh and slumped against the wall.

There was a rumble and crack, then a rush of damp dirt as the stone wall collapsed under his weight. He fell right through it, onto his side, but Octavia jumped over him and through the hole, her hand on her saber. Bright light burned her eyes. They were in a hallway lined with marble walls. The ceiling and floors were marble too. It was lit by electric lights and, thankfully, was deserted.

"Ah! See? It pays to get really angry once in a while!" Modo stood up and began jogging down the hall, Octavia a few feet behind him. She checked her compass. They were traveling toward the palace, were already beneath it, perhaps.

In a few minutes the marble walls turned to wooden panels covered with, of all things, paintings: pastoral scenes incorporating mythological heroes and monsters. One was of a man tied to a rock. Another of a giant holding up the world. A third depicted a man clenching the severed head of a woman with snakes for hair.

The next chamber was populated with an army of bronze and marble statues: men were throwing disks, sitting on thrones, holding spears, while women grasped vases or children, or fixed their hair. Most were naked. If Octavia hadn't grown up in Seven Dials she might have blushed.

Modo rushed up to a wide door covered with ornate carvings.

"Don't just yank it open!" she whispered.

He peeked through the keyhole. "Another hallway," he said. "No sign of— Uh-oh—hide."

The door slowly began to swing open.

49

How Hannibal Was Defeated

Mr. Socrates was nearly out of bullets as the monstrous brigade advanced. They now stood in the midst of his front line. The marines and Association soldiers were reduced to swinging sabers and stabbing with bayonets. It was like pricking giants with pins.

The creatures sent soldiers flying, kicked aside marines, and were able to topple five of the dragoons. Those dragoons who kept their feet exchanged blows with the monsters but were only half as strong.

Mr. Socrates dropped his rifle and drew his pistol, but it wasn't long before it was empty. Not one monster had fallen. All his manpower wasted!

He reloaded his pistol, leaned around a barricade, and fired at the armored monster. The bullets ricocheted off. It was becoming difficult to suppress his fear and revulsion. What had

Hyde done? And how did the little peasant woman, Modo's mother, fit into it? Or Modo's finger, for that matter?

There was a great crash and he saw that the armored monster had cut the barricade in half with his metal claws. Mr. Socrates looked for Tharpa among the slain as he fired his last bullet and unsheathed his saber. No retreat! No, not before these mindless creatures! If this was the end, so be it. He'd go down fighting, like a true Briton.

"Come on," he snarled, "I've got British steel for your innards!"

Another monster came at him from the side, swinging a club, but something else knocked Mr. Socrates down just before the blow landed. He hit the ground hard, his vision blurred. He raised his head, blinking, colors swirling around him. But what was that? Music? He squinted hard, shook his head until he could see.

And there stood Tharpa, alone, in front of the creatures and blowing a trumpet like a madman. He had taken it from one of the sergeants. The Indian had gone barmy.

The monstrosities covered their ears, glaring at Tharpa as he advanced, step by step. One let out an odd yelp of pain and fled, diving into the water. It was followed by another, then another, until all of them had stampeded into the water and disappeared below the waves. Mr. Socrates waited for them to rise again, saw a massive waving hand break the surface, then fall. There was thrashing in the water for a few seconds, then nothing.

Mr. Socrates ran to Tharpa and clapped him on the back. "My man, my man, you're brilliant!" The surviving soldiers cheered. Tharpa beamed.

"It was you, sahib, who once told me the story of how Hannibal and his great elephant army were defeated by Roman trumpeters who let out one big blast of sound. It was worth a try."

"Indeed it was! Though you were horribly out of tune. Perhaps trumpet lessons are in order."

"It may be best to be out of tune, master. Britain has yet to explore horrific noise as a weapon. Perhaps the right frequencies will be more effective than one hundred guns!"

"I will take that under consideration, my friend," Mr. Socrates said, thumping Tharpa on the back again. Then he rallied what remained of his army and turned to the Crystal Palace. It was silent and, he was quite certain, now undefended.

50

To Fight Again Another Day

"It is finished," the Guild Master said.

Miss Hakkandottir looked down from the observation deck and nodded. "Yes, I am afraid the battle is lost."

"Ah, but not the war. Like the phoenix, we will rise again," her master said. "One must know when to retreat. It will take a few years, but I can see my mistakes and I will correct them. Madagascar will be a good home. I have land there for this very eventuality."

"Yes, our future plans are important, but we don't have much time to discuss them right now, sir," she said.

He took one last look around at the smoking ruins of the observation deck. "You are right, Miss Hakkandottir. I put myself in your capable hands."

She led him to the elevator and they took it down to the

basement floor. There, waiting for them, was Dr. Hyde, and three of Miss Hakkandottir's most trusted Guild officers, one of them carrying a limp Madame Hébert. Miss Hakkandottir was tempted to suggest leaving Madame Hébert behind, dead, of course—Modo finding the body would have been a nice blow to her enemies—but she knew that the old woman's chemistry was far too valuable.

She armed herself with one of the officer's pistols, loosened her sword in its scabbard, and led them down the hall. It would take Mr. Socrates and his men at least an hour to break into the palace. By that time they would have boarded the Triton boat waiting in an underground cave and would be well on the way to Madagascar.

At the end of the first hall she opened a wide door, urging them on into the great room that the Guild Master used for meditation; he called it his temple. All she could see were some useless statues. Why had he wasted money on these when he could have bought more armaments?

A birdlike chirp stopped her. She couldn't place where it was coming from, but she knew it was actually human. She signaled the officers, who raised their rifles. "Who is there?" she demanded. The forest of statues did not answer.

Another chirp, this time to her left. She spun, her pistol at the ready. "Show yourself!"

One of the officers fired, chipping the ear off a statue. The report of the gun nearly deafened her. "What was it?"

"Someone moved over there."

"Don't shoot until you have a target."

"Please don't harm the statues," the Guild Master

pleaded, looking rather pathetic. Miss Hakkandottir nearly cuffed him.

Then a statue fell over on the opposite side of the room.

She felt a drop of rain. She touched the damp spot on her face, confused, then looked up. There, clinging to the chandelier, was a man wearing a mask.

51

A Battle Amongst the Gods

Modo did what he had been trained to do. Without hesitation, he dropped to the floor in the middle of his enemies, yanked the rifle from one soldier and knocked him out with the butt end, then broke the gun over the head of another soldier. He threw the pieces at Miss Hakkandottir, striking the pistol out of her hand just as she swung it around to shoot him. Octavia took care of the third soldier and then grabbed Dr. Hyde and held her saber to his throat. Modo's mother fell to the floor.

Modo was face to face with Miss Hakkandottir. "Modo," she said, "how I have longed for this." She swung her metal fist at him; he deflected the blow and she knocked the head off a statue of Zeus instead.

"That's a Polyclitus!" the man wearing glasses shouted.

Modo lost his balance and Miss Hakkandottir delivered a

kick to his midsection that sent him tumbling into another statue. She drew her saber. All he had was his knife. In desperation, he threw it speeding end over end toward her heart, but with her metal hand she batted it aside.

"This time I'll take more than your finger," she said. "I'm not leaving without your head."

"Give it your best shot," he said. As she swung, he lifted a broken arm from a statue and parried the blow. He was surprised at how fearless he felt. She lunged to stab his stomach and he knocked the blade aside, driving it into the wall. It stuck, and as she tried to pull it out, he smashed the saber with the arm of the statue, breaking the blade.

She smacked him in the head with her metal fist. He staggered, swinging blindly, and she caught his fist with her metal hand and squeezed, crushing his bones. She grinned with gritted teeth as she brought him to his knees. Octavia ran across the room, saber raised to slash her, but, with amazing speed, his enemy knocked Octavia aside with her other arm.

"This is for destroying my ship." She tightened her grip; Modo let out a scream. He tried to get up, to push against her, but the pain was unbearable.

Then he saw his mother lying on the floor behind Miss Hakkandottir. She was coming to, fear in her eyes. His heart felt caught in his throat. He gathered every last ounce of his strength and got to his feet, despite his crushed hand. Miss Hakkandottir refused to let go, so he swung his arm with all his might, slamming her into the wall. She still wouldn't let go. Perhaps she couldn't—her hand seemed to be locked. He swung her again and again, knocking over statues. Dr. Hyde was shouting, "Leave her be!" Modo swung Miss Hakkandottir a third time and she flew through the air, screaming obscenities.

Her metal hand was still attached to him, her blood dripping from the wrist and dangling wires.

He pried at the fingers until they loosened and the hand fell off. He didn't dare to look at his own throbbing, mangled fist. Miss Hakkandottir shrieked, "Damn you!" and tried to stand, but couldn't. Dr. Hyde ran and wrapped her stub with a piece of cloth from his shirt.

Meanwhile, Octavia had grabbed a pistol from a fallen soldier. "No one move," she commanded, sweeping the room with it.

Everyone was still. Silent.

Then the man with the glasses fled.

52

Taking the Lift

The doors to the palace wouldn't budge, so they blew a jagged hole in them with dynamite and the dragoons thrust the remaining pieces open. Mr. Socrates sent the dragoons in first, then the soldiers and the marines. When they weren't met with gunfire, he entered. Several dead Guild soldiers lay on the floor. The palace had been deserted.

As his men explored the interior, Mr. Socrates stopped to look up at the giant clock, the symbol of the Clockwork Guild. Beside it was a massive fountain spouting fresh water. Such magnificence, and all from one man's mind. But why a *guild*, then? After all, that meant a collective, several minds working together, didn't it? So once they destroyed this island fortress, would other cells pop up? If so, the Association would silence them all, one by one.

Some forty yards away, a trapdoor was flung open, and a

small man leapt from the hole and slammed the door shut again. He wore glasses and gray clothing; he looked like a clerk, one of many the Guild must employ. Near the door was a spiral staircase, which the man immediately mounted without a glance at Mr. Socrates or his men.

The trapdoor opened again and a short, bulky figure leapt out and sped up the stairs in hot pursuit. Modo!

"Should I stop the little man?" Tharpa raised his rifle.

Mr. Socrates shook his head. "No. Modo wouldn't chase this man for no reason. We take the lift to the top. We'll want to know what this fellow has to say."

53

Cleanup Duty

While the other dragoons cleared the palace, Oppie was assigned cleanup duty around the island. He combed the wreckage with one of the other dragoons and three soldiers, and rounded up all the surviving Guild soldiers. They would be sent on boats to the *Shah* for imprisonment in the hold.

He found himself in the area of the battlefield where he'd left Typhon's body. There was no sign of the creature. He looked back at the *Shah*, now anchored in the bay. One of the ship's cranes was working, heaving a large crate from a boat over to the deck of the ship. *Ah, there we go,* he thought. The marines had already transported the monstrosity to the *Shah*.

"And good riddance," he shouted at the crate, before carrying on with his rounds.

54

Miscalculations

Modo pursued the man up to the highest room in the tower. It was a mess: telegraph machines smashed by the blow of the *Shah*'s guns, shattered glass and burning paper littered the floor. The west wall was in ruins, one section blasted open. This odd man had to be important, might even be the Guild Master. Why else would he have been with Hakkandottir? Did he still have a trick up his sleeve? A means of escape? A hot-air balloon, perhaps? Nothing was impossible, but if a balloon had been tethered to the broken landing post, it was gone now.

"There's no way out of here," Modo said, facing him.

The breeze was warm, rustling and separating the burning papers. The man stood at the far side of the room, blinking as though what was happening was beyond his comprehension.

"So, you are Modo," he said, coming out of his trance.

"Yes."

"A very curious, determined creature."

"I'll take that as a compliment."

"I'm afraid I miscalculated. I failed to foresee this outcome. Plato would be ashamed."

"Who's Plato?"

The man cocked his head. "A philosopher."

"I know, I know. I thought you were using a code name."

He heard a noise behind him. Modo turned to see Mr. Socrates, Tharpa, and several Association soldiers enter the room.

"Your master comes." To Mr. Socrates he said, "A well-played hand."

"Thank you," he replied. "Would you do me the courtesy of stating your name?"

"I am no one," the man said. "Prometheus one day. Midas the next. Yes, that would be a good name for me. A foolish king who could make everything turn to gold but could never eat."

"Come now, the game is done," Mr. Socrates said. "I know a little about you, at least. You were once the Dragon Master of the Red Fish Triad, weren't you? Or should I say 489?"

The man nodded and grinned. So this *was* the Guild Master! Modo shook his head at the thought. This little bespectacled fellow?

"Marvelous! I didn't imagine you or your allies got that close to my old life. You're much more effective than I believed you to be. Another miscalculation. But yes, that number was once me and I was once that number."

Mr. Socrates said, "Please return to my ship. We won't mistreat you. In fact, I'll give you your choice of tea."

"Such kindness," the Guild Master replied. Modo studied him. Sarcasm? He really seemed cavalier. "I suppose logic dictates that I offer up my arms for manacles and bow down to your might."

"There won't be any need for manacles," Mr. Socrates said. "We're all gentlemen here."

"Ah, I am more than that. And I have more names than you will ever know. My father named me Douglas, for one." Then he began dancing around in a circle, flapping his arms like wings, looking every bit the lunatic, until he said, "But I truly am Daedalus."

Daedalus—the Greek scientist who created wings from wax and feathers to escape a prison, along with his son, Icarus. Did the Guild Master really believe he could just up and fly away? As the man began to giggle at his own silliness, Modo glanced out at the airship docking station just to reassure himself it had indeed been broken in half. Then something overhead caught his eyes and he looked up. Man-sized white wings hung from the shattered ceiling.

"To the sun!" the Guild Master yelled, leaping onto an upturned desk and clutching the wings. Modo sprang after him, but the distance was too great. As the Guild Master ran toward the hole blasted in the side of the observation deck, he slid the ragged wings on and leapt toward the sky.

An impossibly large hand shot up from the side of the palace, catching him in midair and causing his glasses to go flying. He was thrown back into the room, landing on his broken wings.

Typhon climbed in and stood over him, a boot on the small man's chest as he writhed around. If the roof hadn't been blown off, the creature wouldn't have been able to stand up straight. Typhon grabbed the Guild Master by his lapels and lifted him.

"Ah, so it is the master of the masters," Typhon said. "Are we standing inside your broken dreams?"

"Put me down, monster!" the Guild Master ordered.

"Correct. I am a monster. But it was you who ordered my creation. You set your doctor and your minions to the task of piecing me together." He paused. "So, tell me, who is the real monster?"

"Put him on the floor," Mr. Socrates demanded. "That man is *my* prisoner." Tharpa and the soldiers raised their guns.

Typhon tilted his head. "Your bullets won't harm me. You cannot wound flesh that is already dead."

"Release me!" The Guild Master was now shouting. "Release me at once! I command you, Typhon."

"I reject that name. And your tinctures and commands no longer work on me. Beg, beg for my forgiveness. Tell me that you accept me as your child."

"I shall not."

"Then are you Daedalus or Icarus?"

Modo didn't like the direction this was going. Icarus had, after all, flown too close to the sun, melting his wax wings and crashing to his death.

"I am Daedalus," the Guild Master cried. "I am Daedalus!"

"You are Icarus," Typhon said. He tore the wing from one

arm and, as though he were tossing away a cockroach, threw the Guild Master over the side of the palace tower to the rocks below.

Everyone else stood there, stunned.

Typhon turned to them and shrugged. "He gave me the brain of a murderer. What did he expect?" He pointed at Mr. Socrates. "I demand safe passage off of this island."

Mr. Socrates looked him in the eye. "It would be immoral to allow you to roam free in the world."

"Then we are at an impasse. I've not discovered my free will only to be forced to surrender it. I see only one avenue of escape." He heaved his bulk toward Mr. Socrates. Tharpa let off two shots, but they only thudded into the creature's flesh.

Modo flew at the monster. He had always been so amazingly strong; surely he could at least come between this thing and his master. But Typhon flicked Modo to the floor. Two more shots from Mr. Socrates' pistol and then the creature had his hand around Mr. Socrates' throat. He jerked him up and squeezed him against his chest. Already Mr. Socrates' face was red from lack of air. "Get too close and I will snap this old rooster's neck. I'll let him go once I've escaped this place. I promise."

He carried Mr. Socrates, who was limp and speechless, into the lift and began his descent. Modo tore down the spiral stairs after them. He shouted at the dragoons waiting below, "Back away! Don't fire!"

Modo trailed after Typhon as they left the palace, staying far enough back so as not to alarm him. Mr. Socrates' face had gone a frightening shade of purple. He saw Octavia running toward them and he motioned her to stay away.

The monster carried Mr. Socrates out into the water and dropped him unceremoniously into one of the Triton boats. He climbed in after him, and after several seconds of experimentation, the boat began to chug out to the ocean.

"You are overly dedicated to your master!" Typhon shouted.

"He is more than my master!" Modo yelled back. What could he do? He had no more weapons. No more words. His hand was broken. Modo pulled up his mask. "Typhon!" he shouted. "You're not the only monster here!" He walked slowly toward the departing boat, the light falling fully upon his face, the waves creeping up his legs, his torso. He began to swim, tentatively, toward Typhon, keeping his face above the surface. "You see," he shouted, "we are both monsters of a kind!" It was a last feeble gesture. Modo hoped to appeal to whatever tiny bit of humanity might still be floating about in Typhon's brain.

Typhon stared at him, bemused. He waved his little finger. "One day I would like to know more about you," he said, "but today is not that day."

As though he had done it all his life, he began piloting the boat into the Pacific. With his enormous bulk it sat heavy in the water. He still had an arm around Mr. Socrates, who was now alert and struggling and beginning to holler.

"Let him go!" Modo pleaded. "You promised to let him go!"

"I did. You shouldn't have trusted a murderer." He paused. "But I shall keep my word."

And so he tossed Mr. Socrates into the ocean.

55

Into Blue Water

Octavia kept her gun trained on Miss Hakkandottir from several paces away. The woman was as pale as the marble statues surrounding her, but her blue eyes stabbed Octavia's. "I will break every bone in your body," she said, spitting out each word, her voice frail.

"Not today." Octavia smiled sweetly.

Dr. Hyde tightened the makeshift tourniquet on Miss Hakkandottir's arm. Then he stroked her red hair, which had fallen out of its braids. "You will live," he whispered. "My love. I will make you beautiful again."

Octavia felt like throwing up. Who would have thought these two could be lovebirds?

Modo's mother had rolled up into a ball at the foot of a statue and seemed to be sleeping. Chloroform? Or exhaustion from the torturous things they'd done to her?

Ah! Relief! A dragoon stooped to enter the door to take in the situation, followed by two Association soldiers, guns drawn. "You must be extremely careful with her," Octavia said, pointing at Miss Hakkandottir. "And tend to Madame Hébert. She'll need to see the ship's doctor immediately." Finally, Octavia scooped up Miss Hakkandottir's metal hand and said with great satisfaction, "I'll give this to Mr. Socrates myself."

Then she ran down the hallway and up a set of stairs into the interior of the Crystal Palace. It was good to see sunlight again, even if it was filtered by the quartz.

No gunfire. The battles were over.

The Association soldiers were standing at attention, uncertain what to do. Through the front gate she spotted Modo walking alone toward the beach. She stepped out of the palace; then Modo turned and motioned her back. But . . . what? Typhon? Was that him out in the boat? And who was he holding against him? Mr. Socrates! He seemed to be struggling, yelling. And now Modo was wading into the water, shouting something at them.

She raced after them, watching fearfully as Typhon dropped Mr. Socrates in the water. Modo began to swim frantically, then dove below the surface.

Octavia dropped Miss Hakkandottir's hand, ran to the end of the half-shattered dock, and dove in. The water took her breath away. She swam hard. She couldn't see Mr. Socrates, only Modo surfacing twenty yards ahead of her and the monster in the boat in the far distance.

She pushed harder, gasping for air. Tharpa had taught

her better, but she was panicking. Then—Mr. Socrates' hand poked out from the water, waving, reaching for the air before sinking beneath the surface again. Modo dove down after his master, and Octavia kicked and kicked until she was closer to them, then dove, down, down, coral and brightly colored fish all around her. Such a beautiful world.

In the coral lay Mr. Socrates—no longer struggling. He gave only an occasional shudder. Modo attempted to pull him up, but with just one good hand, it was impossible. *The meathead will drown along with our master!* Octavia kicked harder and grabbed Mr. Socrates' shoulder, and together they pulled him up.

They broke the surface, the old man between them, pale and limp. A boat was already waiting. Tharpa pulled Mr. Socrates in, turned him onto his side, and began pounding on his back. Modo clung to one side of the boat, Octavia the other, both gasping for air.

After a minute or two, Tharpa let out a noise unlike anything Octavia had ever heard, but she knew its meaning. Overwhelming grief. The language of sorrow.

"Sahib!" he cried out. There had been such devotion between them. Again he pounded his master on the back.

Mr. Socrates gave up the slightest sputter. Then a cough. He began to take in air, great gulps of it. Octavia and Modo climbed onboard and worked on Mr. Socrates, helping him expel the water, as Tharpa piloted the boat toward the *Shah*.

After a few minutes, Modo clutched his hand, grimacing in pain. Octavia stared at him, at his face. She didn't flinch. His eyes were so full of suffering. She studied the water dripping down his features, his patchy red hair plastered to his scalp. His breath came hard through his ragged mouth. She could look at this face.

He turned toward her, caught her looking. She smiled and said, “Next time you should let me do the swimming.”

56

Ever South

Typhon kept one hand on the wheel of the boat, looking back as the *Shah* disappeared on the horizon. Soon the island of Atticus was gone and he was alone on the water. These little boats were fast. They wouldn't be able to catch up with him. He thought of that last view of Modo. That was the young man's name, wasn't it? There had been something, dare he say, touching, about that. He'd shown him his face, and Typhon had been surprised: it was uglier than his own. They were indeed brothers, of a sort. At the least, they shared the same blood. He stroked the little finger on his right hand.

But that world was now behind him. What new worlds, what new places could there be for someone such as he? South was the best direction. South to Antarctica. Maybe there he would find peace: a place where no one would bother him.

He looked at the boat's compass, unsure about the

direction. Still, he was pretty certain he'd find the way. After all, several brains were stuffed together in his skull. One of them would surely contain the map of the Pacific. And with that thought, he discovered a map in his long dead memories. Life was full of little surprises.

He laughed, frightening the seagulls that flew above him.

57

One for the Army, One for the Lord

For the first two days of the journey to Esquimalt, Modo was so exhausted that he mostly slept in his cabin on the *Shah*. The ship's surgeon did what he could for his hand, resetting the bones but predicting he'd never have full use of it again. Modo didn't correct him, but it would be good as new in a few weeks. That was just how his body worked.

He wasn't allowed to see Mr. Socrates, who had not yet fully recovered. Tharpa assured him, though, that sahib had already complained about the quality of the tea, a sign that he was on the mend. When he wasn't sleeping, Modo pulled on his mask and wandered the deck and stared out at the ocean. Or he sat with Octavia, saying little. She too was exhausted. He ate sparingly, the gray sludge still being the only food offered. Only two days out and already he couldn't stomach much more of it.

On one of his visits to the ship's surgeon he discovered that Miss Hakkandottir's life had been saved by cauterizing her stub. "She didn't let out a peep," the surgeon said, amazed. She was now manacled in a holding cell somewhere below deck. Dr. Hyde was in a cell on another floor. Both were guarded by several marines. Modo had no intention of visiting his enemy. He hoped the hangman's rope awaited her and Dr. Hyde.

All of the dragoons were on the *Shah* too, though he rarely saw them. He was happy that Ester had survived and seemed to have no injuries. It wasn't until the third day that he ran into Oppie on the deck, sitting on a crate in the sun. The gash on his forehead had been nicely stitched. "Mr. Modo," he said, with a broad smile. "It's a pleasure to see you, sir. We made it through to the other side."

"Indeed we did," Modo answered. He sat beside him. It was still so strange that this man—who such a short time ago was a small boy—was taller than him. A scruffy beard was attempting to grow on his face. "How are you?"

"All's well. I—I miss my mates. Three of 'em gave their lives, but I guess we all knew our chances going in."

"Yes, you did. You are a very brave man, Oppie."

"Just did my job," he answered. "Some terrible things happened, sir. Truly terrible things." Then he laughed. "But we got the bastards, didn't we, sir?"

Modo could only nod in response, then returned his gaze to the horizon. They were silent for a few minutes. Modo remembered what Mr. Socrates had said about these dragoons. Every week they aged a month. "What will you do now, Oppie?"

"Do, sir?"

"Yes, are you going back to England?"

"I'll be going wherever the army tells me to go, sir," he said.

"You don't get leave? Or perhaps you've done your part? I certainly think so. You could move on."

Oppie looked him in the eyes. "Do you really believe there's a place for me in that other world, sir? My job at the inn again? Ha. No, this is my place now. My home is with my mates in the Lucky Sevens. No one else can wear my uniform, sir. There's still work for the Association to do."

"Yes," Modo said, though he felt for Oppie. "I suppose you're right. But listen, Oppie—you'll keep learning to read, I hope."

"I will, sir," he replied. "That's a promise."

Modo clapped him on the back and strode to the aft of the ship, his eyes set on the direction from which they'd come. How many times had he walked around this ship avoiding his most important conversation? He contemplated the view for several minutes before he found the courage to go down the stairs to the lower deck, past the surgeon's quarters to the recovery cabin. His mother had been here all this time, with reports on her health being delivered to his cabin a few times a day.

He lingered outside her door, having suddenly decided he should be bringing her a gift. She was his mother, after all. But it wasn't as though he could just dive off the ship and return with a bouquet of flowers. She would have to take him as he was. Perhaps she'd see his part in her rescue as a gift; perhaps she'd even be proud of him.

He adjusted his mask, then raised a hesitant hand and knocked. A frail voice said, "*Entrez.*"

He opened the door. Her room, lit only by the light from the porthole, was relatively large for a cabin. It was littered with medical equipment and various supplies. His mother lay on her cot, propped up on pillows, a gray wool blanket covering her legs. He took two steps in and stopped.

Some color had returned to her cheeks, though she was still pale. He didn't know what to say. He stared at her face, looking for familiar features.

"*Parlez-vous français?*" she asked.

"*Oui,*" he said. "*Je comprende.*"

"I am told that you saved me," she said in French. "I remember you, though, as you know, I was not well. I thank you."

"It was my duty," he said. "I was only doing my duty."

"Still, I thank you. It was brave of you."

"Are you feeling better?" he asked. "Are you getting enough to eat?"

"Soldiers bring me horrible food. But the doctor speaks some French. He's not a religious man, but he's kind. He told me my husband is dead. I have not had any tears to weep yet. They will come. I've been praying for his soul. Had I died, it wouldn't have been so bad, to join him again in heaven."

Modo didn't know how to respond, except to say, "I'm sorry for your loss."

"What's your name?" she asked.

"Modo."

"What sort of name is that? British?"

"My name was . . ." He paused. What to say? He began

again. "It's the name my father gave me." He hadn't meant to say father, but trying to explain his relationship with Mr. Socrates was too complicated. "My adoptive father," he added.

She nodded. "He has raised you well. But why do you wear a mask? Were you wounded?"

"I'm disfigured," he said. "At least, some would believe me to be so."

She raised her eyebrows. "How did it happen?"

"At birth," he said. "I was born this way."

Her eyes narrowed. Was she thinking about his birth?

"I—" He had to spit it out. "I know you will find this difficult to believe. But I have learned . . . that I was born in Nanterre. I am your son."

"You're lying," she said. Her eyes grew hard, her face stony.

"It isn't a lie. The nursemaid's name was . . ." He searched his memory. What had Colette said? "Marie. And you left me at Notre Dame Cathedral. You left me there with Father Mauger. Don't you remember?" He hadn't intended to sound so whiny.

"I have no son," she replied. "My husband and I had no children."

Doubt crept in . . . but her eyes were so similar to his. He thought about all the facts. No, she had to be his mother.

"Tell me the truth. You owe me that. Especially now. Did you not give up your son to the Notre Dame orphanage?"

Her face grew tired-looking and she sighed deeply, picking at her fingernails. "I prayed. I asked my God why he had given me an abomination. What had I done to deserve this? And my husband was a good, hardworking man. So it was me, my sinful thinking. Temptations I could not resist in my youth. So I gave the abomination up to the ones who would know what to do with it. It was not a son. And you are not that child. You are not that child. You are only being cruel to me by pretending."

"What year was it?"

She paused to think. "It was 1858."

"And this . . . this abomination, did you give him a name?"

"Why would I? It was a punishment visited on me for my sins. My family disowned me. We chose to change our names. To hide from them and from those who knew about God's punishment. I have been praying for His forgiveness ever since."

"Did you give your son anything?"

"I gave him his life. I gave him back to God."

"And if you could see him again, what would you say?"

"One does not speak to the devil."

He wanted to rip off his mask. Show her his tortured face. Really punish her. The room was blurring.

He breathed deeply, blinked back tears, and summoned all of his courage. "I *am* your son," he said. "It's the truth. Whether or not you are willing to accept it is your own problem."

She covered her face. "Please, go, go . . . stop torturing me."

He thought of changing his shape, of showing her how magical he was, how powerful and strong, but no. It would be a wasted effort.

"I am Modo," he said. "I am your son, who saved your life." He left the room, closing the cabin door firmly behind him.

58

A Vast Departure

The HMS *Shah* landed at Esquimalt in the late afternoon. Already there had been other ships alerted as to the position of the island. Modo wondered if, like the underwater realm of Icaria or the attack on Parliament, this would never appear in the newspapers. The bodies of the Guild's half-men, half-monsters would perhaps be displayed one day in glass showcases. In the short term they would most certainly be shipped to cold storage in the basement of some well-secured building in London. Or maybe in the Arctic, for all he knew, to be dissected and studied. He hoped they wouldn't discover the real secret, as it was in his blood. And his mother's blood too. He wondered what she understood of what had happened to her. Or had she been so drugged that she would only believe it to have been some horrible nightmare? Would the Association ever allow her to live a normal life again?

It wasn't until they docked that Mr. Socrates emerged from his cabin and Modo and Octavia saw him for the first time in four days. Tharpa pushed Mr. Socrates along in a wheelchair, a gray blanket across his legs. He appeared smaller, and more elderly, as though his time underwater had shriveled him up. Mr. Socrates shooed Tharpa away and slowly wheeled himself across the deck.

"I owe you my life," he said matter-of-factly.

"Actually, Octavia and I pulled you out together," Modo said, giving her a nod.

"Yes, I owe my thanks to both of you, though I will take some of the credit for having trained you both so well." A twinkle returned to his eyes.

"We chose how to apply it, though," Octavia reminded him.

"You have free will, too much of it at times." He chuckled hoarsely.

"It is all I have," Modo said.

"Come now, no time to be melancholy. We have accomplished great things. The Guild has been broken into pieces. There may be pockets elsewhere, but they won't dare to rise up again for years. The good citizens of England have no inkling as to what we were up against. Therefore, they will never thank you, but know that you did good work. We're now free to return to London to begin strengthening the Association."

"No," Modo said without hesitation.

"No?"

He had spent last night unable to sleep. His mother's rejection had rattled him, knocking some key part of himself loose. "I'm done with empires, Mr. Socrates. That was my last assignment. I mean to quit the Association and strike out on my own."

"Do you?" Mr. Socrates said.

"You said nothing of this to me," Octavia said, unable to hide her irritation.

"It's only become clear to me now, Tavia. I'm really best off alone."

"You can't just quit, Modo," Mr. Socrates said. "This is not a sporting club. You have oaths to fulfill, duties. There's much work yet to be done."

"Mr. Socrates, I care deeply for you. You're the closest thing I have to a father. But, through no choice of my own, I have given you fifteen years of my life. I want my next years to be my own. I may return one day, when I'm older. But right now I must act alone."

"What madness is this, Modo?" With the help of Tharpa, he rose from his chair and stood shakily on the deck. "I raised you. You would be nothing without me—just a cowering beast."

"Beast?"

"I didn't mean to use that word. I forbid you from leaving me—from leaving the Association. The care, the thought, the years I've put into grooming you, and this is how you repay me? With betrayal?"

"I'm not betraying you. I'm leaving you, that's all."

Mr. Socrates looked at Tharpa. "I have made him too much in my own image." Then he turned back to Modo. "I will not beg you to stay. But know this, Modo: if you walk away from me, you'll regret it. The world out there is cruel. You'll come crawling back to me."

"I must find my own place, sir." He locked eyes with Tharpa, who nodded subtly as though to say *I understand.*

Octavia said, "You're going alone?"

If she came with him, what kind of life would she have? Better for her to stay with the Association. To make a decent living. To find her prince.

"I am," he replied. Then he walked down the gangplank and toward the gates of the naval base.

59

A Warm and Calloused Hand

The cobblestone streets of Victoria were solid under Modo's feet. He felt solid too, even though he wasn't certain about what he'd just done. The decision had come upon him so suddenly and so perfectly that he'd acted on it without the slightest hesitation. He was deeply sad now when he pictured the disappointment in Mr. Socrates' eyes. He'd see him again, he was certain of that, but on his own terms. Living his own life.

Modo didn't have a plan for his future employment. He had the strength to work on the railways. Or in the mines. Or better yet, on a farm in the wild west. He loved the idea of just bending his back to a task without worrying about the fate of the Empire.

A swift step and a hissing noise alerted him, but before he could react a hard blow fell on the back of his head and he collapsed to the ground. He expected a knife between the ribs next. Did Mr. Socrates mean to make sure he didn't leave the Association?

He rolled over to face his attacker. "Tavia!"

Octavia stood over him, her hands on her hips. "You left without me, you . . . you nizzie, you nincompoop!"

"It's for the best."

"For the best? We're friends, Modo. You don't turn your back on a mate."

"But you have a good life with the Association." He was ashamed to hear his voice warble.

"You didn't even ask me if I wanted to go along!" His head hurt. What had she whacked him with? "You made assumptions, you . . . you assumptious ass!"

"*Assumptious* isn't a word!"

"Don't lecture me, you traitor."

"Fine," he said with a huff. He stood, holding his head. "Will you come with me?"

"No. Not now, not ever!"

"Then what are you doing here?"

She took a deep breath, huffed it out and stamped her foot. "Modo, you're so . . . so frustrating! A terribly frustrating, terribly . . . interesting man. And the silly thing is, I can't imagine not being around you. I do love your company."

He got to his feet, dumbfounded. Had she said *love*?

"So?" she said after several seconds had passed. "What are your thoughts? Do you have any?"

"I—I—you know how I feel, Tavia."

"I do? How *do* you feel? Since you're so good with fancy words, tell me!"

But he had very few words this time. "I . . . can't . . . imagine not being around you, either."

"I would like to travel with you. Where, I don't know."

"And what of my face, my looks?"

"Modo," she said seriously, "that will take some getting used to. But I've learned to put up with your personality. I'm sure in time I'll learn to put up with your face, too. Day by day."

"And I'll put up with yours," he retorted. "But there's a further problem: we have no money, no tickets."

She held up a familiar wallet. "I nicked this from Mr. Socrates. My final payment from the Association."

"You shouldn't have done that." Then he laughed.

"There's enough in here for two tickets. Anywhere we want to go, at least second-class."

"Then where would you like to go?"

"San Francisco," she said. "I like the way it sounds. We'll see where it takes us next." She held up her hand. "But first, and this is my only condition, let us go at once to a bakery and eat cake."

"Cake? Why?"

"Because, Modo, I've lost track of the days, but we missed your birthday."

He counted in his head. It was the last day of October. "Actually, Tavia, my birthday is tomorrow." The thought of it, of celebrating his arrival onto this earth wasn't appealing.

Octavia grabbed him by the shoulder, squeezing so hard that it hurt. "Don't go all soft on me, Modo. Don't think about your foolish mother or all those other things. This is your first birthday, and we're going to do it up with style.

Cake today, and cake tomorrow! You listen to me, I'm older than you, and therefore wiser. Are you game?"

She held out her hand. Modo laughed heartily and took it. It was calloused and warm. Hand in hand, they set off in search of a place to celebrate their new, and not so new, beginnings.

ARTHUR SLADE has published several novels for young readers, including *The Hunchback Assignments, The Dark Deeps,* and *Empire of Ruins,* books one through three in the series The Hunchback Assignments; *Jolted: Newton Starker's Rules for Survival; Megiddo's Shadow; Tribes;* and *Dust,* which won the Governor General's Literary Award for Children's Literature. He lives in Saskatoon, Saskatchewan, with his wife, Brenda Baker, and their daughter.

Visit him on the Web at arthurslade.com.